THE LONDONDERRY AIR

Testament of an Ulster Gunman

By Garrad Gawler

COPPERHILL MEDIA
A Division of Copperhill Technologies Corporation
http://www.copperhillmedia.com

THE LONDONDERRY AIR
Testament of an Ulster Gunman
By Garrad Gawler

Published by
Copperhill Media
A Division of Copperhill Technologies Corporation
158 Log Plain Road
Greenfield, MA 01301
USA

Cover Design by Copperhill Media
Original photos acquired through BigStockPhoto.com
Gunman Silhouette At Night - Contributor: miraco
Grunge Union Jack Flag - Contributoir: Sean Gladwell

Disclaimer: There are no such places as Maddenstown, Listober or
Magheraderg in Northern Ireland. The 5th (Co Londonderry) Battalion of the
Ulster Defence Regiment never did have a 'J' Company. While the scenarios
described in this book are loosely based on real events, the characters
portrayed are fictional and are not intended to depict any real person in the
past or present.

ISBN-10: 0-983977569
ISBN-13: 978-0-9839775-6-8

http://www.copperhillmedia.com

Chapter 1 - Charles Cunningham

It all changed for me on a balmy June 1973 afternoon in the County Derry town of Maddenstown. I was a Physics teacher at the local College of Technology. School finished at 3:45, and I had rushed home to my little terraced house on Union Street to listen to the last session of the test match on Radio Three. I didn't own a television, and the reception for Radio Three was poor on the north coast of Ireland. I used to put the radio on the inner windowsill halfway up the stairs where I had found the best reception.

I was sitting in my lounge sipping a mug of coffee when the radio went off station. I came out of the sitting room to climb the stairs to re-tune my little portable when there was a massive explosion from somewhere behind the house. I instinctively put my hands up in front of my face in time to stop shards of glass from the window striking me. My radio came bouncing down the stairs past me. My immediate thought was that someone had thrown some sort of grenade into my back garden. I turned and ran out of my front door where I found that most of the neighbours had done the same. It was difficult to breathe because the atmosphere was full of smoke and fumes. Thousands of tiny pieces of paper, cloth, and plastic were fluttering down around us with the occasional heavier piece of metal.

I saw one of my neighbours ducking as a car registration plate came spiraling down, and then I realised that this was no grenade; it was the aftermath of something much larger. I heard people shouting that there had been a car bomb in Station Street, which was not far behind my house. A few doors up from my home, there was a passageway behind a shirt factory and this led through to Station Street. I joined the throng of people making their way up the passageway.

When I came out onto Station Street, I was appalled by the scenes of carnage that met me. The Laundromat and newspaper shop, which I had regularly frequented, had disappeared leaving a gap on the opposite side of the street. The roadway was cluttered with bricks, parts of a car, and bodies or rather, parts of bodies.

I had taken first-aid courses in the Boy Scouts, in the Officer Training Corps at university and as part of my teacher training but nothing had prepared me for this. Bodies and bits of bodies had been stripped bare by the blast. What really shocked me was the sight of dead and injured people whose flesh had been blown from their limbs but leaving the bare bones still attached to their bodies.

I knelt beside what was left of an old lady. Most of her clothes had disappeared, and her body had been scorched. Her hair had been burnt to a cinder, and her eyes and lips were grotesquely swollen so that her face reminded me of a black and white minstrel. She was still living, and she reached her right hand towards me. I clasped the raw flesh and tried to reassure her that everything was OK and that she would soon be on her way to hospital. I could not believe my ears when she croaked, "Charlie, is that you? My God, my God!"

It was my mother's aunt Lizzie who worked a few shifts in the Laundromat. Many times I had entrusted her with my washing and had received special treatment. I checked her over. Apart from the burns, she had lost the lower part of her left leg, and she was bleeding profusely from her head and upper torso. She gave a croak and then sagged, her hand slipping from mine. I checked her pulse but I knew that I was looking for life in vain. I picked up the remains of a garment that had been blown from the laundry, or more likely from another victim, and I covered her face and breasts.

I stood up, my knees were literally knocking, and I was taking involuntarily deep gulps of air. I looked around. A middle-aged man with an aura of authority had seemed to have taken charge. He was directing people to use doors as stretchers to take the wounded to an assortment of commercial vehicles at the top of the street. I heard the sirens of approaching police vehicles and ambulances. Then a battered old military Landrover pulled up, and I was amazed to see soldiers with rifles getting out. But they were like no soldiers I had ever seen before. They looked very old to me, and they wore olive green uniforms, which I associated with the Yanks in Viet Nam. They looked as shocked and bewildered as the rest of us. This must be the UDR, I thought.

I was ordered to help carry a door supporting a screaming young woman towards an ambulance. She still wore enough clothing to protect her dignity and seemed to have only superficial wounds but, like so many other victims, she had evacuated her bowels. Then my team returned to the scene of the blast to pick up the remains of an unconscious old man who did not seem to have a scratch on him. Then I noticed that he was bleeding from his nose and ears. Soon the only human remains were parts of bodies, and a police sergeant instructed us not to move them.

I staggered away from the scene. Only then did I realise that I had small pieces of glass imbedded in the palms of my hands and that my clothes were sodden with blood, the victims' blood. I knew that there was a chemist's shop at the other end of Station Street. I had my mind set on cotton wool, plasters and TCP. Hordes of other people were walking in the same direction. Nobody spoke. I had heard of the thousand-yard stare, and as I looked around I saw it in the faces of young and old, male and female. Suddenly there was the blast of another explosion on the far side of the town.

Everyone, me included, instinctively ducked. I was thoroughly ashamed of myself.

When I had picked up my medical supplies, I left Station Street and made my way down Church Street before turning into Union Street. I needed a long sweet drink to clear my throat and to combat the early signs of shock. I entered the mini-market and picked up a bottle of Lucozade. I also grabbed a copy of the Belfast Telegraph, an evening newspaper that I rarely bought, but I knew why I had taken it today. The lady at the checkout looked me over intently but we had nothing to say to each other. She was a Catholic but that had never affected my attitude to her in the past two years. Things were going to be different now.

I staggered up the street to number nine and went up to the bathroom where I had a set of tweezers. I was soon confident that I had removed all of the tiny shards of glass from my hands. I took several large swigs of Lucozade and then tore off all of my clothing. I dressed my wounds with TCP and plastered them. I went into the shower and spent a long time scrubbing myself before I felt clean. The plasters had come off by now so I re-applied them and then descended the stairs in my dressing gown. I knew what I had to do.

The Northern Ireland papers always carried a large recruiting advertisement for the Ulster Defence Regiment inside of their front page. Up to now, I had kept myself aloof from the troubles in Ulster but my feelings had changed in the past two hours. I was angry and sickened at the wanton murder of my great-aunt and of the other elderly victims that I had seen on Station Street. I was ashamed of my ignorance of first-aid techniques and of my revulsion at the smell of blood, shit, and roasted flesh. I was deeply ashamed at my reaction to the sound of the second blast, and I was astonished at my first close look at the UDR. Here was I, an able bodied man in his mid-twenties, selfishly following my own desires while a war was going on around me and relying on old guys to defend me.

I studied the advert for the UDR in the Telegraph. I didn't know much about them. I knew that they had been formed to replace the old 'B' Special police force, which had been heavily criticised, by Nationalists and foreign politicians for being biased and amateurish. My grandfather, uncles, and cousins had served in the 'B' specials, which I had always assumed were a cross between a social club and Dad's Army. I had never been attracted to joining them just as I had never joined any of the loyalist marching clubs like the Orange Order and the Apprentice Boys of Derry. It was received wisdom that you could not get a job, nor promotion nor a council house unless you were a member. My parents and I had never encountered any discrimination although none of us were members of any of these organisations.

I was aware that the Catholics of Northern Ireland complained of discrimination in employment, housing, and voting but all of these grievances were easily dismissed by the people that I mingled with. The Roman Catholic Church had chosen to opt out of the state education system to run their own schools, which focused on Irish culture, Irish history, and the Irish language while the rest of Europe was seizing initiatives in the 'white heat of technology'. It was little wonder that Catholics didn't get jobs in the synthetic fibre factories of County Derry because they were not technically literate.

Besides, many jobs in NI gave priority to ex-servicemen who had documentary proof of their honesty and probity. There had never been National Service in NI and many Catholics were reluctant to serve voluntarily in the crown forces because of the Oath of Allegiance. There was no discrimination in the right to vote in NI for Westminster or Stormont elections. The Catholics were out-numbered two-to-one and could never form a majority. True, many young Catholics could not vote in local council elections because only ratepayers could vote. Many Catholic families had five or six children over twenty-one living at home but only the father, who paid rates, could vote. Sure, there was gerrymandering but it worked on both sides and of course, the war cry in Ulster on Election Day was 'vote early, vote often'. I knew a Catholic in Maddenstown who had been prosecuted for personation when he had voted using his dead father's voting card. His defence was "but that's how he would have voted anyway" but it didn't save him from a fine.

To most Protestants the Civil Rights Movement was just a front for the old IRA who had been unable to force the North into a United Ireland after their 'border' war of the 1950s. Now a new type of IRA terrorists, the Provos, were trying not to bomb the Protestants into a United Ireland but trying to "bomb them out of Ireland" as one of their front politicians had proclaimed.

I kept myself well away from it all. I didn't vote; I frequented Catholic businesses and was civil to their Catholic staff. How else could you get a drink or lay down a bet in 1970s Ulster? I taught at one of the few mixed educational establishments in the province. A quarter of the staff and students were Catholics. True, I had no close Catholic friends, and I had never dated a Catholic girl and certainly could never have seen myself marrying one. In my travels I had visited many of the great Roman Catholic cathedrals in southern Europe – Notre Dame, Florence, Sienna, Sorrento, and many others. I was well aware of the influence that the Catholic Church had made on European culture but I always felt that the Catholic Church in Ireland was different. I could not understand the reverence and indeed the fear, which my Catholic pupils displayed towards their priests. I thought that there was a story to be told there someday.

Chapter 2 – The Cunninghams

I was born just after the war and raised in Maddenstown in County Derry. Yes, we called it 'Derry' amongst ourselves only using the term 'Londonderry' when in the presence of Catholics. My father was descended from an old Ulster Scots family of planters. He had volunteered for service in the RAF early in the war and was very disappointed that he had spent the war in England servicing training aircraft and later working on photographic reconnaissance Mosquitoes. A few months before the end of the war he had been knocked down, at night, out on the flight lines by a service jeep. He sustained leg injuries and was invalided out of the RAF with a small pension. He was lucky to get his old job back, in one of the town's shirt factories, before the large wave of returning ex-servicemen came home.

My father had not joined any of the tribal organisations of loyalism. He was not bigoted and often spoke admiringly about his flight sergeant in the RAF who was a Roman Catholic from the Irish Republic. I was well aware that thousands of Irish citizens had joined the British services to join in the struggle against the Nazis. However, Dad was bitter about the support that the Irish government had given to the Nazis, especially accusing them of refuelling and stocking up German U-boats. Many was the argument which we had when I pointed out that the Irish would not have had fuel for U-boats and even if they had, how would they have transferred it in the dangerous coves of the west coast of Ireland? I conceded that villagers had probably sold butter, milk, eggs, and vegetables to the Nazi seamen. He countered that they had probably sold intelligence as well. What intelligence, I had scoffed. Any news about convoy escorts leaving Londonderry was probably out of date by the time it got to the west coast.

Besides, he had replied, hadn't President deValera signed the condolence book for 'Herr Hitler' at the German embassy in Dublin but had not done so for President Roosevelt, and hadn't the Republic of Ireland provided the Blue Brigade to fight for Franco in the Spanish Civil War and later for Hitler? I conceded that for someone who was supposed to be a brilliant mathematician, de Valera had not always acted very intelligently in international diplomacy. Anyhow, I reposted, hadn't the Republic's government turned a blind eye to RAF aircraft overflying their territory to shorten the route of anti-submarine patrols to the Atlantic from RAF Ballykelly and Lough Erne? Didn't they always let downed RAF aircrew escape back over the border to rejoin the fight while continuing to intern captured German aircrew? We could never agree and often found ourselves arguing against our own case.

My mother was a lady of contrasts. She had been born and raised in the small coastal village of Castlerock. Her parents were members of the decent poor, and she was disappointed that her parents could not raise the money for her to take her place training to be a teacher. She left school at fourteen but she was widely read, and she was a deadly whist player. In her teens, she had trained as a cook in a chain of the large tourist hotels across Northern Ireland but after her marriage she cleaned the houses of middle class-ladies and often cooked for them when they were laying on dinner parties. Her social life revolved around the Mothers' Union, the British Legion, and whist drives. She encouraged my older sister Kathy and I to develop a wide range of interests while making sure that we always gave full attention to our schoolwork. Kathy passed the eleven-plus and took her place at Maddenstown High School for Girls. My mother took in sewing and worked into the night to help pay for Kathy's uniforms, books, and extra music lessons.

I passed the eleven-plus in 1958 but I never got to go to the boys' grammar school because my mother died of a stroke a week after we received the letter confirming my success. This event knocked the stuffing out of my father who had now gone onto reduced hours because of his war injuries. I joined a special academic class at the local College of Technology, the Tech, where everything was free.

I received a very good technical and scientific education, and I widened my circle of acquaintances because, unusually, the Tech was both co-educational and mixed in terms of religion. I never, ever recall fearing any examination, and I eventually gained three good 'A' levels in 1965. I applied and secured a place to read Physics at Manchester University where I spent three idyllic years playing poker, boozing, chasing girls, and playing cricket in the summer term. Kathy didn't go to university; her 'A' levels took her into banking where she met and married a Scotsman on detachment to her branch in Northern Ireland. She followed him back to Scotland, leaving my father on his own to look after our large council house. My father's family had come from Coleraine, so he was fortunate to get a transfer to a smaller ex-serviceman's bungalow in Coleraine. It never crossed my mind at the time that the transfer was made easier because both of my grandfathers had been prominent in the ruling Unionist Party, and both had been masters of their local Orange Lodge.

Still, I was glad to get back to uni after helping my dad to move into his bungalow. I had always had a fascination with things military and guns so

I joined the Officer Training Corps and spent many a happy hour on the shooting range but never seriously considered a military career. I made enough money at poker, in my second year, to subsidise a summer spent bumming around the Mediterranean. I had become very aware in my banter with English students, at Manchester, that my technical education had left me very ignorant of the humanities. I took part-time jobs in Nice, Sorrento, and Corfu. I didn't always drink myself stupid; I was a culture vulture, and I took in the lot - the Royal Palace at Monaco, opera in the coliseum in Verona, Mount Vesuvius, and the Amalfi Coast but it was in Corfu that I settled down to spend the last six weeks of my vacation.

I was amazed to find that they played cricket on Corfu and had done for 150 years since the Royal Navy had been based there in the Napoleonic Wars. I wandered down to the Esplanade one Saturday afternoon to find a cricket pavilion and a game in full swing. I was further surprised to find out that both teams were made up largely of Corfiats with a few long-term resident Brits. I had a few beers and got talking to some Englishmen who told me that they were to hold a game on a private estate on Sunday afternoon. When I learned that they were short of players I volunteered my services. They were reluctant at first. An Irish dosser who could play cricket? I exaggerated my exploits at Manchester University and managed to convince them to take me on after hinting that I had taken the wicket of a former England player who had turned out for a Lancashire eleven. I didn't tell them that he was in his fifties and half-pissed at the time and had actually hit his own wicket. They gave me directions and told me how to get a bus out to the estate.

Next morning I hunted out a pair of nearly white trousers and a long-sleeved white shirt. I had no suitable boots so I wore a pair of Bondu boots. I walked down to the square and caught a bus out to the gates of the estate. As I was walking up the avenue, a shooting brake stopped, and one of my drinking companions of the day before gave me a lift. We came out of the tree-lined avenue, and I was astonished to see a Victorian colonial mansion with a well-tended cricket pitch to the front. I was assigned to one of the teams, and I told the captain that I never could bat so he put me in at number eleven. My team was not very good and we had just made 83 when it was my turn to bat. I was duly out first ball, and my teammates could hardly disguise their scorn as I walked back to the pavilion. The ladies offered us cucumber sandwiches and glasses of Pimms and what ladies they were. It seemed as if we were back in the nineteen-twenties with their silk dresses and the genteel conversation.

"Played for Manchester University, did we?" brayed one of my teammates. "I take it that you didn't open the batting." This brought a ripple of laughter. I made an extra effort to make myself useful in the field throwing myself at the ball when others might have let it run by. I reckoned that I had saved about ten runs when I took a difficult catch at the boundary. Our bowling was flagging when I persuaded our captain to give me a couple of overs. I bowled my usual medium pace but with a very good line and length and soon took four wickets including the opposing captain. This helped us to win by three runs.

After that my place was assured, and it opened a whole new social world to me. I played every weekend and sometimes on a Wednesday afternoon, but I was also invited to dinners and beach parties. My hosts were mainly English ex-patriots but a few Corfiats and mainland Greeks were also in our sporting and social circle. I also made use of my skill at whist, taught to me by my mother, but I never did get hooked on bridge. The real money was to be made at the late-night poker sessions, and I was soon able to give up my bar jobs. I made a point of sometimes bluffing outrageously to give them a chance to get some of their money back and, I made myself a reputation as an easy mark at snooker that was sometimes able to win luckily but only when the money was right.

All things considered, I was well ahead financially whilst making myself pleasant company. The women were out of my league but I did receive the occasional invitation from a bored wife, which I fended off graciously. My father had warned me that 'hell hath no fury like a woman scorned'. He had also told me how to get rid of the 'ladies of the night', and there were plenty of them in Corfu, without giving offence by simply telling them that I had no money.

I returned to Manchester for my final year when I got stuck into some serious studying. I never did have a serious girl friend at uni; it was the cricket in the summer term, which just stopped me from getting a first when I graduated in 1968. I spent that whole summer playing cricket, whist and poker in Corfu, and when the season ended I decided to have a gap-year. I had enough money saved to visit mainland Greece, more Greek islands, the Turkish coast, and finally Israel.

When I eventually returned to the UK in the spring of 1969, I realised that I would always need a long summer break, so I rejected industry for a career in teaching. I applied to Manchester again and enrolled for another year to take a Post Graduate Certificate in Education. I was lucky to get a job for the summer painting radio towers on RAF stations, which paid very well because of 'height and danger'. I needed transport to move around and landed on my feet again when a corporal at RAF Lyneham sold me his Morris Traveller at a snip when he was unexpectantly posted to a small island in the Indian Ocean. The woodie became my pride and joy.

I went home for a week with Dad in September and then returned to do the PGCE course, which I breezed through. I knew my subject inside out; I got hooked on Psychology, and I was surprised to find that I loved teaching young people. When it came time to start applying for a job, I was very conscious that my father was aging rapidly. He always sent me the local newspaper, and I noticed that there was a post advertised for a Physics teacher at the Tech. I sent off for an application form which I filled in and posted back straightaway. I was surprised to be invited for an interview a week later. I'm not saying that the interview was a formality, but I was well qualified, an 'old boy', and the Chairman of Governors had marched in the same Orange Lodge as my mother's father.

I received dispensation to move in with my father as his carer but I knew that it would never work out. In September 1970 I began my teaching career at the Tech, and I looked forward to a job that I loved with plenty of time for poker, whist, cricket, beer, and horse racing to fill my spare time. After a year, I took, what was then, the massive step of applying for a mortgage, because I had a good salary and enough in my poker nest-egg for the deposit on a small Victorian, terraced two-up and two-down in the centre of Maddenstown. It had just been renovated with the addition of a modern kitchen downstairs and a beautiful black-tiled bathroom above it. I had a wonderful life without a care in the world, apart from Dad, until the day of the bomb!

Chapter 3 – Basic Training

One morning in, early August, the postman brought me a buff OHMS envelope. I opened it excitedly. I was instructed to report to the UDR barracks at the old school on Magilligan Road. I was to be prepared to spend five days training, and I should bring a packed lunch daily. I was still on my summer break from teaching, so that did not pose any problems.

The following Monday, just before eight o'clock, I drove up to the main gate of the UDR barracks which was in a disused primary school whose perimeter had been sealed off with a high panelled wall with coils of razor-wire on top. A notice proclaimed that this was the home of 'J' Company of the 5th (Co Londonderry) Battalion of the Ulster Defence Regiment.

There was a sangar at the main gate, which was protected by sandbags. When I stopped, a rifle poked out of a slit, and a soldier came through a smaller door set into the main gate. I showed him the letter inviting me to attend, and he told me where I should park after I entered.

The gate was swung open and I drove through to park on what must have formerly been a playground. The soldier had followed me in and he came up to me to direct me to the front door of the old schoolhouse. I was met by a corporal who checked my name against a list on a clipboard. He led me to a rest room where there were two other young civvies being spoken to by a very tall, smart looking soldier in his mid-fifties.

"Sir!" the corporal barked. "This is Charles Cunningham, come to join."

The tall man looked me over, and I instinctively stood to attention and pulled my shoulders back.

The corporal told me that this was Company Sergeant-Major Dougan and that I should address him as 'sir' ".

"Well, Cunningham, you look like an ex-serviceman. What regiment?" asked the CSM.

"No, sir, I did two years in the Officer Training Corps at Manchester University," I replied.

"Sweet Jesus! The OTC, still we won't hold that against you," Dougan said with a twinkle in his eye.

He told me to take a seat while we waited for two more recruits to join us. I looked around at the two who were already there. There was a young chap aged about eighteen and a big ruddy-faced man of about forty. We were soon joined by two other young men in their mid-twenties.

"Right! Listen up," said the CSM. "We are going to take you to Derry to collect your kit. Then you're going to Shackleton Barracks at Ballykelly to start basic training. Report here in uniform at the same time tomorrow, and we'll get you sworn in by the Major."

We were herded out to a battered old army mini-bus. I was concerned to see that the driver was an old civilian, and our only protection came from one soldier carrying a sub-machine-gun.

We set off to Derry, twenty miles away. I was relieved to see that we met an army mobile patrol every two miles or so, who gave us a toot. We did not go into Derry but pulled into the old naval barracks at HMS Sea Eagle, which, I noticed from a large board, was now called Ebrington Barracks, home of the 5th (Co Londonderry) Battalion of the Ulster Defence Regiment.

We pulled up at the edge of a parade ground outside of an old redbrick building, which was labelled as a clothing store. We went in, under the supervision of our guard and were marshalled along a counter that ran the whole length of the building. Behind the counter there were a corporal and an old civilian in a dustcoat. As we moved along the counter, we were asked for our vital statistics and given a kitbag, two pairs of boots, plimsolls, steel helmet, webbing, three khaki shirts, two pairs of long johns, socks, scarf, beret, you name it.

We were then ushered into a room where our guard ordered us to change into uniform.

"Keep on your own underwear but change everything else," he bellowed. "Put on the dimpled boots, and don't attempt to put on the puttees."

As usual, the army had only two sizes – too big and too small. We joked at the sight of each other and exchanged items in some cases for a better fit.

The supply corporal came in and laughed his head off. "Anybody want to come back out to change anything?" he asked.

One chap had discovered that he didn't really know his shoe-size, so he went out to change his boots. Another guy decided that he needed much larger shirts. Eventually we lined up for inspection. We had been issued with the old pattern NATO style, olive-green, battle dress. We looked a sight. Our guard showed us how to fix our badge to our rifle-green berets and how to wear the beret with the badge over our left eye and the beret pulled over to the right.

The corporal came back in with a clipboard and told us to sign for the 'Queen's uniform' and warned us to look after it.

We stuffed our civvies and extra gear into our kit bags and ambled out to the mini-bus. As we did, we were confronted by a sergeant wearing a much superior uniform with a scarlet sash.

"What the fucking hell have we got here?" he roared. "What a fucking shower! Is this Ulster's last line of defence? Is this NATO's fucking western flank? God help us!"

His beret was dark blue, and he spoke with a northern English accent; he must have been a regular.

"Get them into that fucking bus and off my fucking parade ground!" he shouted to our guard, but I could see that it was all an act. When we got into the mini-bus, our escort told us that we had just met Staff Sergeant Warburton of the Prince of Wales' Own Regiment of Yorkshire but now attached to our training team.

We drove back a few miles east to what used to be RAF Ballykelly a famous Coastal Command air base. As we drove in, I saw a sign saying 'D' Company of 5 UDR and calling the base Shackleton Barracks.

We pulled up outside of an old office block and we were led into a rest room to be given cups of hot, sweet army tea. We were sprawling around on armchairs when a sergeant with a crown above his stripes came into the room. I had the sense to spring up to attention, and the others followed my lead.

"Stand easy, lads, sit down. I'm Staff Sergeant Montgomery. I'm from 'J' company but I have been detached to the battalion training staff. I will be training you for the next five days. We're just waiting for some more recruits from Derry to join us, and then we'll make a start."

He sat down with us and quietly asked us questions about ourselves. We learned that he had been a regular in the Royal Irish Rangers and had been called out of retirement to help set up the UDR. He came over as an intelligent, quietly spoken man in his late forties. He showed us how to wind our puttees around our ankles and how to tuck the tapes on the inside of the legs.

"That's a lot smarter looking, and it will support your ankles and keep out the wet," he told us.

We were joined by six other, new recruits from Derry. Altogether we were a cross-section of Ulstermen but I was pretty sure that there were no Catholics in our squad.

Staff Montgomery, as we learned to call him, took us outside and began to teach us the rudiments of foot drill. He told us that we would not be issued with weapons until we had been sworn in.

We learned how to form a double filed squad according to height, how to 'dress' ourselves, which meant spacing ourselves out properly and how to quick march and slow march. Then he took us into a makeshift classroom where he issued us with a notebook and a pencil. He taught us about the history of the regiment and how it was organised. We also learned how to recognise and speak to people of different ranks.

We stopped and had our lunch. A civilian lady arrived and poured large cans of sausages and baked beans into a massive saucepan. She issued us with billycans and ladelled large servings into them. I picked out the sausages, which I gave to my comrades, and I dipped my cheese-rolls into the beans.

The lady topped up the urn of tea by the simple method of pouring in a packet of loose tea and the contents of a two-pound bag of sugar. She finished off by pouring in cans of condensed milk. She turned up the heat and was soon serving mugs of army tea, which was surprisingly good.

After lunch, Staff Montgomery came back and told us that we were going out for more drill. We formed up the squad or section as he called it, and we were taught how to salute and how to dismiss. We soon learned why, when we were joined by an officer in combat uniform wearing the crown of a major.

We went through our drill, marched past with eyes right, and dismissed with 'officer on parade' when we gave him a salute. He expressed his satisfaction and thanked us for giving up our time. Staff Montgomery gave him a very smart salute, and the major left us.

"That was Major Roper-Wickham, the battalion training major. He's a regular on attachment to us, and you'll notice that he's not too proud to wear our green beret," said the staff sergeant. "Right, back to the classroom for first-aid instruction."

At four o'clock the staff sergeant informed us that we would be sworn in at our company headquarters the next morning and would then be issued with self-loading rifles.

"Then it's back here for rifle-drill, and if the weather is OK, we're off to the range in the afternoon." Then he dismissed us.

When we went outside, the mini-bus was waiting for us. We drove back to Maddenstown, and then I drove home in my uniform. I was very self-conscious about getting out and walking fifty yards to my front door,

14

carrying my kitbag. I went in but now I realised that lots of my neighbours now knew that I was a part-time soldier.

I reported bright and early next morning in my uniform. When the others arrived, we went to get our photographs taken for our ID cards. Then CSM Dougan joined us and told us that we were going to be marched in to meet Major Crawford the company commander.

The CSM and the five of us crowded into what previously must have been the headmaster's office. Willie Crawford was seated behind a desk. I knew all about him. He was a director of the family business, which was a large milk processing plant on the outskirts of town. As a young man he had won the Military Cross in the Korean War where he had served as a lieutenant in the Royal Ulster Rifles. I also knew that he had served with my grandfather in the Ulster Special Constabulary - the 'B' Specials – in the mid-fifties campaign against the old IRA.

Major Crawford welcomed us and gave us a pep talk, and then we were formally sworn in on the Bible. It was easier for me to go with the flow and pretend that I was a Christian. The major then came around from behind his desk and shook hands with us individually. He made chitchat, and when he heard my name he mentioned that he had served in the 'B' Specials with my grandfather.

He warned us to be careful about our personal security, especially to check under our cars. He told us that the UDR were no longer permitted to take their rifles home, another concession to nationalist politicians, but that he would support our applications for licences to carry a personal firearm – a small calibre pistol.

We were marched out and gathered in the rest room where CSM Dougan handed out applications for firearm certificates.

"OK, last thing, lads," he said. "You'll all need to get a haircut. It doesn't have to be US Marines style. If you go to Tommy Batchelor on Station Street, tell him what you need; you can trust him."

Then came the moment that we had been waiting for. We were taken to the armoury where we were issued, and signed for, our own 7.62mm Self Loading Rifle and two magazines. No ammunition yet, of course. I was very proud of my rifle, which was a brand new example with a black fibreglass stock and butt. The last four digits of the serial number had been stencilled in white on the inside of the butt, and I had to memorise it.

Then it was out to the mini-bus and on our way to Shackleton Barracks. Staff-Sergeant Montgomery was there to greet us, and the Derry boys were already in the tearoom. When break was over, we were taken into the classroom where the staff sergeant showed us how to strip, clean, and re-assemble our rifles.

One of the young lads from Maddenstown, Noel Gibson, kept getting things wrong but he kept us amused with a string of banter. Montgomery took this in good spirit and patiently guided young Gibson until he got it right.

Then it was outside for drill with the rifles. I had mastered rifle-drill in the OTC with the old Lee Enfield .303 inch, which had served the British Army for eighty years. But this was different. Because the SLR had a large carrying handle and had a twenty round magazine, it was not possible to slope arms. We marched with the rifle at order arms by our side and carried it, less formally, by the handle.

After lunch we were marched for the best part of a mile to a firing range. We were given thirty rounds and told to load fifteen rounds each into the two magazines. It was good practice not to fill a magazine to full capacity, which would strain the spring. Then we went in groups of four to the firing position. We were taught how to fire while standing, kneeling, and lying down. The targets were only twenty-five yards away so that our rifles could be zeroed. When we had fired twenty rounds, the range sergeant studied our grouping and then produced a tool to adjust our sights.

I had achieved a very tight grouping but slightly off-centre. Now when I fired the remaining ten rounds, I put them all through the bull in the chest of the Russian soldier target.

"Where did you learn to shoot, soldier?" asked the range sergeant.

When I told him that I had been in the OTC he replied, "Well, they're not completely fucking useless then. Well done, we'll make a marksman out of you."

I noticed with surprise that all of the other recruits had peppered their targets all over. When young Gibson came to shoot he even managed to hit the wooden stake that supported the target and had brought it down.

"Thank you very fucking much for destroying the Queen's property!" shouted the range sergeant, which provoked a round of raucous laughter.

"I was aiming for the stake," protested Gibson to further jeers.

Before leaving the range we attested that "I have no live rounds or empty cases in my possession, Sergeant!"

We marched back to the classroom where we cleaned our weapons. We were told that it was a punishable offence to hand in a dirty weapon.

Staff Montgomery made us strip and re-assemble our SLRs again and again until four o'clock. Then the mini-bus arrived to take us back to Maddenstown but we were not allowed any ammunition. So if we get ambushed, I thought, we have got only one man with a loaded weapon.

I drove home and got out of my uniform. I prepared my evening meal, and then I spent an hour with my notebook going over everything, which we had been taught so far. I watched my newly acquired TV for a couple of hours and then had an early night.

Wednesday morning came quickly; it was a beautiful day when I drove into the barracks. I signed for my weapon and was also given a flak jacket but no ammunition. An hour later we were in the classroom in Ballykelly with the staff sergeant. He used diagrams and models to instruct us how to set up a VCP, a vehicle check point. He explained the positioning and the duties of every member of a VCP. He issued each of us with a yellow card that explained the circumstances under which we could fire our weapons.

"But I warn you lads, don't count on it if it gets to a court of law. My best advice is only to shoot at a definite target if the terrorist is about to do something that endangers your life or some other person's. Fire two rounds at their chest, don't fire to wound, never over their head and never into a vehicle or house unless you can see a target," he emphasised.

Then we marched off to a proper rifle range. We were issued with the usual thirty rounds and we fired at targets at 50, 100 and 200 yards. I was pleased to confirm that I was the best shot in the cadre as the range sergeant called the section.

We marched back for lunch, which was the same as the previous two days. Staff Montgomery mingled with us informally while we ate. He told us that it was very unlikely that we would ever have to fire our weapons in earnest, and if we did, it was most likely to be at a range of twenty-five to fifty yards. This consoled some of the lads who had not made a great showing on the range.

Then we were taken out to practise setting up VCPs. He showed us how to attach one end of the rifle-sling to the butt of our rifle and how to fix the other end securely around our right wrist. He called Noel Gibson out to the front of the section and grabbed his rifle from him. Young Gibson had attached the rifle-sling to the stock of his SLR near the barrel. The staff sergeant was able to pull the rifle away from Gibson and point it at him.

"Bang, bang, you're dead!" shouted the staff sergeant.

Staff Montgomery explained to us that in the early days of the troubles, a young regular soldier had made the same mistake when confronting a mob in Belfast. One of the crowd had grabbed the rifle and turned it on the soldier and killed him. The terrorist had then taken the SLR off the body and disappeared into the crowd before the rest of the platoon could catch him.

Montgomery then called me out. When he grabbed my rifle he couldn't turn it on me because there was not enough slack between us. He had made his point and most of us never forgot it.

We had two Landrovers and a civilian car and drivers at our disposal, so we spent a couple of hours driving around the airfield and the admin buildings setting up VCPs at various points. We were taught how to address the public and what to look out for. We learned to watch drivers when we asked them for their vehicle number because criminals and terrorists who had stolen vehicles often wrote the registration number on the sunshields and looked up to read them. We learned never to open the boots of cars and always to get the driver out to do it. Staff Montgomery also showed us how to search men for suspicious objects.

"What do we do with women?" asked Noel Gibson.

"Leave them to a Greenfinch," replied the staff sergeant and then seeing the look of bewilderment on our faces went on to say, "We are recruiting female members called Greenfinches. Juliet Company hasn't got any yet but you Derry boys must have seen them."

Then he produced a sack and took out a weird object. These were caltrops, a set of metal spikes clustered in fours so that when thrown on the ground one of the three-inch spikes was always pointing upward. Forty or fifty of these were threaded onto a chain attached to a rope. The rope lay across the road at the front or rear of the VCP. If a vehicle tried to drive through the VCP without stopping, a soldier pulled the rope that pulled the chain and caltrops in a barrier across the road. The theory was that the tyres would be punctured.

When we returned to the classroom, Staff Montgomery made us sign for two magazines and thirty rounds. He told us that we could take them home but should bring them every time that we were on duty. We loaded fifteen rounds in each, because magazines were never fully charged to ease the strain on the spring. He took us outside where there was a sandpit. He showed us how to load the magazine with the rifle pointed at the sand but he cautioned us never to cock our rifles unless directly ordered to.

We boarded the mini-bus. I wasn't sure whether or not I felt safer with five of us with loaded rifles. We handed our rifles into the armoury at Maddenstown but kept our magazines. When I got home, I spent twenty minutes practising emptying and loading the mags. Then I spent another twenty minutes drawing plans for VCPs for various road configurations from memory. I must have listened to my lecturer on the psychology of learning when I did my PGCE at Manchester University.

When we arrived at Shackleton barracks on Thursday morning, we were surprised to find Staff-Sergeant Warburton waiting for us in the classroom with the Derry lads.

"Right lads, Staff Montgomery can't be with you today, so you've got me. Let's get outside and find out what you can do."

We went outside and formed two ranks. Warburton brought us to attention and to order arms. He gave us a right turn and then marched us off. As we were marching he sidled up beside me and whispered into my ear "Just like little guardsmen."

"Fucking railway guardsmen!" he roared.

He gave us thirty minutes of close-order drill marching fast and slow. Inevitably, young Gibson was soon out of step and received a tongue-lashing.

He halted us and gave us a left turn. Then to 'at ease'. He inspected us minutely. Kneeling down to see if the laces of our boots had been threaded army fashion and how neat our puttees were. Then it was our rifles. He cocked, hooked and looked at each rifle but he couldn't fault us for cleanliness. He looked disappointed as he marched us back to the classroom.

In the classroom he ordered us in turn to blindfold ourselves with our scarves. Then we had to empty our magazines and then reload them against the clock. He taught us how to strip our SLRs and reassemble them while we were blindfolded.

"Remember, 90 per cent of your duties will be at night," he told us.

After a lunch-break we were herded back into the classroom where Staff Warburton told us to sit at attention. He opened the door, and in strode a captain wearing a UDR beret.

"Relax, lads, sit easy, and get your note-books out. I'm Captain Blair Leslie; I'm the Intelligence Officer with 'A' company. I want to spend some time giving you advice about your personal security."

He told us that, so far, the UDR had lost three times as many members off duty as on duty. He warned us about vehicle security, postal security, and home security. He showed us simple techniques for checking our cars, opening post, and securing our homes. Two of the Maddenstown lads lived on farms, so he spent some time focusing on farm-gates and machinery.

"Now I want to turn to kidnapping. The regiment has lost a dozen members who have been kidnapped and tortured to death."

He warned us about entering Republican areas. Some of the lads were drivers who had to deliver to remote locations. Captain Leslie's advice was to carry a personal firearm and to reach for it when first accosted by strangers.

"Never let yourself be kidnapped easily. Start the fight at the first approach. Even if you don't have a pistol, pretend that you do, pretend to reach for it, better to be shot there and then than to be tortured. If you are taken and tortured, remember two things. You will talk and you will die. Spin them a load of shit. If you know any Republican sympathisers give up their names as informants. Sow dissent among them. But remember, you will die so don't get taken."

The room had become deathly quiet. I looked around. The faces of my compatriots were in stone.

"Last thing," said Captain Leslie. "Most of you lads are under thirty, and you are mostly unmarried. This is mainly for the Derry lads. Maddenstown is a protestant town but Derry is fifty-fifty. It has to be said. Ninety-nine per cent of Republican supporters are Catholics. When you go out to get pissed, and you are hitting the dance halls and discos looking to get your leg over, be very suspicious of that Catholic girl who gets very friendly too quickly. I know that it's bollocks over brains, and you won't be thinking about it but please, ask yourself. Is she in a higher league than the girls you normally go out with? Why is she so keen for you to take her home or to go out to the car park?

Another thing. Do not carry your personal firearm when you are going out drinking. You are more likely to hurt yourself or some innocent by-stander, or you are likely to lose it. Or worse still, you'll pull it and end up getting shot by the security forces. There has been only one occasion where an off-duty UDR man used his pistol successfully against a terrorist."

He thanked us and wished us good-luck. Warburton gave the captain an immaculate salute before he left us. We had another half hour of rifle drill before the staff sergeant dismissed us. As he left us, he warned us that on Friday we would be tested on everything we had been taught. I spent the evening going over my notes. I was confident. For Christ's sake, I had passed a Physics degree with honours.

Next morning we drew our rifles and formed up to wait for the mini-bus. Corporal David Pollock of the permanent base guard supervised us as we loaded our weapons at the sandpit. Unusually, Corporal Pollock joined us on the bus. On the way to Ballykelly, he told us that he had done nine years as a regular with the RAF Regiment and had seen action in Aden.

When we got to Shackleton barracks we were guided into the classroom. I was surprised to see that Corporal Pollock had joined us and that the Derry contingent had also brought a corporal.

Staff Montgomery addressed us. "I trust that you had a pleasant time yesterday with Staff Sergeant Warburton. He tells me that you are just about ready to take your tests. As you can see, we've got Corporals Pollock and Henry with us today. They are going to put you through your paces, so that I can observe, and it will also give them practice for their sergeant exams. OK, outside for foot drill."

Corporal Pollock gave us thirty minutes dressing, drilling, marching, saluting, and presenting arms. Then Corporal Henry marched us to the rifle range. We had to fire five rounds standing, kneeling, and lying down. I was very happy with my performance. The corporals watched closely as we stripped our weapons and cleaned them. We had to reload the empty magazine blindfolded against the clock. Again, I was very happy but I could hear other people dropping rounds and swearing.

"Don't put a fucking dirty round into your magazine!" shouted Pollock. "It will jam just when you need it." I assumed that he was bawling at Noel Gibson.

We marched back to HQ and had the usual lunch, and then it was into the classroom again.

Corporal Henry took us while Pollock and Montgomery sat at the back of the room.

"Right, lads, I'm going to take you over basic procedures and knowledge before Major Roper-Wickham tests you, and you do a written exam."

Corporal Henry made us strip and re-assemble our weapons and empty and re-fill our mags while blindfolded. Then we were sat at separate desks.

"I'm going to ask questions around the class. I will point at a specific man. If he gets it wrong or can't answer, I will point to another man and so on. Don't shout out or whisper the answers; it might get to you anyway."

He asked us questions on regimental organisation, first-aid, army law, VCP management, names of post-holders in the company, and the battalion and basic radio procedures. I had no problems but I noticed that others sometimes stumbled. Meanwhile, Pollock and Montgomery were taking notes. This went on for an hour, then we were sent for a tea break while Staff and the corporals stayed behind in the classroom. We were called in after thirty minutes. I looked around. I expected to see exam papers on the desks, and I looked in vain for the major.

When we were sitting, Staff Montgomery took over. "Has anyone seen the major?" he asked.

We all answered in the negative.

"That's right, he isn't coming. You've had your test, and you have all passed. Some with flying colours," and I sensed that he was looking at me, "And some just made it. No names, no pack-drill. Well, lads, welcome to the family, have a good weekend because you will be expected to do duties next week. Good luck!"

We turned to congratulate ourselves. I was to find out later that this was a common practice in the army, to use a practice session as the real exam because the candidates were less nervous. Corporal Pollock rounded us up and took us out to the mini-bus. I had a chance to thank Brian Montgomery and shake his hand before we mounted up. His last words to me were, "Give it six months and then apply for a commission. We need keen, young, intelligent officers. I fear that things are going to get worse. I hope that you are giving me the orders some day." He was still chuckling as I stepped up into the bus.

When I parked the woodie in Union Street, I pulled my shoulders back and looked people in the eye as I strode to number nine. I reckoned that I deserved a few pints, and I planned my evening accordingly.

Chapter 4 – First Duty

School restarted on the Monday, and I was due to perform my first duty on the following evening. I could not relax throughout the weekend. As I tried to mark a sixth-form Physics test, which I should have done over the holidays, I found that I was not taking in what the students had written. I was clutching a script but staring through it as I worried about how I would live up to expectations. Would I know what to do if we made contact? Would I let my compatriots down? I couldn't even concentrate on the racecards when I made my usual Saturday morning visit to the bookies. I couldn't sleep as I wondered whether I had made the correct decision to join the UDR. On Monday I had managed to struggle through a day's teaching but had been thrown off balance by a conversation with Linda May.

Linda was a recently appointed teacher in the English department. She was a few years younger than I, and although she was a local, our paths had never previously crossed because she had attended the girls' High School. She was a very attractive girl, tall, slim, and athletic with a dark brown pageboy. I was definitely interested and had caught her eye across the staff-room a few times. We were placed in the same tutor-team, which had led to me getting to know her.

One evening, we had a tutor-team meeting after school. Afterwards, we walked out to the car park together, and I heard her gasp when she noticed that her old Austin A40 had a flat.

"I've got a netball match at the High School," she wailed. "I play for their staff team even though I work at the Tech. What am I going to do now? I'm not in the AA."

"Don't worry," I said. "I'll do it, and you'll be on your way in ten minutes."

I opened the tailgate and lifted the carpet. Fair enough, she had a spare tyre that was reasonably inflated but I couldn't find a tyre-lever or a jack. I went to my old woodie and got out my tools and my trusted jack. The nuts on her wheel were so rusted that I had to stand on the arm of my wheel wrench to budge them. When they were loose, I took off my jacket and crawled under her heap to find a secure jacking-point. I jacked the A40 up and had soon changed the wheel.

"There, that will do you but you will have to put some air in this tyre before much longer. I'll take your flat to the garage and get it sorted out, and I'll swap them back tomorrow."

"Thank you, Charlie," she gushed. "Whatever would I have done without you?" She leaned over and pecked my cheek, giving me a whiff of her alluring perfume. "Look at your shirt; you've ruined it, and it's all my fault."

I sent her on her way and no, I didn't take the opportunity to ask her out when I swapped the tyres back again, even though she appeared keen and had hinted that she wasn't seeing anyone. Another of my priggish principles was not to get involved with work colleagues.

On the Monday before my first duty, I ran into Linda as we shared adjoining playground duties.

"What happened to your lovely hair, Charlie? Isn't that a bit severe?"

"Oh, it's just something that I had to do," I said airily.

"Don't tell me you have joined the security forces, Charlie! Now we'll never get together. My brother is a reserve police officer and me and my ma worry every time he's on duty. I couldn't face another one to worry about."

I tried to make light of it. "Don't worry about me. I've joined the UDR but I intend to keep my head down."

The bell sounded before we could say anymore.

I didn't get a chance to speak to Linda on Tuesday. I went home straight after my last lesson to get my head down for a couple of hours. Of course, I couldn't sleep but I felt rested. I made myself a good feed of pasta that would release energy slowly over the next ten hours. I made myself cheese and pickle sandwiches and a flask of coffee. Then I got dressed. I rejected the long johns. I polished my boots. I checked that I had fifteen rounds in each magazine, made sure that my puttees were neat and checked my beret in the mirror, UDR badge over my left eye, all OK.

At seven-thirty I went out and got into the woodie. A couple of neighbours gave me a second glance but it must have been common knowledge by now that I was a 'UDR man'. I drove through the one-way system but was not aware of other drivers giving me a sideways look. I had no bother getting into the base. The permanent staff all knew my car by now. I parked and took a couple of minutes to pull myself together, and then I walked into HQ. It was a hive of activity. One section from each of the three platoons had turned out for duty along with others looking for a spare duty. I wasn't sure what to do when a tall, good-looking soldier approached me and stuck out his hand.

"Hello, Charlie, I'm Lieutenant Roddy Houston in charge of 33 Platoon. You're with us. Come and meet the lads."

I later discovered that things were usually free and easy with first name terms in the UDR. I knew Roddy by reputation. He had been a well-known athlete in his younger days, and I knew that he now taught at a primary school in Coleraine. He introduced me to my Section Commander, Corporal John Madison, who I did know. Years ago he had played in the same flute marching band as my cousins. He was in his early forties, carrying a lot of bulk, which I later found out was mostly muscle. Young Noel Gibson turned up a few minutes later, and he was also assigned to Madison's section. The UDR was a light infantry unit. There were eleven battalions in Northern Ireland. A battalion of about one thousand men was divided into between four and nine companies unlike regular units, which had three or four rifle companies. Each company was commanded by a major and was divided into between three and five platoons of about twenty-five men. A platoon was divided into three or four sections of about eight men led by a corporal.

I was shown where to draw my rifle and flak jacket. I braced myself for going up country to face the IRA but the whole evening was an anti-climax. I learned that it was my section's turn to guard the base until four o'clock. The base emptied quickly as the other sections jumped into Landrovers and headed off to set up VCPs throughout the east of the county, to patrol the town, or to guard vital points such as police barracks or electricity generating plants.

Madison told me that my duties would alternate between patrolling the perimeter, manning the gate, and checking the identity of entrants and taking my turn in the sangar to cover the other guy at the gate. I was paired up with Alfie Thompson who was an old hand. He took me out to the sandpit to load our weapons but he warned me not to cock it because they were very wary of an accidental discharge, which had killed soldiers in the past.

The next hour was boredom mixed with apprehension. Alfie told me that there had never been an attack on the base but warned me that other UDR bases in the province had been attacked. He reckoned that it was unlikely that anyone could actually gain entrance to the base. An attack was more likely to be a bomb thrown over the wall or a massive truck bomb let off beside the perimeter fence.

After an hour we went to the rest room. There was a big turnout from our section, that evening so we were not required for another hour. I was given ring binders full of details of local players in all of the paramilitary groups, but mostly Provos, to get familiar with. I was surprised to note a few guys who I had been to school with. The security forces were obviously picking up a load of intelligence about local activists; in some cases they were suspected of having taken part in specific operations.

Then it was our turn to man the gate. Alfie said that he would check the cars in, and I was to cover him through a slit in the sangar wall. The sangar was a breezeblock built hut half in and half out of the boundary fence beside the main gate. It had been sheathed with a double bank of sandbags, especially the windows, but a slit had been left big enough to take an SLR. Outside of the main gate, there was a square with rows of small cottages forming two sides. The cottages were festooned with union jacks and Ulster flags. The third side of the square, to my right, was a low stonewall that was the boundary of a copse of trees. Alfie warned me to keep my eyes on the wall whenever he exposed himself but once again assured me that there had never been an attack.

The hour dragged. Only two vehicles had entered the base. One was a new Landrover being delivered to the company, and the other was an officer from another platoon coming in to do some late admin.

We had another hour off in the rest room. Some of the guys read paperbacks, some swapped war stories, and a few snoozed. Then Alfie and I went out to patrol the perimeter again. As we ambled around, Alfie told me his story. He was forty-two, married with two kids. He had a small dairy farm near Limavady. He had been a 'B' Special policeman since he was eighteen and had been one of the few permitted to transfer to the UDR probably because he had never had the time to join the Orange Order. He surprised me when he told me that he did four duties each week because he relied on the money. It had never crossed my mind that the UDR got paid the same rate as the regular army. He also told me that he had been awarded the General Service Medal but it was no big deal because most of the company had it after serving for twenty-eight days.

We went back to the rest room and got our heads down until the end of the duty. The other sections were returning to base by now, and the permanent cadres were turning up for their day duty. I managed to get my rifle signed in before the rush, and I pulled out of the gate at five past four. I was in bed at four-thirty and very conscious that the alarm would ring at seven o'clock.

I felt reasonably refreshed as I taught my morning lessons, then I went to the staffroom. It was our habit to listen to the one o'clock news on an ancient radio. We were all shocked when we heard the leading story about the deaths of a UDR soldier and his daughter who had been blown up in their car outside of Garvagh. No more details were available.

I managed to get through the afternoon and resolved to turn out for duty that evening although it was not my section's turn. As I hurried out to the car park, I ran into Linda May who was leaning against my car. She appeared to be very distressed.

"My God, Charlie, isn't it dreadful," she sobbed. "I implore you to get out before you are sucked in. That man must have been from your battalion; you are all sitting ducks!"

I opened the car and got her to sit in the passenger seat. I reached her my crisp handkerchief and tried to calm her down. I told her that I wasn't going to take chances and that I was very aware of my own security.

"But you never even checked under the car before we got in, and I bet that you don't even carry a gun." She reached over and patted under my left armpit. I managed to get her calmed down and went round to let her out. She put her hand to my cheek and said, "Remember what I told you, Charlie. I was hoping that we would get somewhere but don't ask me while you are still in the UDR."

I went home and listened to the six o'clock news. I was totally shocked when the name of the murdered UDR soldier was announced as Brian Montgomery, my trainer at Ballykelly. It appeared that Brian left the house each morning at 8 o'clock to take his eight-year-old daughter to school before he went on to work at Ballykelly. He was renowned for meticulously checking his car with a mirror for underneath because it was parked overnight in his driveway. It appeared that this morning, he had been distracted by a bogus telephone call just as he left the house. The caller claimed to be a police officer that wanted Brian to call in to the police station immediately about a hit-and-run accident that his car was supposed to have been involved in.

There followed the usual parade of politicians condemning the attack and calling for tighter security, police appealing for information, and finally a Republican leader regretting the death of the child but warning that people who joined the security forces were putting their families at risk.

When I entered the base that evening, I found the car park full and had to be directed to the old school's tennis court, which was being used for the overflow. Inside the HQ was chaos. Half of the company had turned out. We were called to order by the CSM, and then the major addressed us.

"This was a foul deed; the scum must have known that Brian took his daughter to school. I want half of a section to guard Garvagh police station so that the officers can get on with this investigation. I want another half section at Kilrea police station. I want a full section to go up the Glen to set up

VCPs. I need people to guard vulnerable points all night - electricity stations, bridges, and the houses of prominent people. That includes Catholic politicians to show that we are even handed, and because I fear that some Loyalist hot-heads may be looking for revenge." He turned to a big, florid-faced corporal from another platoon. "Dougie, I want you to take your section into Kilrea and turn it upside-down."

There was a big cheer from the company. Then Lieutenant Houston came over to me and said, "Well done, Charlie, for turning out again tonight. I'm afraid that you will have to stay and guard the base with Andy Clark's section." He must have read the disappointment in my face. "Don't worry, you'll get lots of chances to go out. Next week you are on bomb patrol down the town."

The funeral was to be on Friday; Brian's wife wanted a military funeral with the full works. I arranged to take a day off work. There was no chance that I would take part in the funeral because I didn't have a 'best' uniform yet but I was detailed to help guard the area around the church just outside of Garvagh. My section was assigned to a ridge overlooking the church from two hundred yards away. Other sections manned VCPs in a ring around the area. We were supposed to look away from the church but it was very unlikely that terrorists would attack the funeral, so I was able to sneak glimpses of proceedings.

Hundreds of people attended the funeral and many had to stand outside while the service was relayed to them on loudspeakers. There appeared to be representatives of the police and from every regiment stationed in the province, each wearing their unique regimental dress. There was an audible sigh from the congregation when Brian's coffin was carried out by eight NCOs from 'J' Company, followed by four young men carrying the smaller coffin of his daughter. I was gutted when I saw Brian's sixteen-year-old son supporting his mother as the firing squad fired three volleys over the graves. I resolved, one way or another, to get back at the organisation responsible for the atrocity. So the Republican spokesman thought that the families of security men were legitimate targets; perhaps someone should make the families of terrorists' fair game.

Chapter 5 - Gawker Gallagher

I first met Danny Gallagher when I was a student at the Tech. Danny was an insignificant little runt who had shared many classes with me. He hung in there by the skin of his teeth and managed to scrape enough 'O' Levels to get a job as a local government clerk with Maddenstown Borough Council. Gawker had acquired his nickname because he wore glasses with very thick lenses. He often had to bend over his desk so that his eyes were a few inches from the textbook. A teacher had once shouted at him to 'stop gawking at your book' when he should have been looking at the board. Since then he had never lost the name 'Gawker'. I had not heard of Danny for almost ten years until one Friday evening before we set out on a UDR local bomb patrol when we were briefed on local houses of interest.

It appeared that someone at the Town Hall had been stealing from other employees' bags and desk drawers - money, jewellery, expensive pens, and chequebooks. The mayor authorised a search of the employees' private lockers by the sergeant-at-arms. Unsurprisingly, he didn't find any stolen items but when he searched Gallagher's locker, he found bags stuffed with electronic gear and Republican literature. The RUC were called in, and Gallagher was very soon lifted for questioning.

Gallagher was charged with involvement in terrorism and had appeared at the courthouse that morning. Unusually, Gallagher had pleaded 'not guilty' and had engaged a solicitor to defend him. Real, died in the wool Republicans never made a plea, they just refused to recognise the court.

Gallagher's defence was that he was building a model railway layout, which he was adapting to control electronically. I laughed when I heard this. My recollection was that Gallagher couldn't solder two wires together when we did Electronics at the Tech. His solicitor also made the point that the original search was illegal. The upshot was that the magistrate dismissed the charges.

The company intelligence officer, Captain David Armstrong, gave us this briefing. He told us that the gallery of the courthouse had been packed with local Republican sympathisers who had erupted with glee when the case was dismissed.

"Now listen up. Maybe Gallagher is innocent but he has made himself a target for local loyalist yobs or, he was lucky and he is a player, in which case we need to let him know that we are onto him," said Captain Armstrong.

He tasked us to swing by Gallagher's house regularly to keep an eye on things. We mounted up and drove down to the town square. Four of us got out and walked a bomb patrol through the commercial part of town. We met up with the Landrovers an hour later, then drove out to the Ballypatrick housing estate. We swung past Gallagher's house or rather his parents' house. Things were quiet, so we moved on and drove over to Limavady Street, the heart of Loyalism in the town. Four of us got out at one end of the street, and the Landrovers drove on to set up a VCP just outside of town.

Limavady Street was a prime target for the IRA. It wasn't barricaded because it was a main thoroughfare but it displayed all of the symbols that Republicans hated. The Orange Hall, a Free Presbyterian Church, red, white, and blue kerbstones and murals of King Billy on gable ends.

We walked the length of the street and had to suffer verbal abuse from drunken yobs. They claimed to be Unionists and Loyalists but they did not have the guts to join the part-time security forces. Not that most of them would have been accepted. They were the dregs of Ulster society. In the region of the UK that gained the highest educational successes and with the lowest, general crime-rate, these lowlives were mostly illiterate and many had picked up low-level criminal records.

We reached the far end of the street where we rendezvoused with the Landrovers returning from the VCP. We returned to base for refreshments but our break was interrupted by the duty comms corporal who alerted us that there was a mob outside of Gawker Gallagher's house. We jumped into the Landrovers and set off for the Ballypatrick estate.

The mob had barricaded one end of the street with two burning cars. Four of us jumped out and pushed our way past the hooded yobs that offered no resistance. We sprinted down to Gallagher's house and found a dozen young men shouting taunts and throwing pebbles at the house. They wore NATO jackets, just like ours, and jeans. Many had tartan scarves tied around one wrist and they were all hooded.

Just as we got there, someone threw a petrol bomb, which broke against Gallagher's door and burst into flames. Our brick was led by Corporal John Madison who pulled out his personal radio and called for police, ambulance, and fire brigade.

A lanky youth came to the front of the mob and attempted to light a second petrol bomb with a cigarette lighter. Madison shouted "British Army, drop the bottle!" but the yob ignored him and the crowd jeered. The bomber succeeded in lighting the rag around the neck of the milk bottle. Madison shouted, "Drop it, or I fire!" The bomber raised his arm to fling the bottle and then, to my surprise, John Madison fired a single shot from his Sterling. It

30

appeared to hit the youth in the chest. The youth dropped the petrol bomb, which broke and ignited and then he fell into the pool of burning petrol. Bobby Craig and I reached the youth simultaneously and pulled him clear of the flames. Bobby got down and sprawled over the bomber and succeeded in smothering the flames.

The crowd had run away by now and the bomber was screaming. That's a good sign, I thought, at least he's alive and breathing. At that point a police car and a fire engine had raced up from the other end of the street. A fireman gave the door to the house a few squirts from a hand held extinguisher. The petrol on the road was out by now.

John Madison was bringing an RUC sergeant up to speed when an ambulance pulled up. The bomber was loaded into the ambulance, and our corporal told Bobby and I to get in, too. As we sped along with the siren blaring, a medic treated the superficial burns on Bobby's hands and face. We soon arrived at Coleraine hospital where the bomber was taken into a theatre.

Bobby went off for further treatment while I sat in reception guarding his SLR. Twenty minutes later, an RUC Inspector turned up and told me that he intended to take a preliminary statement from me. I outlined the night's events as I recalled them.

"Are you absolutely sure that your corporal warned the young man before he fired at him?" asked the Inspector.

"Absolutely, he identified himself, and then he warned the bomber that he would fire."

"The alleged bomber," said the Inspector with a grin. "We don't know yet that Wilton threw the first petrol bomb, and he certainly didn't throw the second one."

"Wilton?" I asked.

"Yes, George Purcell Wilton aged seventeen."

"Jesus wept, I used to teach him." I remarked. "Not too bright. How is he? Do we know anything?"

"He'll live, he was lucky. The bullet was deflected by a rib, and it hit another rib, then came out. He's got two broken ribs and a minor flesh wound," answered the Inspector.

At that point a UDR sergeant from the Coleraine Company came in.

"We're here to take you and Bobby Craig back to Maddenstown. Is he fit to travel?" said the sergeant.

"Yes, he should soon be out." I turned to the Inspector, "Can we go now?"

"Yes, but you will all have to be interviewed formally at Maddenstown in the next couple of days," he informed me and then disappeared into the hospital.

Bobby came out to reception with his hands and face painted yellow. I reached him his rifle, and we went out to be taken home.

When we went into the rest room we met the others from our section.

"Where's John?" I asked. We were told that John Madison had been taken in by the RUC. The general consensus was that it had been a 'good' shooting and that John had stuck to the yellow card.

I went home thinking about how my first confrontation had been with so-called Loyalists and that the first shooting that I had witnessed had been against a young yob whom I used to teach.

Next morning, as I sat eating my cornflakes, I was called to the front door. It was a young RUC constable who reached me a summons to appear at Maddenstown RUC station at two o'clock that afternoon. I was annoyed that I would miss the big chase at Haydock on TV; I reckoned that I knew the winner.

I walked around the corner, in good time for my interview, and approached the sandbagged sangar outside the police station. I showed my summons and was let in through the front door. The desk sergeant sent for an Inspector who took me into an interview room. Another Inspector, the guy I had met at the hospital, was seated behind a desk. I was invited to sit down, and the local inspector joined his colleague from Coleraine.

Inspector Butler, the local man, then invited me to go through the previous night's events, which I did.

"Well, it looks like we've got a problem here," said Butler. "We've got witnesses who say that there was no warning given before the shot."

"I suppose that these are credible, upstanding, neutral citizens?" I put to him.

"No. These guys were part of the mob, I'll give you that, but they are very insistent that there was no warning."

"And what does the rest of the patrol say?" I asked.

"You guys had plenty of time to agree on your story," said the Coleraine Inspector.

"So it comes down to who you believe?"

"No, it comes down to who the judge believes," said Butler.

"This is bullshit," I protested. "Has Corporal Madison been charged?"

"Not yet. Are you sure that you don't want to change your statement before we take it in writing?" asked Butler.

"No way, let's do it now. I know what I saw and heard."

I wrote my statement, following their guidance, and then we all signed it. I went home with a dull ache in my stomach. Maybe we should have let Wilton throw the petrol bomb. Why were we rushing in to defend a possible Provo activist? Why the hell had we rushed away from our tea and sandwiches? I had joined up to get at the Provos, not to defend them.

By mid-September I was fully back into the swing of teaching at the Tech, and that was when it really hit me that holding down a demanding full-time job while serving at night in the UDR was stressful and tiring. I resolved to limit myself to one full night duty per week when I had to teach the next day, a short training evening on Thursdays, and a day duty at the weekend. By the end of September, I had tasted every type of duty. My favourite was country mobile where we went out setting up VCPs all over the east of County Londonderry, checking police stations, electricity sub-stations, and the homes of vulnerable people. My least favourite duties were guarding the electricity generating plant at Coolkeeragh near Londonderry and Saturday duties guarding the entrances to the city of Derry. Nights spent guarding the base were just boring, and local bomb patrols were amusing but I didn't rate them as part of the struggle against the PIRA.

On a rare Friday or Saturday evening, I played poker with old mates, or occasionally I went to a dance or a disco but I soon discovered that women lost interest very quickly when they heard that you were in the UDR. I tried to have a meal once each week with my father. The novelty of the UDR soon wore off when I realised that we were not there to take the fight to the terrorists. I rationalised that the boring day-to-day duties, which we did, released regular soldiers to carry the fight to the terrorists. It was years later that I learned that it was only the SAS who were truly pro-active. Also, Captain Armstrong, our intelligence officer, explained the true value of our efforts to the new recruits at a training evening.

By us setting up routine VCPs and carrying out bomb patrols, the terrorists could no longer carry out random attacks or move arms and explosives around as they felt like it. The risk of getting caught was too high. Now they had to carefully plan the timing of operations and movements to avoid UDR VCPs and patrols. This gave the opportunity for informants and

MI5 plants to tip the army off with precise information about timing and locations, and this was the source from which most arrests were made. It made me feel a bit better but I really wanted to make contact with the bastards.

Chapter 6 - Cynthia

I arose early on a Saturday morning in late October. I was excited because I had been invited by my platoon commander, Lieutenant Roddy Houston, to go for a morning's range practice out at Castlerock. I drove up to the barracks and went in to sign on. The place was crowded. One section of 34 Platoon had arrived to do guard duty, and another section was preparing to go to Derry to guard the gates into the city.

A dozen or more of my platoon had arrived to go shooting. All of the recent recruits were there but there was also a good turnout of old hands. Roddy came down from the Major's office with a clipboard, and he led us into a classroom. He called the roll and then told us to draw our weapons, and he made sure that we had brought our thirty rounds of ammunition for personal protection.

"I will bring a couple of bags of ammunition for us to shoot off." He turned to Sergeant Maguire and said, "What goodies have you got for us, George?"

Sergeant Maguire held up a Chinese copy of the AK47 assault rifle and an old Thompson sub-machine gun.

"I've also got a collection of pistols and some Schermuly flares. Everybody will have some fun."

We were to travel in an old mini-bus escorted by one Landrover. We travelled down the Glebe and made our way down to the sleepy, seaside village of Castlerock. We drove through the village and up over the railway tunnel entrance until we came to the gate-lodge of the avenue leading up to Downhill Castle. The gates were chained, so we parked and dismounted. We gained entrance through a pedestrian gate. Two guys were left to guard the vehicles.

Roddy had a key for a door in the high wall opposite the lodge. This door took us through to the moors. It was an area that I knew well because my mother had come from Castlerock. My sister and I had often been brought up to the moors to roam and to explore the castle.

There was an old 'B' Special firing range with a firing slope and butts for targets 300 yards away near the cliff-edge. Roddy also had a key to a small hut built into the wall. He picked four privates under Lance-Corporal Jim Toy to man the butts. They went into the hut and emerged with some NATO targets and a box of metal plates. One guy also carried a pot of white paint, a tub of glue, and strips of paper. The detail headed off down to the butts.

Roddy turned to me, "Charlie, I hear that you're a crack shot and don't need so much practice. I want you and Tim to go up that hill and guard our left flank." Tim was one of our Catholic members. He was in a different section but I recognised him as a local bus-driver.

"You're to warn off any members of the public who are straying in this direction. Jim will put up red flags, but I want you to be on your guard because we are sitting ducks down here."

Roddy must have read the disappointment in my face. "Don't worry, I'll relieve the pair of you after an hour. You'll get your turn to shoot." We turned away and clipped our magazines into our SLRs.

I was able to show Tim a path that curved gently through the gorse to the top of the hill. I knew of a little cave-like inlet, which was shielded by a thick bush. We went in there and sat down on fallen rocks. We could easily see the approach to the hill from one side, and we could also observe proceedings down at the range. Tim and I agreed to take it in turns to stroll around to the other side of the hill every ten minutes.

The shooting soon started. Details of four men at a time lay down to fire at the white metal plates that had been lined up along the front of the butts. Red flags had been erected at the shooting point, at the butts, and on both sides of the valley. I noticed that the coastguard station, further to the east of the range, was also flying a red flag.

Near the end of our stag, it was my turn to stroll around to the far side of the hill. As I stood up to come out from behind the bush, I noticed a man about twenty yards from me. He was lying in the long gorse observing the shooting party through binoculars. I almost missed him because he was wearing an olive green NATO jacket similar to ours, brown corduroy trousers, and a gamekeeper hat. One leg of his trousers had ridden up displaying a red sock, which caught my attention.

I stalked up behind him, and when I was five yards away I cocked my rifle. He looked around in astonishment.

"British Army," I said. "Stand up, sir, and put your hands up."

He got to his feet and raised his hands.

"I hope that gun is not loaded, young fella," he said in a New England accent.

"Believe me, it's loaded and I know how to use it."

"Well, don't point it straight at me then," he pleaded.

"If you keep your hands where I can see them, you'll be alright," I replied.

I shouted for Tim who came out with a look of amazement at the sight.

"This is private property, sir, leased to the British Army. What are you doing here, spying on us?" I asked.

"Believe me, son, you're making a big mistake," he answered.

We shouted for Roddy's attention and ordered the stranger to make tracks down to the firing party. Roddy and George Maguire came to meet us; they both carried Sterling sub-machine guns.

"For Christ's sake gentlemen, you don't need to point all of that hardware at me!" squawked the Yank.

Roddy asked me to pat the suspect down. I reached my SLR to Tim and frisked the stranger. There was nothing obvious but I removed his binoculars. We escorted him down to the shed where Roddy asked him to identify himself. He produced an International Driving Licence under the name of Patrick Michael McShane. It stated that he was a citizen of the USA, and we worked out that he was thirty-five.

"Look, before you go any further, contact this number." McShane pulled out a card in a plastic cover. Roddy examined it and said, "You might be a diplomat to the Irish Republic but you've got no immunity up here."

"They claim all thirty-two counties," he sneered. "Look, you're bluffing, son, and you're out of your depth. Take me to a police station."

Roddy and George went into the shed to consult. McShane turned to watch the shooting that had carried on.

"Very good shots but not much else. Isn't that what somebody said?" he commented.

"Wrong," I replied. "That was about the old 'B' Specials, not us."

"Is there any difference?" he came back.

"Oh yes, for instance, Tim here is a Catholic. But be assured, we are very good shots," I said.

Roddy came out and asked Tim and me to accompany him. We took the suspect back to the Landrover, which was guarded by Alfie Thompson. McShane seemed reluctant to get into the back of the vehicle.

"I'm an American citizen and you can't do this to me," he protested.

"Don't worry, we'll fly the stars and stripes if you've got one. The Provos don't kill Americans," said Roddy. "Get in the fucking Landrover or you'll walk!"

We drove down to Castlerock police station where the RUC sergeant listened to our story. He allowed the Yank to make a phone-call but we all listened in. He seemed to be talking to his superior. He said that he had been out bird watching when he was arrested.

"You haven't been arrested," interjected Roddy.

The Yank handed the phone to the RUC sergeant who identified himself. He listened for a while, and then said, "I think that the UDR were entitled to bring this man in for questioning. If you are going to vouch for him then I'll see that he is released."

He put the phone down and then turned towards the Yank.

"You've got to agree, Mr McShane, that your actions were suspicious if not to say stupid."

The Yank turned red and said, "Well I want my property back."

We gave him his card, licence, and binoculars and then led him out to the Landrover.

"Where's your car, sir?" asked Roddy.

He told us that his car was parked at the other gate-lodge at the Lions' brae.

Roddy got into the back with us and we set off. "Spot any curlews?" asked Roddy, innocently.

"Fuck you," replied the Yank.

"It's lucky that we caught you and not some of the boys in the UDA or UVF. They don't like the way you Yanks are sending money and arms to the Provos," commented Roddy.

"I know nothing about that," replied McShane. "My government is working hard to stop all that, and you guys are supposed to be our allies."

"It seems to be a bit one-sided to me," responded Roddy.

We pulled up at the Lions' Gates, so called because the large gate pillars had the figure of a lion on top of them, or rather, one did, and the other lion was lying broken in pieces at the foot of the pillar. It was believed that the Earl of Bristol, who was the Bishop of Derry, had procured the lions on his travels in Europe in the 18th Century.

A Porsche hardtop with southern plates was parked in off the road. We let McShane go and waited until he drove off in the direction of Coleraine.

"He's fucking Cynthia!" snarled Roddy.

"Yeah, I noticed that he didn't have CD plates, sir," I replied.

"Diplomat, my arse," said Roddy.

"Who's Cynthia?" asked Tim in bewilderment.

"CIA, the company, the Central Intelligence Agency," replied Roddy.

"What are they doing up here?" asked Tim.

"They're in every country in the world, looking after America's interests, sorry, looking after their own interests," answered Roddy.

"They are very interested in Northern Ireland at the minute," I explained. "Do you remember Billy McKinley on that BBC panel show?"

Billy McKinley was the spokesman for one of Ulster's myriad of loyalist political parties. The only facts that I remembered were that it started with 'U' and it was pretty extreme.

"McKinley advocates an independent Northern Ireland. When he was asked how it would be viable without subsidies from the mainland he replied that Russia would be very interested in a deep water port like Belfast on the western flank of NATO," I told Tim.

"The Yanks are shit-scared about what's going to happen here. Remember, every British battalion that's sent to Ulster is one less in Germany which the Yanks will have to replace themselves."

"Good analysis, Charlie," said Roddy. "But a united Ireland, a neutral country, would also suit the Yanks."

We arrived back at the range, and Roddy sent Tim and Alfie in to have a shoot.

"I didn't like to say in front of Tim, but have you noticed that every CIA agent you ever read about or seen in the movies had a Fenian name," said Roddy confidentially.

"Who knows what they are up to over here but I don't consider them to be our friends. You want to read the shit they write about the UDR in New York and Boston newspapers."

"Oh, I'm well aware of it, sir," I told him.

"Come on Charlie, let's give you a chance to see what you can do with the SLR at 300 yards, then I'll let you shoot some captured weapons."

We had a break for tea and sandwiches, and then it was my turn to join a detail to shoot. We had to shoot five rounds at the plates lying down, five rounds kneeling, and five rounds standing up. I very quickly knocked down four plates with my first five rounds, and then I had to wait while the others finished firing their rounds. We were ordered to stand at order arms while the butt party ran out and touched up the plates with white paint and stood them up again.

When the red flag was re-raised at the butts, we were ordered to kneel and fire at will. I soon despatched another four plates.

When we fired from a standing position, I found things not so easy. The SLR wobbled, and I reckoned that I had hit only two plates with my five rounds. We were marched off and invited to recharge our magazine with fifteen rounds from the hessian bag.

"You've got a good eye, Charlie, but you want to build up those muscles in your arms," remarked George, our platoon sergeant.

"Some of us stay behind after training on Thursdays to do a bit of gym work. Why don't you join us?" I promised that I would.

Then it was time for us to walk down to the butts to have a go at firing the captured weapons. We put up the standard NATO targets on poles and took it in turns to fire at them from twenty yards with the Kalashnikov AK47 assault rifle and with a variety of American and Soviet block pistols. Then we had a go with an old Thompson sub-machine gun but we were allowed only three rounds each. It was no longer used by the provisional IRA who had plenty of American money to purchase Soviet block weapons, on favourable terms, from Libya.

We spent a lot of time learning to strip and re-assemble the AK47 because it was the weapon, which we were most likely to come across. We learned how to make it safe, and we were reminded that we might have to fire one in an emergency.

Then we moved onto the Schermuly flare. It was a long cardboard tube with a trigger at the base. It fired a parachute flare 300 feet into the air. It was used for illumination and as a danger signal. Some of the members who lived out in the country had them attached to their houses. Their families were trained how to fire them from a button, in an emergency, in the hope of attracting local friendly forces.

"I'm experimenting with setting one up in my car to fire through a hole in the roof," said Roddy.

40

We all laughed. "No, seriously, I've cut a circular hole in the roof and attached the rocket under it. I've covered the hole with light card and sprayed it the same colour as the car. I can fire it from a button on the dashboard but I'm having problems with a trigger mechanism which would fire it if someone interferes with the car."

As a Physics teacher who taught Electronics I was intrigued, and I told him that I would look into it.

We spent the next half hour stripping and cleaning all of the weapons that we had been firing. I sat on a mound of earth with Alfie Thompson exchanging small talk while we cleaned and oiled a couple of old pistols.

"What do you think of that old Webley?" he asked me.

"Well this one must have seen service in the First World War; it's marked with a government arrowhead and dated 1913," I replied.

"True, but it does the job. I bet you found that it was accurate. You can't beat a revolver for close range work. They very seldom jam, not like that Russian shit automatic."

One of the Makarov automatic pistols had jammed when we were firing it. Our best efforts could not clear the jammed round, and it would have to be sent to the armourer at battalion HQ in Derry.

"I heard that you got turned down for a licence to carry a personal weapon," said Alfie. "How would you like me to get you one of these?"

"Oh yeah, and how are you going to get me a licence?" I joked.

"No, I can't get you a licence, but I can get you a .38."

"Where did it come from?" I asked suspiciously.

"Last summer we searched an old barn outside of Dungiven. We found about a dozen firearms and some detonators. Let's say that it didn't all get handed in. Some of the guys in our section carry a 'throw down'. It's an expression used by American cops. If they shoot someone carrying out a crime and then find that the criminal is not carrying, they plant the 'throw down' on them."

He must have read the expression on my face. "I'm not suggesting that you carry it as a 'throw down', just for personal protection on your way back from duty late at night."

"How did the gun get into the hands of terrorists?" I asked him.

"Well, it was definitely a Provo dump. It's got British Army markings, they must have got it from an arms raid on a barracks in the old days," responded Alfie.

"How much?"

"To you, twenty pounds," laughed Alfie.

"Yeah, and ten pounds a round," I came back cynically.

"No, I'll throw in six rounds buckshee, you just want it to scare people off," said Alfie. We agreed the deal and Alfie promised to deliver it at the next training evening.

"Right, let's tidy up and head off," shouted Roddy. "I want to divert to Articlave and put on a show of force for the locals. It's a very loyal, wee town and an obvious target for a Provo car-bomb or drive-by shooting. We want to let any Provo sympathisers know that we're keeping an eye on Articlave."

We drove out of Castlerock and turned left towards Coleraine. We were in 'E' Company territory but we knew that they wouldn't mind. We entered Articlave. The kerbstones were still painted red, white, and blue from the marching season. There was a staggered crossroads between the church and the orange-hall. There were fifteen of us, so plenty of personnel to set up a VCP on all four approaches to the crossroads.

The people we stopped were very friendly. They shouted comments such as, "You're far from home, George, what are you doing around here?" and "Have you boys got nothing to do in Maddenstown, there's no Provos around here. They're too fuckin' feerd to come near us."

It was all very good-natured, and after an hour we headed off home. I was back in my house in time to watch the football results on my new little black and white TV. I mentally reviewed the day. What was that Yank up to? My only regret was that I had not been able to have a bet. A Saturday without a bet. Unheard of. The UDR was starting to impinge in all aspects of my life. Still, I consoled myself with the thought that I had probably saved myself a few quid.

As I get older, I notice that events and places in my life often come back to haunt me. About a month later, on a Saturday evening, I switched on the local TV news. I was appalled by the lead story. A different platoon of the UDR from Maddenstown had gone that morning for a day's shooting on the range at Castlerock. When the first detail of four men lay down to fire, they had activated a pressure switch, which had ignited a large bomb beneath them. Two members had been killed outright and two severely injured. Others had received lesser injuries.

My thoughts returned immediately to McShane. Had he passed on information to the Provos? Perhaps not, surely it was common knowledge that we used that range. In any case, what had Cynthia to gain from such an

42

action? Perhaps McShane was a rogue member with his own agenda perverted by the propaganda, which gullible New Englanders lapped up. I put my plans for the evening aside and got into my uniform. As I walked down to my car, an elderly couple approached me.

"Isn't it a crying shame about what happened at Castlerock today?" said the old lady.

"Good on you, son," said her husband. "If I was twenty years younger, I would join you. I hope you get them."

I parked the woodie behind HQ because the car park was full. I went in, signed for my weapon, and entered the rest room. It was packed. The atmosphere was tense and angry. There were members from all three platoons and some of the permanent staff who normally worked day shifts. The major himself came in and addressed us.

"It was a damned dirty deed, men. I want maximum effort tonight. I want two different country mobiles and a local bomb patrol down the town on top of our usual commitments to guard the base and to relieve the artillery chaps at the power station. I want you to go into Republican areas and disrupt their lives as much as possible. Search their cars minutely, arrest anyone who obstructs you but stick to the law. Watch out especially for gunmen. They will be expecting our response. Over to you, Roddy."

Roddy Houston, my platoon commander, took centre stage.

"Right, listen up, 33 Platoon, I have counted twelve of our men here. If any of you permanent staff want to join us, that's OK with me, you're very welcome. We're going to Listober to set up a VCP right in the centre of town. I want you to give them the run-around. Annoy them as much as possible but stay within the law."

He looked at the clipboard in his hand. "We have ten left from 34 Platoon because Captain Armstrong has taken four men to the power station. I want the rest of you to form a country mobile to beat up the Limavady, Dungiven, Ringsend triangle. Don't go into Dungiven but put up lots of VCPs in the country roads. Don't worry about treading in D Company's territory; they are going to concentrate on the coast. You guys that are left from 35 Platoon, I'm sorry for your loss. I want you to do a foot patrol around the town tonight. The Provos will think that we are stretched elsewhere and will let our guard down in Maddenstown. They always like to follow up one success with another very quickly. So keep your eyes peeled. You'll have to take the mini-bus because we are short of Landrovers. OK, mount up!"

We went outside to load our weapons. With the permanent staff there was fourteen of us in the patrol. We were allocated three Landrovers, and we were soon pulling out of the base.

Listober was a Nationalist town about three miles south of Maddenstown. We pulled into the town centre and set up wooden signs on all four entrances to the square. We parked one of the Landrovers across the entrance to the car park opposite the chapel. There seemed to be a Saturday night mass going on.

As usual, I was ordered to cover the searchers at one of the roads into the square. I took cover in a shop doorway and checked my surroundings. There were just too many windows overlooking us. Any one of them could have concealed a sniper. Not long after there was a tremendous commotion in the car park. The churchgoers had returned to their cars but they couldn't get out. Sergeant Maquire came over to us and ordered us to abandon the checkpoint.

"Come and help us control the crowd," he said.

We went to the centre of the VCP where the parish priest was arguing with Roddy.

"I'll let them out, one at a time, when the cars have been searched," explained Roddy.

"You're only doing this in revenge for what happened at Castlerock today," accused the priest.

"This is just routine," answered Roddy. "Surely your parishioners had nothing to do with it. I'm quite sure that you were in there praying for the souls of those murdered men. You must know that one of them was a Roman Catholic."

The priest had the grace to look embarrassed.

"Look, it's in none of our interests to provoke a riot," said the priest. "Some of those old ladies have been sitting in that cold chapel for over an hour."

"OK," said Roddy. "Ladies first, you go and decide who comes out first; we're not going to search old ladies."

It took ten minutes for the car park to clear. Meanwhile we had ruined some other residents' evening by detaining their cars unnecessarily. Others were pissed off because they couldn't get into the car park to leave their cars while they went to one of the two lounge bars in the square. A gang of youths had gathered and were taunting us. They sang:

"We killed one. We killed two.

We killed two cunts more than you.

With a knick-knack paddy-wack

Give the dog a bone

Provos two, army none."

One of them threw a bottle at us but Corporal Jimmy Christie expertly kicked it in mid-air so that it deflected through the windscreen of a parked car. There was a massive cheer from the UDR members.

"Nice one Jimmy, why don't you sign up for Derry City? They could use you," commented someone.

The priest began to protest to Roddy but he said, "Go and collect the parts of the bottle and take them to the RUC. You won't find any of our fingerprints on them."

He turned to us and shouted, "Mount up lads. Let's get out of this fucking dump!"

Two minutes later we were headed out the road to Limavady. We stopped and set up a VCP for half an hour. One friendly soul told us that he had been stopped three times that evening on his way back from Derry. Then we headed back to Maddenstown for refreshments. We went out again later and set up a VCP on the coast road between Downhill and Benone. It was all very unsatisfactory, and most of the guys were despondent when we returned to base.

"When are we going to get a chance to get at the Provos, sir," asked a young private soldier whom I didn't know.

"You know that's not our role, lads," replied Roddy. "We are here to guard the population and to deter the terrorists from moving arms and explosives around at night. We are a re-active force. Sure we can take them on if they attack us but we can't go out looking for them. That's the job for others like the SAS."

"More like the UVF," someone muttered cynically.

I drove home and was in my pit by four-thirty. I lay pondering whether it was worth it. Surely there must be another way to get at active Republicans?

Chapter 7 - Dougie Tennant

It was a cold, wet, Wednesday evening in February, and I had turned up for an extra session with a different platoon because they were doing my favourite duty, country mobile.

There was a very strong turnout, ten of us under Corporal Dougie Tennant, a guy who had impressed me on training days. Dougie was a man after my own heart; he was only interested in taking the fight to the enemy.

We pulled out of HQ in two Landrovers, and I congratulated myself for being in the leading vehicle with Dougie. As soon as we left the main gate, he instructed the driver to head for Maghera.

"We're going to go up the glen and stir things up," said Dougie.

Half an hour later we were past Swatragh, and we turned off the main Coleraine to Maghera road. We drove about four miles up the glen then swung to the left into a country road that followed a valley into the southern Sperrins. Dougie instructed the driver to pull over then the other Landrover pulled up behind us.

"Bale out lads!" shouted Dougie. I was surprised because we were not in the usual configuration for a vehicle checkpoint.

Dougie waved to the guys in the other Landrover to get out to join us. We all gathered around Dougie.

"Right, here's the plan. Alan, you're in charge of the Landrovers. Take two men in each. You're going to go back to the main road and go on for about three miles. You will then pull into a country road on your left signposted for Ardpenny which is actually this road which forms a loop."

He continued, "You will make a lot of racket, stopping every few hundred yards and pretending to search roadside ditches. Don't go through any gates. They could be booby-trapped. This is real Indian country. Don't touch any parked cars or farm machinery. Shout lots of orders, give the impression that there is more than four of you."

He pointed to me and four other privates.

"You guys will follow me. We're going to carry on walking up the road. Well spaced out, dead quiet, I will take the point, I've got a red torch. I'll stop any vehicles, which approach us. Reggie, take the spot-light."

He handed a powerful torch to Reggie who was a former pupil of mine. He was eighteen but looked fourteen.

He turned to me, "Charlie, take the rear, keep your ears open for any vehicle coming up behind us. Let them pass you but give me a whistle; you can whistle can't you?" We all laughed.

"I will stop them, and Mervyn can search them. Charlie, I'm relying on you to cover us. Everybody understand?"

The two Landrovers made a job of turning to get back onto the main road. Dougie turned to us that were left and told us to cock our weapons, something that we never did in my platoon. The six of us set off up the loop road with Dougie leading the way and the rest of us well spaced out. I brought up the rear.

It was a dirty night, very cold with beating rain, which soon made our berets sodden and trickled down our necks. We trudged on quietly for about a mile when Dougie stopped and gestured for us to gather round.

"Look and listen," he said, pointing up the valley.

We could see farmyard lights coming on all the way up both sides of the valley, and we could hear dogs barking, doors slamming, and a strange clashing sound.

"What's that noise?" I asked Dougie.

He laughed. "They're banging dustbin lids to warn their neighbours that the army are out and about. Good! That means that Alan's doing a good job. Let's see who he has flushed out."

We carried on for another half mile when I heard shouting from the front of the patrol. I ran up to join them.

"What's happening?" I whispered.

Dougie replied, "We met a young lad running down the road. When he saw us he jumped that wall into the field below."

"Put the spotlight on," he ordered Reggie.

Reggie scanned the field with the powerful light, back and forward, left to right. Suddenly, a young man stood up from behind a trough.

"Don't shoot!" shouted Dougie, then he turned to the young man.

"British army! Come forward slowly with your hands up."

The young fellow walked towards us with his hands up. When he got closer we could see that he was literally shaking with fright and crying. He came forward to the wall and tried to climb up over it.

"Give him a hand, Charlie," said Dougie. "Make sure that he can't grab your rifle."

I transferred my SLR to my left hand and reached over the low wall offering my right hand to the youth. He grabbed it, and I pulled him over. He was crying his eyes out.

"Calm down, young fella, we're not going to hurt you," said Dougie.

"What are you doing out here in this weather without a coat? What's your name? Where do you live?"

He told us that his name was Cormac O'Hara and that he was sixteen and a student at Magherafelt's Catholic grammar school.

"You're a long way from home," observed Dougie. "What brings you out here?"

He told us that he had ridden out earlier, when it was dry, to meet the daughter of one of the farmers up the valley.

"I was courting her in an old cow-shed."

"How romantic," observed Dougie.

When all hell had broken loose he had ran for it leaving the bicycle at the farm gate. He told us that he was scared of the girl's brothers.

Dougie called me over to one side. "What do you think, Charlie?"

"I'm inclined to believe him. He's terrified. Does he have any identification?"

We returned to the lad and told him to turn out his pockets. He had a dirty handkerchief and a few coins but he was able to show us a battered school bus pass with his name on it.

"I live three miles out of Maghera, and I get the school bus," he informed us.

"OK," said Dougie. "Mervyn, have you got your usual vacuum flask in your kitbag?"

Mervyn gave the young chap a mug of hot, sweet tea, which seemed to help him gather himself together.

"Right!" said Dougie. "The Landrovers will be here in a minute. We'll go back and pick up this young fella's bike, then we'll take him home."

No sooner had he spoken than the two Landrovers pulled up. Dougie explained the situation, so the Landrovers had to turn around again as best they could.

We took young O'Hara with us in the leading vehicle.

"Give us a shout when you can see where you left your bike," shouted Dougie into the back of the vehicle.

The young lad leaned over the front seat between Dougie and the driver. Soon we came to two large white almost conical gateposts that marked the entrance to many Ulster farms.

"Here we are!" shouted O'Hara. We stopped, and I got out with him. Sure enough there was an old bicycle lying in the ditch beside one of the gateposts. I helped him lift the bike into the back of the Landrover, and then we jumped in.

We drove on along the loop road. All of the farms were lit up, and there seemed to be lots of activity in the yards. We carried on through the little village of Ardpenny and out to the main road where we turned right and headed back to Maghera.

A few miles down the road, the young lad leaned over to talk to Dougie.

"Please don't go into our farm. Me da will kill me. Drop me here somewhere. Please, sir."

"OK, pull up," laughed Dougie. "Why don't you take that young lassie of yours to the pictures next time?"

I helped the young fellow out with his bike and waved him goodbye as we sped on into Maghera.

It was past eleven o'clock when we pulled into the joint Army, UDR, and police base in Maghera. We cleared our weapons and made our way to the rest room to eat our supper and get dry in front of a large stove. I noticed that Dougie slipped off down the corridor, which led to the Intelligence Office. I was well into my cheese and pickle sandwiches when Dougie rejoined us.

"He seems to check out. There's nothing known about him or his family," he told us.

"Ah well, that's our good deed for the day," said Mervyn.

"I'm not here to do fucking good deeds," said Dougie sourly. "I'm here to do bad deeds to bad people. We'll go up the glen again just when they think that things have settled down. Eat up! Have a piss. Mount up."

We left the base and headed back up the glen. After a few miles, we swung right this time, up a fairly broad road. We came to a junction with a narrow, steep road coming down from the mountains. Dougie called us to a halt, and we straddled the junction to set up a VCP. Dougie ordered me to go up the narrow road about fifty yards, where it started to bend out of our sight.

"Take a position in the field up that hill," he ordered me. "Keep an ear out for anything coming down that road and cover us."

After about twenty minutes, we had stopped only one vehicle on the main road, when suddenly it became very busy, and all of the other guys were fully engaged in stopping and searching.

I heard a car coming down the side road; it was a new VW estate edging down the narrow road. The driver slammed on the brakes when he saw the VCP. He attempted to do a three-point turn but ended up with his rear wheels hanging over the ditch. He revved up but the wheels could not find any purchase. He turned off the engine and then switched on the interior light. I could see that the driver was a middle-aged man and that there did not seem to be any other occupants.

I made my way down the slope and climbed over the wall of the field. I approached the driver's door apprehensively. This would be my first solo contact with the public. I knocked on the driver's door, and he looked up startled; he immediately locked the door. I noticed that he was pulling out sheets of paper from the glove compartment, which he crumpled up and threw into the foot-well of the passenger side.

I watched in amazement as he took out a lighter and set fire to the bundle of paper. I tapped again on the window with the muzzle of my rifle but he ignored me.

At this point Dougie appeared at my side, and I told him what was happening. Dougie carried a Sterling sub-machine gun, and he banged the butt fiercely against the window.

"Open the door or I'll blow your fucking head off!" he roared.

The car was filling with smoke, and the driver was obviously feeling the effects. He opened the door and staggered out coughing and wheezing.

"Get in and grab those papers!" shouted Dougie.

I crawled in and managed to retrieve a good handful of the papers, which were only singed. Dougie attempted to interrogate the driver but was getting no response. He called Mervyn up to take the driver to the Landrover.

I smoothed out the papers and handed them to Dougie who got out his torch. The papers seemed to be lists of peoples' names – Catholic names – with numbers beside them. I went in again and looked in the glove compartment. I pulled out a cloth bag with a drawstring. I got outside and opened it; it was full of rolls of banknotes and hundreds of loose coins.

"Look at this, Dougie," I said. "There must be hundreds of pounds here."

"What the fuck is going on here?" asked Dougie. "What is this fucking merchant up to?"

We made sure that the fire was out, and we called up two of the other guys to help us get the car out of the ditch.

"Charlie, I want you to drive this heap along with us between the two Landrovers. We'll take this guy back to Maghera to get him looked at properly. It's your collar, so I want you to go down and arrest him formally."

We went down to the VCP where I found the suspect sitting in the back of one of our vehicles. He was a skinny, dark-featured man of about forty-five. He was wearing an expensive looking blue suit and a smart, sheepskin jacket.

I ordered him out, and I formally arrested him on suspicion of terrorism, under the Northern Ireland Special Powers Act. I warned him that anything he said could be used in evidence against him but he didn't say a word.

I returned to the car, which I drove down to take its position between the two Landrovers. They had turned around so that we were now facing back towards Maghera. We set off and were soon inside the compound.

Dougie and I escorted the prisoner to the holding area where I was left to guard him with Dougie's personal 9mm Browning pistol.

Dougie soon returned with a sergeant from the army's Special Investigation Branch of the Military Police accompanied by an RUC inspector.

We took the prisoner to an interrogation room where the inspector asked me to outline the events of the arrest. Dougie then put in an account of his involvement and reached the inspector the bundle of scorched papers and the bag of money.

"There's seven hundred and sixty-four pounds and thirty-five pence in that bag," he asserted.

Dougie and I were then ordered to leave the room.

We went back to the rest room and got stuck into mugs of hot tea and the remains of our sandwiches.

"I think he's a collector for the IRA," declared Dougie.

I agreed that, that was what his behaviour and the evidence suggested.

After another half hour, the SIB sergeant came to join us. He did not look pleased.

"I wish you lot would stop harassing the local population," he said in a Welsh singsong. "It makes life difficult for those of us who are trying to win hearts and minds."

You've got to be fucking joking!" exploded Dougie. "What were the lists of names and all that money about? Would you like to explain his behaviour?"

"Don't speak to me like that, corporal!" snapped the sergeant. "He's a respectable solicitor from Strabane. He's the treasurer of the local GAA football club, and he has been out collecting subs."

"Oh yeah?" said Dougie. "He lives in Strabane, forty miles away, yet he's the treasurer of the local Gaelic football club. You will be checking that?"

"Don't try to tell me how to do my job, corporal,"

"And how do you explain his behaviour in the car?" asked Dougie.

"He was carrying a lot of money, and he was scared that you lot were going to rob him," countered the sergeant. "It has happened before."

"That's an outrageous slur!" I shouted. "That's the type of Republican propaganda that we have to put up with but you don't have to take it in."

The sergeant turned to address me. "Ah yes, you're Private Cunningham. You made the arrest, so you can escort Mr Mulrane off the premises. Be polite, be professional," he sneered.

I went out to the corridor where the suspect was standing smirking. He was with the RUC inspector who looked at me and shrugged apologetically as he reached me the car keys.

"Follow me, Mr Mulrane," I said.

We went outside to his car, and I reached him the keys. "Follow me over to the main gate slowly."

"You're fucking joking, aren't you?" It was the first time that I had heard him speak.

"I'm not leaving until I've searched this fucking car. You boys will have planted something and you'll have another patrol down the road waiting to search me," he said.

"Please yourself," I replied, "But be quick about it."

He spent nearly twenty minutes searching his car minutely. He popped the bonnet and searched the engine; he even unscrewed the top off of the air-filter. Then he popped the rear door and lifted the carpet. He took out the spare wheel and searched the wheel-well and his tool case.

He moved on to the interior, shifting the seats and searching under them and in the crevices. He lifted the carpets, he pulled down the sun-shields and he searched the glove compartment. Then he got down on his knees, with his nice suit in the wet puddles, and checked under the chassis.

He seemed to be satisfied, so I spoke, "Haven't you forgotten something?"

"What are you fucking on about?" he enquired.

I reached him the bag of money. "Do you want to count it?"

"Don't get fucking smart with me, sonny," he said. "Don't worry, I'll make sure that the money's put to good use."

He paused, "And remember, I know where you cunts come from."

He waved the scorched papers and said, "These aren't the only addresses that we've got, so watch your fucking back."

"And you watch your fucking back," said Dougie, stepping out of the shadows with his SMG which he had been covering me with. "And now we know your fucking address and what you're up to. You might have pulled the wool over that Welsh idiot's eyes but we're on to you now. So get in the car and get to fuck out of here before you have an accident."

Mulrane looked around nervously and then got into his car. I guided him to the main gate and waved him goodbye, sardonically.

"He's a fucking member!" said Dougie as we walked back to the rest room. "That was a good arrest, Charlie, it's just that the regulars and the police are frightened to take these people on. Wait and see, we're being sold out behind our backs."

We joined the others and sat down together.

"Two things," said Dougie quietly. "We normally tell you not to mention the things which we do to your family and work-mates. This time I want you to let it slip out, especially if you work with Fenians. But tell them he was carrying three thousand pounds." We all laughed.

"Number two, I got the RUC inspector to photocopy those lists for us. They should make interesting reading."

Then he shouted, for all to hear, "Mount up, we're wasting our fucking time around here." We went outside and charged our weapons then climbed into the Landrover to go home.

This turned out to be another incident, which I had put out of my mind when it was brought back to me in horrific circumstances. About a month later, I had reported for duty with my own section, when Dougie Tennant beckoned me out of the rest room to the corridor.

"Have a read of this," he said, reaching me a newspaper folded to an inside story. I took it and saw that it was the previous evening's Belfast Telegraph.

I quickly scanned the article. It described the mysterious shooting to death of a well-known Strabane solicitor, Donal Mulrane, aged forty-seven. It appeared that Mr Mulrane had been invited to a meeting to draw up a will at a remote farmstead near Newtownstewart, and when he got out of his vehicle, at least two gunmen had sprayed him with automatic weapons killing him instantly. Police were baffled by the circumstances because the farm had been deserted for months. Mr Mulrane's secretary had told them that he often carried large sums of money, and she was sure that it was a robbery. A police spokesman said that they were not ruling out terrorist involvement from either side and that they were following an anonymous phone call, which had suggested a drug involvement.

I returned the newspaper to Dougie who was beaming. "Who do you think did that?" I spluttered.

Dougie put his finger up along his nose. "Well, we know that he was a player. Did some of our boys get him, or did word get around that he was skimming the Provos?" He laughed. "It was probably the bhoyos; they figured that Mulrane was keeping half of the money for himself."

I wasn't sure whom Dougie meant when he had said 'our boys' but I was left with the feeling that he knew more about it than he was letting on to me.

"Oh yeah, Dougie, I believe you," I countered.

"I swear, I know nothing about it," smirked Dougie.

Later, as I lay in bed waiting for sleep, I felt good that someone had taken positive action but, on the other hand, maybe the Provos had punished Mulrane and planted the drugs story, in which case it was down to Dougie's suggestion that we spread the idea that Mulrane had been carrying thousands of pounds and was ripping off the IRA.

Chapter 8 – The Electric Range

It was 33 Platoon's turn to guard various vulnerable targets in County Londonderry for a week. I went in on Tuesday evening and set off on a two Landrover patrol with six other members of the platoon. I was in the second vehicle with Joe Gilchrist driving and Corporal John Madison beside him in the left-hand front seat. I was in the back with Noel Gibson, the young chap I had done my basic training with.

Unusually we headed east towards Coleraine. John Madison turned around towards us in the back and informed us that 'E' Company in Coleraine were short handed and wanted us to relieve them of some of their duties. Eventually we pulled into the UDR base at Laurel Hill where Madison and Sergeant George Maguire, the patrol leader, from the front vehicle, went into the 'big house' to be briefed.

When Madison returned, he told us that both vehicles would head down to Kilrea where the guys in the front vehicle would pull off to relieve the RUC guard on the home of the local MP who lived in a large farmstead just outside of the town. We were to go on into Kilrea police station and then do a foot patrol through the town until midnight, then we would spend the remainder of the evening guarding the RUC station while the police went out to show their presence.

We drove into Kilrea past the Marian Hall, which was used, mainly by Roman Catholics, for social occasions. Gibson and I sat close to the open rear with our rifles at the ready. As we entered the town proper, the Landrover bounced over a sleeping policeman. I heard a clatter on the road behind us.

"Fuck's sake! I've dropped my rifle!" shouted Gibson.

I shouted for Joe Gilchrist to stop and then to back up. When we got to the rifle, Gilchrist didn't hear our shouts for him to stop and, inevitably, the Landrover drove over the weapon. Gibson and I jumped out. I nervously covered Noel whilst he crawled under the vehicle to retrieve his weapon. Luckily it was a dirty Ulster March night with the rain coming in swirls so that there was nobody about.

We jumped back into the Landrover where Gibson secured the strap to his right wrist, as he should have done at the start of the patrol. We drove on and then entered the RUC station. We went into the rest room where Corporal Madison went to town.

"You fuckin' idiot!" he roared. "How many times have you been told to strap your weapon to your wrist? This is a Fenian hole. Real Indian country. Anybody could have ran out and picked up the fuckin' gun and then turned it on us. Let me see it."

Madison inspected the SLR and then said, "There doesn't seem to be any damage to the furniture." Gibson's SLR had a wooden walnut butt and stock unlike mine which had black maranyl, a synthetic hard nylon product, dimpled to make it more secure to hold.

"Right! I'm going to say no more about this, and I warn the lot of you to shut up about it. Let's get out on foot-patrol."

Just then a RUC constable came into the room and sheepishly asked, "Does anybody own this?" He held the magazine from an SLR in his hand, and only then did we all notice that Gibson's rifle was without a magazine.

"Some old guy has just brought this to the front door. He's a friendly prod. You're lucky, it wasn't one of the local taigs or you would never have seen it again."

John Madison thanked the police officer profusely with embarrassment and asked him not to report it.

"It belongs to this young idiot." He pointed at Gibson who was on the verge of tears. "We normally don't let him out, and this will be the last fucking time that he does a patrol!"

We checked our gear and then left the station to walk into the town. There were two of us on each side of the road. The corporal led Joe Gilchrist on the right hand side, and I followed about ten yards behind Gibson on the left. I was relying on Noel to check to our front and to look up to the roofs on our right. I turned around every few yards to cover our rear. The rain had got heavier, and there was nobody about. We got to the other side of town without meeting a soul. We had passed two bars but they were very quiet with no music. There were a few cars parked at odd angles in the side streets but our orders were not to touch them.

We turned back, walking into the rain this time, but the town seemed to be deserted. We got back into the rest room and took off our sodden berets, scarves, flak jackets, and Nato jackets. There was an ancient coal stove in the rest room, so we hung our duds off chairs around it. We were soon stuck into our mugs and rolls.

At eleven o'clock an RUC sergeant came into the room; he seemed to know John Madison.

"That was a damned bad show, John, with Brian Montgomery and his wee girl. I was first on the scene, and it wasn't pretty." He told us. "I had to stop Brian's wife from cuddling the remains of her daughter. There wasn't much there. Just a head and the rest like a ragdoll."

"Any clues?" asked John.

"Nothing specific, but the word is that it was INLA and not the IRA."

INLA was the Irish National Liberation Army, a Republican group that was even more extreme than the PIRA.

"Anyway, we're off to do a foot patrol around the town. I'll leave a constable on the front desk. Could one of you cover him when he goes out to open the gate and could you always have one man up in the back sangar? We've had intelligence that some day they are going to throw a bomb over the back fence. The trouble is that they sometimes send youngsters to play with balls in the backfield. We don't want any unfortunate incidents."

John Madison looked at me and said, "Come on, Charlie. Grab your kit." He led me to the back of the station and out into the backyard. We climbed a set of steps into a sangar built from double layers of breezeblocks with an outer layer of sandbags. There was hardly room for both of us with our flak jackets on.

The front of the sangar had three slit windows, one pointing out to a well-lit field and one at an angle at each side. They had thick glass with sliding panes.

"I wouldn't count on the breeze blocks or the glass stopping a bullet from a modern high-velocity weapon but they should stop shrapnel from a home-made bomb," said John. "There's a button here to press if you want to alert us. I'll send somebody to relieve you after an hour. It won't be that fucking spastic Gibson."

We both laughed, and then he was off down the steps leaving me on my own. I have to confess that this was the first time that I was really scared during my service in the UDR. The field rose up behind the police station to a housing estate about two hundred yards away. A sniper could have a field day here, I thought. I was a sitting target. My other concern was what to do if someone approached the sangar. How was I to know if it was a bomber or a kid trying to be brave? The field was harshly lit up by two banks of lights on pylons on either side of the sangar. The light was so intense that it was difficult to discriminate between hummocks of grass and someone crawling towards the station.

I rested my rifle on the front windowsill which I had slid open. The rain had eased but now there was a freezing wind. I checked my watch. 11:35, only fifty-five minutes to go. I should have had a piss. I resolved to piss out the back of the sangar if I really had to. I imagined how it would look if I was shot in the back, lying there with my dick in my hand.

I froze. Was that someone crawling through the field? No, it was only the grass ruffling with the wind. I considered cocking my SLR but I knew that it was against standing orders. I checked my watch again. Christ, it was only 11:40. Now my knees were knocking with the cold. I stamped my feet for warmth. I found my thoughts straying. Was this what I had joined up for? I knew that somebody had to do it but I had imagined that I would have been engaged in more pro-active operations against the terrorists.

I resolved to give the UDR a year of my life, and then I would seriously consider leaving this country. But what about my father? No, I had to stay here. I knew that I was pissed off because of my lack of social life. No decent girl wanted to know a chap who was in the security forces. Perhaps my best chance was in finding a girl whose father was in the security forces but, of course, he wouldn't want her mixing with a target.

I checked my watch. 11:49. Now I really needed a piss. It was a struggle to open the fly of the NATO trousers but I managed it. I closed the window and then turned around to piss out into the yard. A swirl of the wind blew some of it back around me and into the sangar. I laughed hysterically and then rearranged my dress as the notices in public toilets say. I opened the front window and rested my SLR on the sill. No danger of it falling out because the strap was securely fixed to my wrist unlike young Gibson. 11:56, my watch informed me. Christ! I wasn't even halfway through my stag.

Suddenly I was aware of a group of men leaning against the fence behind the housing estate and waving in my direction. Above the wind I heard snatches of shouts. "RUC bastards!" and "UDR wankers!"

My guts were churning. Was this a diversion? I checked the sides of the field but spotted nothing. After a few minutes, the shouters drifted away. It was now 12:05. I stamped my feet and then jumped up and down but my toes felt like blocks of ice. I didn't even smoke. Was smoking allowed in the sangar? I doubted it. I resolved to bring my Thermos if I ever had to do this duty again. But I didn't intend to do this duty again. I would be very careful about picking my duties in future. I thought that I heard someone coming through the yard behind me. I checked. It was only 12:16 but it turned out to be Joe Gilchrist. He was early.

"What's that fucking smell? Have you had a piss in here, Charlie? It's a good job you didn't need a shit."

I was so relieved that I couldn't return his banter. I left him to it and returned to the rest room. John Madison looked at me quizzically.

"Nothing to report, corporal. But I could make a few suggestions. How about a seat and a can to piss into? A set of night-glasses would be useful as well."

"Have your piss before you go out. You know what the Duke of Wellington said. A wise man pisses when he can; a fool pisses when he must. No seat, we don't want you sitting down and then falling asleep. Do you know how much a night-sight costs? We are only allowed one per company and I haven't got it."

I put my feet up to the stove and got out my last cheese and pickle roll and poured a mug of tea from my Thermos. The time passed much faster in the rest room and soon the RUC patrol returned. A policeman relieved Joe Gilchrist from the back sangar, so we hung around until near two o'clock before we went out and mounted up.

Corporal Madison had contacted the other half of the patrol on the radio. We drove into the MP's farmyard where the others were standing outside of their Landrover waiting for us. Sergeant Maguire took over and informed us that we would set up a VCP at the bridge at Swatragh before returning home.

The rain had ceased and the wind had blown the clouds away by the time we got to Swatragh. We parked the two Landrovers at angles to each other to form the classic VCP on the bridge. I walked to one end of the bridge and found the perfect cover in a hedge to take on my customary role of cover for the searchers. The Moon was out now and I had perfect vision of the VCP. Swatragh was a Republican hotbed, and I heard the abuse that the searchers got from the few night owls which we stopped. After an hour, George Maguire shouted, "Mount up!" and we were soon on our way to Maddenstown. I asked myself what we had achieved but couldn't satisfy myself. An hour later I was in bed between cold sheets with icy feet.

On Thursday evening I went in for a two hour training session. I watched as Corporal Madison struggled to teach my section how to measure the distances between contours on a map to produce a sketch of how the horizon might appear.

"Charlie, help me out here. I know that you teach Maths as well as Physics." I went up to the blackboard and sketched a horizon with hills of various sizes. Then I showed them how to mark off heights at every hundred feet to produce a set of contours. It was standard educational procedure to teach a concept from two opposite directions. The section soon started to get my drift.

"Charlie, you should take your Lance Corporal's exam," suggested Jim Toy.

"He can't," retorted John Madison who appeared to be miffed. "He hasn't served six months yet."

"But he could put in for a commission," interjected our platoon Lieutenant, Roddy Houston, who had been watching us from the doorway. "He's got a degree and I would recommend him."

We left it at that and went down to the basement, some to go to the gym and others to have a .22 rifle competition, which I won with ease because Sergeant Maguire had gone to do some paperwork.

As we were preparing to leave the building Roddy Houston shouted, "Is there anybody here who has not been on the electric range?"

Noel Gibson and I put our hands up and four other recent recruits in the other sections also indicated.

"Well, I want you in on Saturday morning ready to go to Magilligan. I have managed to get us a slot. Now don't let me down because this might not come up again for six months."

Saturday morning came and I was soon travelling in the mini-bus with Lieutenant Houston and five other recent recruits including Noel Gibson. I noticed that Gibson had his rifle strap correctly fixed to the point under the butt and to his right wrist. We pulled into the old army camp at Magilligan and parked outside of the headquarters building. We were led into a classroom by a sergeant from a regular regiment. Six privates were already sitting at desks, and I recognised some of the Derry boys with whom I had done my initial training.

"I'm Sergeant Hardieman from the Green Howards!" he bawled. "I'm your range-master today."

He went on to explain about how the electric range worked. We would walk through it in pairs with loaded rifles. Some of the terrain would be rural lanes and other parts would lead through farmyards or built-up areas. We could expect targets to pop up at anytime. Some of the targets would be full-size cutouts of civilians and some could be of terrorists carrying or pointing arms or flinging a nail-bomb.

We would score points by 'killing' terrorists and lose points by missing them or by hitting civilians. He warned us to be extra careful not to shoot our companion nor himself and Lieutenant Houston who would be trailing close behind us. He cautioned that some of the targets could pop up as we were passing them. The remainder of the cadre, as he called it, would be following further behind.

We all went out and clambered into the back of a three-ton lorry. We were joined by a UDR lance corporal that I had never met. He was carrying a pot of glue and a sheaf of strips of paper. I noticed that he also carried a Browning 9mm automatic pistol in a shoulder holster. Sergeant Hardieman drove us through the sand dunes for the best part of a mile before we stopped at the entrance to the range. He ordered us to fix a magazine to our rifles but not to cock them. He pointed to two of the Derry lads and told them to start walking.

The sergeant and Roddy Houston followed the pair and the rest of us came in a gaggle behind. Nothing happened for two hundred yards, and then I heard a shot ring out. One of the Derry lads had fired a round.

"You fucking moron!" bawled Sergeant Hardieman, "You nearly killed Old Mother Riley. It's a good job that you fucking missed. Now get a bloody grip!"

We gathered around the target, which had swung up. It was a picture of an old woman carrying a bundle of sticks but it was unmarked.

"Carry on! And keep your bloody eyes open," ordered Hardieman.

We carried on for another three hundred yards without incident, and then the Sergeant called us to a halt.

"Let's have two more Derry men," shouted Hardieman and two volunteers stepped forward. We proceeded for just fifty yards when both point men opened up and fired multiple rounds. Hardieman called us all up to inspect a target painted as Clyde Barrow, of Bonnie and Clyde fame, with a wide-brimmed hat and pointing a Thompson sub-machine gun. It had been hit four or five times. The artist must have been influenced by the movie because I knew that the Barrow gang actually carried Browning Automatic Rifles not Tommy guns.

"Well done lads, you've just killed a terrorist," observed Hardieman. The lance corporal stepped forward and proceeded to paste squares of paper of the appropriate colour over the bullet holes.

"Next two. Let's have some Maddenstown men," shouted Hardieman. Noel Gibson immediately pushed his way to the front but I held back. No way was I going to get anywhere near Gibson with a loaded rifle in his hands and raring to shoot.

We carried on for another two hundred yards. By now we were in an urban area with mock house and shop fronts on either side. I was at the front of the trailing gaggle, and I was in a great position to see a gunman suddenly looming out of an upstairs window. There was an explosion such as I had never heard before and then there were peels of hysterical laughter from Gibson and his companion. Sergeant Hardieman was ranting and raving and when I got up I saw that Roddy Houston was struggling to keep a straight face.

"You've ruined the Queen's fucking property, you idle little man. When was the last time that you cleaned that fucking barrel?" ranted the sergeant.

It helped to confirm to me that regular NCOs could not complete a sentence without using a profanity.

The barrel of Gibson's SLR had split into 4 parts like the leaves of a half-eaten banana. The working parts had also blown backwards and were drooping over the butt. He was obviously shocked but I could see that he had come to the same conclusion as I had. The wheel of the Landrover in Kilrea had deviated the barrel slightly but enough for a bullet to jam near the muzzle. The expanding gas had nowhere to go. Luckily, young Gibson was unhurt.

Our Lieutenant escorted Gibson back to HQ to get checked out and, no doubt, for an investigation. The rest of us carried on. The course was more or less circular and soon we were back at the start. In the centre of the range was a tall tower with an office on top. The sergeant noticed me staring at it.

"That's the control tower. The controller can observe the whole range, and he activates the targets electronically when he chooses. When we go around again, he might select the same targets or ones that we haven't encountered yet. It's your turn next, so keep on your toes."

I hadn't gone fifty yards before a child popped up from behind a bush but neither my companion nor I were fooled, and we held our fire. We carried on into the town when suddenly a pram appeared from behind a shop but the woman in a headscarf pushing it was pointing a pistol at us. I quickly cocked my weapon and put two rounds into her upper body, my companion fired as well and managed to hit her head.

"Good shooting, lads," said Hardieman. "Where did you learn to shoot?"

I told him that I had served in the Officer Training Corps at Manchester University.

"What did you shoot with? The old .303? Good, it has transferred well. Next two."

We carried on until everyone had had a go, and I was looking forward to tea and wads. But no, Hardieman sent us around again, this time not to shoot but to pick up any cartridges that we could find at the edge of the trail. This gave me a chance to examine some of the targets. They were attached to coils of wire, which were buried under the trail and obviously led back to the control tower. The targets were retained in their hidden positions by levers, which were controlled electro-magnetically by the wires. Springs pulled them up into their exposed positions. I hadn't noticed that the lance corporal pulled down the activated targets, after gluing the holes, to lock them down again.

We drove back to HQ to hand in the spent cartridges and to replenish our magazines. As usual we had to swear that we had only thirty rounds in our possession. We had our tea and wads, and then we had a quick debrief where Roddy revealed that he had charged Gibson with destroying government property through negligence. He and John Madison were to appear in front of the major on the following Saturday morning. I was called as a witness, and I got the clear impression that Lieutenant Houston was not pleased with me.

I was slightly worried about my part in the incident in Kilrea but I rationalised that I had been ordered by a superior officer to keep quiet about the affair. The following week, 33 Platoon was on base guard, which I found intensely boring. I decided to attend on Monday night when a different section of 33 was guarding the base, so I volunteered to go out with a section from 34 Platoon who were under strength.

We headed off in two Landrovers through Limavady and on towards Londonderry. We pulled in through the gates of the large power station at Coolkeeragh. We relieved a section of regulars from the Royal Artillery who acted as infantry in NI. Sergeant Archer split the section into two bricks. He led me and two other guys, who I knew vaguely, on a patrol around the plant. I was concerned that the whole power station was lit up by powerful lights on towers. We walked up a central road between different modules of the power plant. Ahead of us I could see a fence with a housing estate behind it.

"Don't worry, lads, that's a Protestant estate, so you are not going to be fired on," said Sergeant Archer. I wasn't persuaded. What was to stop an IRA active service unit from driving into the estate and firing at us who were perfectly illuminated targets. The plant was surprisingly large, and by the time we had been around it twice an hour had elapsed. We went back to the rest room in the admin block.

The other brick headed off on foot patrol, and we got stuck into our tea and wads. Suddenly, the door flung open, and in stamped Staff-Sergeant Warburton from the training staff.

"Attention! Officer on parade!" he shouted. We dropped our wads and sprang to attention. Ducking through the door came an apparition. He was six foot four and wore a brown beret with a gold-bullioned, star pointed badge. He wore a jungle camouflage jacket over beautifully cut and pressed cavalry twill breeches. In his left hand he carried a gold-topped ebony swagger stick, and he waved effeminately, with his right hand, at us to sit down.

"Good evening, gentlemen. I am your new Battalion Training Officer, Major Cadogan-Bentinck of the Coldstream Guards. I have only started work today, and I would like to get to know what sort of chap joins the UDR. When I point at you, could you please tell me your full name and what your normal occupation is."

He started with me. "Private Charles Cunningham, sir, and I am a Physics teacher at Maddenstown Technical College."

"Robin Kennedy, sir, and I teach History at Coleraine Academical Institution."

He turned to the young fellow behind me. "Private Gerald O'Farrell, sir, and I am a Ph.D. student at the New University in Coleraine."

Then it was the sergeant's turn. "I'm Robbie Archer and I'm only a fuckin' bin-man but I'm the one with the fuckin' stripes, sir!"

Even Staff-Sergeant Warburton joined in the peel of laughter.

"Quite right, sergeant. You are the most important man here," nodded the major. "OK, I get the picture. Could you get onto your radio and inform your walking patrol that Staff and I are coming out to find them."

There were some light-hearted moments with the UDR but it became serious again on Saturday morning. I drove through the gates at ten to eight and parked the woodie. As I made my way towards HQ, I was met by Corporal Irvine consulting a clipboard.

"Wait outside the orderly room and smarten yourself up. You will be called in after Corporal Madison. Make sure that you've got your story right."

I went inside and took a chair beside John Madison who was sweating profusely.

"I should have charged the little bastard there and then. Watch out! Here they come."

The Company Sergeant-Major marched Gibson and a private from 35 Platoon, who was the prisoner's escort, past us and stopped outside of Major Crawford's office. The door opened and Corporal Irvine gestured them inside.

"Prisoner and escort, quick march!" roared the CSM, and the door slammed behind them. Five minutes later, Corporal Irvine came out and told John Madison to march in. After another five minutes Madison came out trembling, then it was my turn. I was marched in and stood to attention in front of the Major's desk. Lieutenant Houston stood behind him and the CSM to one side of the desk. The bareheaded prisoner and escort stood to one side of the room, and Corporal Irvine sat on a chair taking notes.

The major looked over his glasses at me. "Private Cunningham, tell us your version of the events surrounding the rifle in Kilrea."

I told them that the rifle had been dropped when we went over a hump and that the Landrover had backed up over it. I confirmed that the SLR had not been attached to Gibson's wrist. I told them that we had inspected the rifle in the police station and concluded that it was undamaged. I also confirmed that the weapon had exploded when it was first fired at Magilligan.

"And you didn't think to report this incident to your platoon sergeant or officer when you had a chance? You let Private Gibson carry a suspect weapon onto a firing range."

I attested that I had been ordered by Corporal Madison not to speak about the incident. I was marched out.

Ten minutes later, the CSM, Gibson and his escort marched out down to the rest room. Gibson looked shocked. The CSM returned and addressed John Madison.

"Corporal Madison, you are charged with failing to report damage to government property and with conduct prejudicial to good order and discipline. March in!"

When Madison was marched out, he was literally shaking. We made our way down to the rest room where Noel Gibson was sitting crying. The escort told us that Gibson had been admonished and ordered to pay forty pounds towards the repair of his SLR. I thought that he had got off light.

I turned to John Madison and tried to explain that I had simply told the truth but he didn't hold me to blame. He told us that he had lost one of his stripes for six months and had been fined twenty pounds. It all brought it home to me that we were members of an armed service and that we weren't just here to play soldiers. I also felt that I had let down Roddy and the Major. I reckoned that I could kiss a commission goodbye.

As I went out to the car park, I was intercepted by Alfie Thompson who was doing a Saturday base guard duty.

"Charlie, I've got something for you. Come over to my car."

I followed Alfie to his old rusting Ford Anglia. He looked around us nervously, opened the boot and gestured for me to look in. He opened an old biscuit tin and took out a bundle wrapped in an old towel.

"There you are, just what you ordered." He unwrapped the towel to reveal an old .38 Webley. I reached in and snapped it open. It contained six rounds so I spun the chamber. It moved sweetly. I checked the firing pin and found it to be fully intact.

"Twenty pounds to you, cheap at twice the price," said Alfie. I asked him whether he had any more rounds but he could not help me.

"You don't need any more. You just want to scare off casual intruders or UDA shites if they get nasty at a roadblock. If you run into the real bhoyos you want to provoke them into firing at you because you don't want to get captured."

Luckily I was carrying a wedge because I intended to go to the bookies and the supermarket later. I reached him twenty pounds and re-wrapped the piece in the towel. I made my goodbyes and opened the woodie. I stuffed the bundle under the front seat and drove off to number nine. I decided to take the piece to bed with me. I stuck in down beside my toes; it felt good. I imagined an intruder coming into my bedroom but I was a very light sleeper, I would hear them before they got to my room. Plenty of time to pull out the .38. Six live rounds. I didn't believe in that nonsense about keeping an empty chamber under the firing pin. I slept like a log.

Chapter 9 - The Year of the Strike

One week followed another. I usually did two night duties and one training evening each week. About once a month I went training on a range at the weekend. My resolve to do something about my social life had slipped below the radar.

I woke up one Saturday morning after a night guarding a large electricity generating station near Derry. I promised myself that I would go out that evening. After I had done my normal Saturday chores, I wandered down to the bookies. I placed my bet, and then slipped through the back door into Brennan's Bar. I had a feeling that I would bump into Dave Maxwell who had shared a desk with me at the Tech when I was a teenager. We had drifted apart when I went off to university, and Dave had become a draughtsman in a Coleraine engineering company. We had met occasionally since I took a job at the Tech because Dave still lived with his mother in Church Street. Dave was a devotee of the ponies and could usually be found darting between the bookies and the bar on a Saturday afternoon.

Sure enough, Dave was there, propping up the bar near the TV waiting for the first race. I sidled up beside him and muttered in his ear, "How's your luck?"

Dave seemed delighted to see me. We had always been on the same wavelength at school, and he was unattached like myself. Dave and I were both members of Maddenstown Rugby club although neither of us played the game. I did play cricket in the summer months on the pitch behind the clubhouse, and Dave made regular use of their squash court.

"How are you going to spend your winnings tonight?" I asked him.

He told me that he had nothing planned so I suggested that we shared a taxi out to the club, which was running a disco in their function room. We agreed that I would call round at his mother's house at half-seven, and then we would ring for a taxi.

Dave knew that I was a member of the UDR and was very supportive. He had toyed with the idea of joining the police reserve but had done nothing about it. We had a few pints and watched our horses lose, and then we staggered off to our respective homes.

I put my head down for a couple of hours, and then cleaned myself up carefully. I put on a pan of pasta to boil and made a cheese sauce out of a packet. I heated up a saucepan of chopped tomatoes garnished with herbs. I drained the pasta, mixed it with the tomato sauce and poured it into a large bowl. I covered it liberally with the cheese sauce and then got stuck in. I intended to lay a good foundation for the drink that I was going to shift that evening. I cleaned my teeth and then headed off round to Dave's house.

We arrived at the clubhouse just after eight and hit the bar. I decided to stick to Tennents ordinary for the time being and Dave started on pints of Guinness. The rugby first team had played at home that afternoon, and many of them had obviously gone straight to the bar afterwards. Dave and I knew most of them but they were mainly ex-pupils of the grammar school.

The crack was good, the bar became packed, and we could hear the throb from the disco next door. After an hour's drinking, Dave and I made our way into the darkened function room. The music was deafening and strobe lights were flashing. I thought that I might be getting a bit old for all of this. Dave was much taller than I, and he stooped to tell me that he had spotted two girls who were not dancing. He led the way through the ranks of dancers to the far side where he approached two young women. He spoke to a tall, thin girl who seemed to know him, and they danced off into the crowd.

I was left with a cuddly blonde who looked expectantly at me. I jerked my thumb towards the dance floor, and she very quickly pushed past me to join Dave and his friend. Luckily, dancing skills were not asked for. There was only room to shuffle our feet on the same spot and to gyrate our bodies. When the set finished, the four of us headed off to the little bar inside the function room. Dave bought a round of drinks, and I introduced myself to the blonde.

She told me that her name was Greta Baxter and that she knew who I was because I taught her sister at the Tech. Greta was twenty-one, and she worked as a secretary in one of the town's shirt factories. She had attended the Tech but after I was a pupil and before I was a teacher, so we had missed each other.

The next set was a slow dance, so I put my arm around Greta's waist and held her other hand while we shuffled around the floor. We were not exactly dancing cheek-to-cheek, more like my chin to her forehead, but it worked. I looked over and saw that Dave and his friend were also in a tight embrace.

At the end of the set I bought a round of drinks, and I was amused to find that Greta and her friend, Bobby, were shifting brandy and Babycham, a potent mixture, but they seemed to be able to handle it. We alternated sets of dancing with rounds of drinking until eleven o'clock. I think it was one of the girls who suggested that we got a taxi before the rush started and went back to their flat for a nightcap.

The girls shared a flat on the top floor of a terraced house in Station Street. They turned down the lights in the lounge and put on Jim Reeves. They seemed to be well stocked with bottles of shorts and mixtures. I sat on an armchair and nursed a whiskey and ginger. Greta came unbidden and sat on my lap. She was very affectionate, and when I came up for air I noticed that Dave and Bobby were no longer with us. Well, good luck to him, I thought, but I don't really want a quick jump. I had got past the stage where I would go out with more or less any girl as I had done as a teenager. I hoped that I wasn't becoming a snob but I felt that Greta was not up to my expectations. I had to be honest with myself. I was looking for a life partner. I got through the next hour snogging and drinking. I didn't want to take it any further.

Dave and Bobby came out of the bedroom and asked us if we wanted coffee. Greta put the main lights on and joined Bobby in the kitchen. I looked over at Dave who had a contented grin on his face. We drank our coffee and kissed the girls goodnight. I managed to avoid Greta's suggestions for a future meeting. I told her that I was very busy with the UDR. She seemed to lose interest after that revelation although I knew that she came from a Loyalist family. I supposed that girls didn't see UDR men as long-term prospects.

Dave and I parted out on the street. Before we went our separate ways, he confirmed that he and Bobby went way back. We shook hands and promised to meet up at the bookies the following Saturday.

I joined my platoon for duty on Tuesday night. My section was detailed for 'bomb patrol'. This meant that we would patrol the town and local area in Landrovers sometimes getting out to do a foot patrol to show the flag, reassure the local loyalists, and discourage republicans from setting up shootings or laying bombs.

We left the Landrovers with their drivers parked in the main square. The reserve police officers on the barricades had let us enter the town centre. John Madison was our corporal, and he led the four of us on a foot patrol through the town. We checked shop doorways in the commercial sector and then headed down to Mountjoy Park. This was a well-known meeting point for local teenagers who often gathered to play guitars and drink cheap wine. We soon encountered a group sitting on the walls of a small stone bridge over the stream, which meandered through the park.

"Hello, sir!" shouted a teenage girl who was obviously the worse for drink. I recognised her as Janice Conway a student in my commercial arithmetic class.

"Are you playing soldiers, sir? Can we play?" she continued. I knew that it would ruin my credibility at the Tech but I grabbed the bottle from her and poured it into the stream.

This provoked a barrage of complaints but I noticed that John Madison had also grabbed a bottle and was pouring out the contents. I wasn't sure of the legal position but I reckoned that the teenagers were not going to make any complaints to the police. I heard a commotion behind me and turned around to see Noel Gibson and a red-haired teenage yob fighting over possession of a bottle. John Madison strode towards them and slapped the lad across the face. He took the bottle and poured its contents over the lad's head.

"Do you think that we haven't got better things to deal with than to sort out you little shites?" he roared. "Now fuck off home before we run you in. I know your father," he said to the red-haired lad. "I bet he's fucking proud of you."

The teenagers moved off reluctantly. One of them turned around and shouted, "We'll get you, Gibson, when you're on your own!"

This wasn't exactly what I had joined up for.

We moved on back to the town square and mounted up. The police let us out at the barricade and we headed off to Downhill, a sleepy seaside village. We set up a VCP at the bottom of the hill down into the village. We were a hundred yards from the hotel, which was holding its usual Tuesday night country and western dance. I stood behind a low wall to cover the VCP and listened to the strains of a poor Patsy Cline imitation.

Still, I thought, young people were in there enjoying themselves, and I was out here groping a rifle. It did concern me that patrons could park their cars right up to the front door. This was Loyalist territory, and the Provos could easily have parked a car-bomb next to the hotel. I made a mental note to inform our intelligence officer.

I was woken from my thoughts by John Madison shouting for us to mount up.

We followed the coast road all the way to Ballykelly and entered Shackleton Barracks where we took our refreshments in the same room where I had done my basic training. Then we drove inland to Limavady where we did a foot patrol through the town. It was all very quiet. We mounted up and set up VCPs every mile along the road back to Maddenstown. There were very few cars on the roads, and most people were very co-operative.

This is a waste of time, I thought. We are never going to stop a car carrying arms or explosives. The Provos aren't that stupid. Why weren't we doing something more pro-active? I knew that the establishment didn't want us to come into direct contact with the Republican population. They were prepared to spend millions maintaining thirty thousand reserve police officers and UDR soldiers just to keep us under control. The UDA marches in the early seventies had demonstrated that one hundred thousand Loyalists were prepared to go onto the streets. The government had obviously gambled millions of pounds just to keep control of thirty thousand of the more ardent Loyalists to direct them away from the Republicans.

We were back at base by four o'clock, and I was in my bed twenty minutes later. I couldn't sleep. I was due to teach Janice in the morning. No doubt she would tell her mates and my name would be mud. I hadn't been in the UDR a six months but I had my doubts already.

In December 1973, Mervyn Rees, the Secretary of State for Northern Ireland, coerced Loyalist and Nationalist politicians to meet in England to reconcile their differences. They came up with the Sunningdale Agreement, which was designed to lead to power sharing. Unfortunately, a Labour politician once again showed that he had completely misjudged the mood of the people of Ulster, especially the Loyalists. Politicians, paramilitaries, trade unionists, clergy, and ordinary people formed the Ulster Workers Council, which called for a general strike beginning in mid-May of 1974.

The strike received massive support from the Loyalist people, and this had serious consequences for the security forces. Up to now, I had always found that most of the Loyalists that we encountered were generally supportive of our efforts even when they were held up at VCPs or searched entering Derry. That all changed. I sensed a new mood. Loyalists were more likely to be critical because they saw us as part of the hated establishment.

I also encountered many more UDA barricades, even in broad daylight, as I travelled to and from work and to the UDR. Eventually the petrol stations ran out of fuel as they received no deliveries, and I had to purchase cans of army petrol at the base. Then the power strikes began, which affected TV and radio and the street lighting. There were no postal services. I always felt fairly secure when I was on duty but I had some scary moments travelling home in the early hours of the morning when I came across paramilitary barricades.

There was also a new phenomenon. UDR members were accosted at their front door by Loyalists looking for their weapons. The paramilitaries soon caught on that we no longer took our rifles home, and they began to demand personal protection pistols. We were split in our response to this.

Some members agreed simply to hand the weapons over while others like myself vowed to use them, but I was never put to the test.

After two weeks the power sharing executive collapsed, and Rees imposed direct rule from Westminster. After that we gained the impression that the Labour government were washing their hands of the Protestants of Northern Ireland and that included the UDR. There seemed to be increasing measures to prevent us from meeting the Republican section of the community face-to-face. My application for a commission was turned down because of lack of funds, and I never bothered to apply to become a lance corporal. I did my three duties a week for the rest of the year, and I didn't even go on the summer training camp in England because I went for a two weeks holiday in Corfu at the same time.

I spent Christmas Eve of 1974 with my father, and then I did seven duty nights in a row to help to relieve the married members. My New Year resolution was to widen my social life, to make an effort to meet single girls who were not put off by my membership of the UDR.

The first couple of months of 1975 continued with the same pattern of '74. Mervyn Rees introduced legislation to tighten up on gun ownership and membership of shooting clubs. For Christ's sake we scoffed, there were more illegal guns per head of population in Ulster than in the USA. The Protestant paramilitaries geared up their campaign of killing innocent Catholics in retaliation for the murder of soldiers and policemen. The PIRA lapped it up; they simply killed more defenceless Protestants. I was particularly incensed by the death of a 16-year-old Air Training Corps cadet who triggered a bomb when he did his officer a favour by opening their training hut. Is there nobody in this country with the intelligence and resources to take the fight directly to the terrorists, I asked myself?

Morale in the company reached an all time low with the murder of two of our members while off duty. In February, the Provisional Army Council proclaimed that they were resuming their on-off ceasefire while all sorts of secret talks were held with Protestant clergymen. We assumed that the Provos were also having secret talks with the Labour government. Meanwhile, the UDA and UVF carried on a blood feud, which was really a fight for the control of crime in Loyalist areas. The Irish National Liberation Army continued their feud with various factions of the IRA. We had been ordered to keep a low profile in Republican areas and to concentrate on holding the ring between the various Loyalist feuding groups.

Some of our members started to take chances, which they would not have done ordinarily. Jack Hutchinson, a guy who I had shared a sangar with on many occasions, was a gentle giant. Some might say, he was a bit slow-witted. He drove a lorry for Maddenstown Council in the town where he lived with his mother. He had found himself a girlfriend, one of the few Protestants who lived in Listober, a Republican town a few miles south of Maddenstown. Jack started to visit his girlfriend regularly, spending the evening at her family home on the outskirts of Listober. It was my habit to listen to the BBC Ulster news on the radio while taking my breakfast before setting off for college. One morning in early March I was sickened to hear that gunmen had sprayed Jack and his girl with automatic weapons as they were kissing goodnight in the doorway of her home. They were both pronounced dead at the scene. The Provos denied responsibility, blaming the attack on the INLA who in turn blamed the PIRA.

Less than a week later, Terry Farrell, one of our Catholic members, went to a dance in the Marion Hall in Kilrea with three Catholic friends who weren't members. At the end of the evening they couldn't locate him and assumed that he had gone off with a 'hard blonde ticket' that he had spent most of the evening dancing with. Next morning his mother rang the police in Maddenstown who contacted the UDR but there was no sign of Terry. Further investigation revealed that Terry had been issued with a 9mm Browning for his personal protection, because he was a Catholic, but it was found in his bedroom; he had not taken it with him. An investigation by the RUC could not find anyone who knew the identity of the blonde or at least who were prepared to say anything. All of the UDR companies in East Londonderry were called out to assist the police and soldiers from a squadron of the Dragoon Guards in searching the area. We broke every rule by entering barns, pigsties, cowsheds, and deserted cottages but there was no trace. One training evening, Captain Armstrong, our Intelligence Officer, told us that the RUC had been given word by a go-between that the PIRA were not responsible for lifting Terry.

Then in early March, the Coleraine Chronicle received an anonymous telephone tip-off that a body could be found in a ditch beside the Limavady to Dungiven road. A Felix, or bomb disposal team was called out from Derry to check that it was not a trap, and then George Maguire volunteered to identify the remains. He reported that he was 99 per cent sure that it was our colleague Terry. This was later confirmed from his dental records at the post-mortem, which also revealed that Terry had received a terrible beating before being shot in the back of the head.

Terry did not receive a military funeral at the request of his parents. They feared that his Catholic school friends and distant members of his family would be intimidated by Republican paramilitaries from attending if there was going to be a military presence.

About twenty members of the company met that night in the Londonderry Arms in the town square to see Terry off. The mood was initially sombre but the evening ended on a high once the drink had disguised us.

As the year progressed the government continued to release hundreds of Republican detainees in response to the PIRA ceasefire. There were no PIRA spectaculars but the tit-for-tat killings between the various factions on both sides continued on a daily basis. My life had slipped into a routine of work and duties. Despite my New Year resolution my social life was non-existent.

Chapter 10 - Dominic McGann

I attended a two-hour training session on a Thursday evening in April. My section did a lesson on map work led by our platoon commander Lieutenant Roddy Houston. Then we went down to the .22 range with other sections from the platoon. We had a lot of fun in a competition, which involved knocking over five matchboxes at twentyfive yards with single-shot BSA .22 match rifles. We were given ten rounds each, and there were points for matchboxes down and rounds left. I was not surprised to win my first two heats, which put me into the final against three other shooters. I ended up runner-up to George Maguire, our platoon sergeant, who was a crackshot from the old 'B' Specials.

We finished earlier than usual, and Roddy called us together to address the whole platoon. He told us that he wanted volunteers for a special mobile patrol on Sunday. We would be setting up VCPs between Derry and the border near a town called Letterkenny in the Irish Republic. About a dozen of us put our names forward.

I decided to devote a day to myself on the Saturday. I cleaned the house and did my laundry, and then I headed down to the bookies at the end of Union Street. I studied form for about half an hour and then picked four horses for a Yankee with singles. I went next door to the pub and ordered a pint of Tennent's and a cheese and potato pasty.

The pub was getting very busy because the racing was due to start on the TV. I ate my pasty and lowered my pint while I watched my first two selections run like tugboats. I ambled back up Union Street to number nine where I stretched myself out on the sofa to watch my other two donkeys on TV. I got one winner, which didn't quite cover my total outlay, but I was happy. I rationalised it that I had bought some useful information for the future.

My thoughts kept straying to the next day. I realised that we would be going into real Indian country but I had no idea what to expect. Hopefully we were going to make contact and get into some serious action against the Provos. Would I be up to it?

I resolved to stay in and rest that evening and keep off the drink. There was a good movie on TV. I knew that, at my age, I should be out in the bars and discos sniffing out totty but I needed to be fully alert on Sunday. I finished the evening watching the football, and then I crawled into my pit.

Sunday morning came quickly. It was cold, dark, and drizzling at six in the morning. I made up a flask of soup and cut myself a pile of cheese and pickle sandwiches. I decided to carry my piece in the car. I got into my uniform, pulling on the long johns for the first time. I made my way down to the woodie, gave it a quick check, and then drove to HQ. I was in good time but the car park was already almost full. I was surprised to see a Shorland armoured car parked with the usual assortment of Landrovers and mini-buses. The Shorland was an armoured Landrover with a turret on top. The General Purpose Machine Gun, called the gimpy, could be mounted in the turret to give heavy support fire.

I drew my SLR and a flak jacket and squeezed into the rest room where there was thirty-plus members drawn from all three platoons. I learned that 34 platoon were putting up two different country mobile patrols in our area, 35 platoon were providing base guard and a local bomb patrol while my mob, 33 platoon, was forming the special mobile for the border. There must be something on, I thought, for such a big effort.

The officers came down to join us, and David Armstrong, the Intelligence Officer, told us that the regulars and the police were carrying out a large search operation in Derry that day. They had also been given intelligence that the Provos were preparing a spectacular somewhere in our area today but they had no further details.

"Be specially alert," he warned us and then sent us on to our various duties.

Nine of us were detailed for the special mobile, eight from my section led by our platoon sergeant George Maguire. I had mixed feelings when we went outside, and I discovered that we had been allocated two patrol Landrovers and not the Shorland. I had a fear of being confined in constricted spaces even though the Shorland offered greater protection.

We set off for Derry. I wondered whether we would have to go through the Bogside to get to the border near Letterkenny. My geographical knowledge of that area was rather limited. I supposed that if the police and regulars were searching in Derry it would be in the Bogside, and they would not want us showing up. Once we had got across the Craigavon Bridge over the Foyle, I was happy to see that we swung west and took a circular route around the maiden city, which took us onto the Letterkenny road.

We sped along a country road with tall, thick hedges on both sides. I was in the second Landrover driven by Alfie Thompson with Lance-Corporal Gordon Morrow in the front passenger seat. Jimmy Patton and I occupied the two seats nearest the rear facing each other. We started down a long incline, and I turned to look behind me through the wire-meshed windscreen. I could

76

see a wooden trestle supporting three aluminum milk churns on the left; a familiar sight at farm entrances in Ulster. I turned away to look out of the back when I heard a massive explosion, and our Landrover came to a sudden stop as it smacked into the rear of what was left of the leading patrol vehicle. Jimmy and I had been thrown in a heap on the floor beneath the bench seats.

We immediately came under heavy machine-gun fire. The makrolon armour was useless. As I looked up, I was horrified to see Gordon's head disintegrate as it was hit by a heavy round. Alfie was lying slumped over the steering wheel. His left arm was shattered. I crawled to the back and jumped out of the Landrover. Jimmy followed my lead. We rolled into the ditch at the left-hand side of the road. The machine-gun fire continued to pepper our Landrover. I could see that the leading Landrover had been blown over on its side and was slewed across the road. It was a wreck; nobody was getting out.

Jimmy and I crept along the ditch away from the scene. We passed a hedge, which separated the field that was the source of the gunfire from another field. We spotted a gate to the second field and crawled under it. I could see that the hedge separating the two fields was growing out of an embankment about two feet high. Jimmy and I crawled over to it and lay down behind the embankment.

The machine-gun fire had stopped, so I peeked over the embankment and through the hedge. I saw that the adjoining field sloped up to a ridge, and there appeared to be figures up there. I whispered in Jimmy's ear suggesting that we crawled up the side of the hedge until we could get a shot at them.

We crawled about halfway up the hedgerow until we came to a gap. There was a water-trough forming the barrier so that animals from both fields could use drink from it. When we looked over it we saw two men walking down the field carrying AK-47s. I nudged Jimmy and told him that I would take the nearer one. I cocked my SLR and stood up to challenge the men.

"British Army! Drop your weapons!"

Both men turned sideways towards us and opened fire from the hip. Jimmy and I returned the fire, and both men went down. I was sure that I had hit my man in the chest at least once. I became aware that Jimmy was screaming, so I looked sideways to see Jimmy going down with wounds in his abdomen and legs.

A burst of heavy machine-gun fire riddled the trough in front of me so I leapt to my left to get behind the embankment. I crawled further up the field while the machine-gunner sprayed the hedge above me. I got to the top of the ridge, and I risked a look through the hedge.

Two men dressed in camouflage smocks were serving a large machine-gun on a small bipod. I reckoned that it was an American M-60. The weapon jammed or ran out of ammunition, so I fired two hasty rounds in their direction. They both got up to abandon the machine-gun. One of the men pulled a pistol from his smock and fired a couple of rounds at me. One of them hit the plastic stock of my SLR shattering it. I was aware that I had been hit in the head and face and I had a shard of plastic sticking out of my upper right arm. I pulled it out and almost fainted with the pain.

My rage pulled me together, so I burst through the hedge to get a better shot. The pistol shooter had run over the brow of the hill by now and was making for a Morris van parked in the gate to the field. The other machine-gunner had fallen over. When he got to his feet, I saw that he was a teenager. He started to run to the van but half turned towards me with a black object in his hand. I fired at his upper torso just as he turned away, and he went down on his face.

The van's engine was roaring as the driver tried to get away but his rear wheels were struggling to get a grip in the mud. I fired two rounds through the rear windows of the van but the driver managed to get it through the entrance to the field. As he turned right onto the road I fired two more shots through the driver's door. I was sure that I had hit the van but it sped off towards the border.

I ran over to check the teenager. I pulled him over to get a look at him. He was about sixteen with a narrow face, which betrayed years of poverty and neglect. What the hell had brought him to this field where his last contribution to this world was the murder of decent family men? One of my rounds must have hit him because he was stone dead but I could not find a wound. I ran back down the slope and found that the guy that I had shot was dead, and the other terrorist was in a bad way. I flung their AK-47s over the hedge. My main concern now was to help Jimmy. I went over and scrambled over the trough. Jimmy was unconscious. His trousers were soaking with blood, and his face was the colour of cheese sauce. I struggled to remove Jimmy's flak jacket so that I could open his NATO jacket. I had to keep wiping blood from my right eye. I undid Jimmy's belt and rolled his trousers down. He was a mess. Both legs had taken a round from the M60, and he must have taken another round in his abdomen. I pulled a bandage out of my kit bag and struggled to remember what I had been told in the first-aid lessons. I was attempting to apply the bandage to one of his wounds when I heard the whack-whack from the blades of a helicopter.

A Wessex was landing at the top of the ridge and soldiers were jumping out. They wore the badge of the Royal Greenjackets and seemed to know how to take control. A sergeant ran down to me and took one look at my efforts and then detailed a soldier to take over from me. He carried a large first-aid kit and seemed to know what he was doing.

I briefed the sergeant on what had happened, and he started shouting orders. He sent three men down to the Landrovers and two others over to the downed AK-47 men. He got onto his personal radio and then looked me full in the face.

"What about you, mate, you don't look too good, how are you feeling?"

I told him that I was fine but that a lot of my compatriots were dead and dying.

He replied, "You don't look fine, you seem to have taken some hits." He took out a bandage, opened it and doused it with water from a flask. He wiped my face and the top of my head. "You've been hit on your head and jaw but not by bullets. How did that happen?"

I pointed to my SLR, which he picked up. The stock was shattered; there was not much of it left on the right-hand side.

"Christ, you were lucky," said the sergeant. "It seems to have deflected a round, and you got cut up by the splinters."

I could hear sirens, and I looked down to see police cars, ambulances, and army Landrovers lining up behind our vehicle. I was aware that the Greenjackets were carrying wounded men, including Jimmy, to the helicopter, which soon took off and banked away towards Derry.

I was examining my SLR when a corporal wearing the brassard of the Royal Military Police came and took it from me. He put it into a large plastic sheath along with my other magazine. He asked me for my name which he wrote on a label laced to the bag. He did the same with Jimmy's SLR and asked me for his name.

Then I was lead down to one of the ambulances where a medic from the RAMC cleaned up my facial wounds and patched them. He took off my flak jacket and cut open the upper sleeve of my jacket. He cleaned and bandaged the wound. He asked me if I was in pain, and I had to admit that I was feeling it now. He gave me two painkillers and two other tablets that he said were antibiotics.

I was then conducted to a police car by an RUC sergeant. I was driven to a police station in Derry where a doctor examined me again. He put a couple of stitches in my head wound and three under my jaw. He examined my arm and re-patched it.

An RUC inspector came into the room and asked me if I felt up to making a statement.

"You don't have to," cautioned the doctor. "Why not wait a couple of days until you're feeling better?"

I replied that I seemed to be the only one who could tell them what happened and that I'd better get it done as quickly as possible. I was taken into an interview room where a captain in the regulars and a RUC inspector cautioned me.

"Why am I being cautioned?" I asked.

"You told the sergeant that you had killed two men; it's procedure," replied the inspector.

They took me through my version of the events, taking notes but saying nothing. When I asked about the boys from my platoon, they told me that there had been four killed and four severely wounded and myself. Three terrorists were dead; one had died in the helicopter.

I was then taken to a canteen where I was given soup but I couldn't move my jaw to chew the sandwiches. A constable came in and told me that a UDR Landrover from Maddenstown was waiting outside to take me home.

I went outside and was met by Captain David Armstrong and three lads from 35 platoon. I got into the back of the jeep, and Armstrong jumped in with me. A private, who I did not know, took the rear seat to guard us. On the way back, I told the captain everything that I could recall. He told me that George was dead along with Corporal Clark and private Connell from the leading vehicle. Gordon Morrow I knew about. Three others were in hospital in Derry. They had found a command wire leading to the site where the churns had been.

The private who had been on guard at the rear of the vehicle turned and said, "You'll be getting a medal for this."

"More like a murder charge," I answered.

"No, no," interjected Armstrong. "Those were righteous killings. These guys were Provo terrorists."

We pulled into HQ at Maddenstown. The mood in the rest room was sombre. The sergeant major shook my hand. He was a decorated hero from the Korean War but I felt a fraud when he congratulated me. I said that I was fit to drive the woodie home because I didn't want to risk someone else finding my piece stuffed into the driver's seat. I was accompanied by a UDR Landrover until I parked outside the mini-market. I assured the corporal in charge of my escort that I was OK to get to my front door without help. I didn't want them to see me getting the .38 out from the seat.

It all hit me when I crawled into my pit. My face and arm were throbbing. I was shocked by the carnage that I had witnessed, and I was angry and apprehensive about how I had been treated in the RUC station. I realised that there was no way that I could work the next day; I would have to ring in the next morning.

When I woke, I felt like I had been in a train-wreck. I staggered downstairs, and I rang the Tech. I took two more painkillers and crawled back to my bed where I soon fell into a deep sleep. I was woken by heavy banging at the front door. I slipped into my dressing gown and stumbled down the stairs. It was Linda May.

"Jesus, Charlie! What's happened to you?" She pushed past me into the dining room. She told me that the Principal had given her permission to leave at lunchtime to find out how I was. She knew about the ambush from her brother Michael, and she told me that she had lain awake all night worrying whether I was one of the fatalities. The Boss had told the staff about my condition after he had got the details of my phone-call.

Linda insisted on making me a light lunch, which we shared. I caught her studying me anxiously, and I laughed.

"Relax, Linda, I'm hardly touched. This will all heal up. I got off light. Think about the lads who didn't make it," I tried to assure her.

"Charlie, give it up. You've done your bit. Ask me out again when you've left the UDR. You know that I fancy you."

I laughed again. "It wouldn't make any difference. This battalion has lost three former members to the IRA. They've got long memories or else their intelligence is out of date. I can't leave now. I've got a score to settle."

"But at least you wouldn't be putting yourself in danger, and you would have more time for your social life. I never see you out anywhere these days," she sobbed.

"Do you really care that much?"

"I do Charlie, you know I do."

"Look, tell the boss that I will be back in a few days time. I promise, I'll listen to what you said but I've just got to get back to bed now," I told her.

She kissed me on my good cheek as we parted at the front door. I pulled myself up the stairs and crawled into bed. My head was spinning with conflicting thoughts. I wanted to get back into the saddle as quickly as possible but I realised that it was holding back my social life. Did I really want to chase Linda? Maybe I should get out of this God-forsaken country.

By Thursday I was back at college where the plasters on my head and chin excited lots of comments from staff and students alike. It was common knowledge by now that I was a soldier in the UDR. Some of the Catholic teachers were a bit standoffish, and I heard whispered derogatory comments from some of my Catholic students. On the other hand, a couple of the Catholic members of staff were friendly and asked after my health.

On Thursday night I turned up for a training evening but I was intercepted by Corporal Irvine who led me up to the office where Captain Armstrong was waiting for me. He asked me how I felt but his attention seemed to be elsewhere.

"Private Cunningham, I have to inform you that you are suspended from duty pending further investigation of the events at Ballylisson on Sunday," he said formally.

He stood up and came around the desk. "Sorry about this, Charlie; it's procedure. As far as I'm concerned, you did everything by the book but the RUC in Derry are saying that you shot an unarmed man and that you fired at a vehicle."

He reached out and patted my uninjured arm. "Go home and get the events right in your mind. You're going to have to go to Derry to be interrogated again. Don't worry; I'll drive you there, and if you need a solicitor, I've got my cousin Reggie lined up. But it won't go that far."

I was marched out and had to hand over my identification card to Corporal Irvine. I got into the woodie and drove home with thoughts racing through my mind. I had joined up to get at the Provos. I had volunteered for the duties, which made that most likely. Then I had been given the opportunity. I thought that I had done well. Now here I was possibly facing charges. I remembered Carson Boyd, my aunt Sadie's husband, warning me that the government didn't really want the UDR to come face to face with terrorists. They wanted us to put on a show to reassure Loyalists and to control the very men who were most likely to take the Provos on. Surely there were other avenues for tackling the Provos. I wasn't interested in harming Catholics. I looked on all religions with bemused contempt. I couldn't join the UDA or the UVF. There must be people who were interested purely on taking on Republican terrorism. I shook my head to put such thoughts out of my mind, and I concentrated on driving to number nine.

I went to Gordon Morrow's funeral as a private citizen. I was sickened by the sight of his widow and two young sons weeping uncontrollably at the graveside. I visited Alfie in hospital where I was relieved to hear that he wasn't going to lose his arm but he told me that he had no intentions of staying in the UDR.

I concentrated on my teaching career for the next two weeks, and then I had to report to the UDR doctor in Coleraine to get my stitches out. He seemed to know all about the ambush, and he shook my hand and told me to keep my chin up. Yeah, so that the girls can see my scar, I thought as I drove back to Maddenstown.

I settled down to spend the evening planning lessons and marking but I was soon interrupted by someone banging on my front door. I opened it to find the RUC inspector who had sat in on my interrogation about the Danny Gallagher incident. I invited him in, and we took seats in the lounge. He enquired about my health and then he reached me an envelope.

"You are asked to report to RUC headquarters in Derry at 10 o'clock next Monday morning. This is part of the investigation into the deaths in that incident in Ballylisson. You can bring someone with you. I understand that Captain Armstrong will accompany you. You are not under arrest but you will be interviewed under oath."

"Yeah, I was expecting this," I said.

"If it's any consolation, the lads at the barracks think that you did a good job. Just remember that if someone points an object at you under those circumstances, then you are entitled to think that it is a weapon. But I never said that. Good luck."

I showed him to the door, and then went back to read the contents of the envelope. It confirmed what the inspector had said.

That evening, Captain Armstrong phoned me and offered to drive me to Derry. We arranged for him to pick me up at number nine at eight o'clock on Monday morning. I had a nasty feeling that the shit was going to hit the fan, so I went to the bottom of my garden and dug a pit about three feet deep. I greased the .38 and wrapped it in an old towel, and then I placed it at the bottom of the pit. I shovelled in half of the soil that I had dug out. Then I took a gallon can of engine-oil out of the shed. It had only about a pint still in it. I poured the oil into the pit, and then I jumped all over the can until it was flat. I placed the can into the pit and then shovelled in the rest of the soil. I had no interest in gardening but there were plenty of weeds to choose from. I dug some up and replanted them over the pit.

I kept my head down on Saturday; I didn't even go to the bookies. On Sunday morning I went for a run along Castlerock beach out to the Barmouth. This was where the River Bann entered the sea. There were two massive piers on either bank, and I walked out to the end of the west pier. Even though the sea was moderate the waves were throwing large blankets of spray over the end of the pier. A very dangerous place, I had been brought up to be aware of, because the end of the pier was like an ice-rink. I couldn't help thinking that it would be an ideal place to make an end of things if I had to. I had resolved that I would never do time in a Northern Ireland prison.

I gathered my thoughts and ran back to Castlerock. I got into the woodie and drove to my father's place in Coleraine to make his Sunday dinner. When I had washed the dishes, I sat down with him and brought him up to speed on the events of the last two weeks. He wasn't a well man but he had all of his mental facilities.

"You have nothing to worry about. Tell the truth. Those chaps weren't innocent; they were murderers. Big boys' games, big boys' rules. You were trained, armed, and paid by the government to do exactly what you did do."

"I have a feeling that the government never really expected us to take the Provos on face to face. They're happy with the idea that we are targets."

I hugged my da as I left. I wondered whether I would ever see him again. I reached him a sealed envelope and said, "If anything bad happens give this to Kathy." The letter explained to Kathy all about my financial affairs and how to wind them up.

"Don't be daft. I'll see you next Sunday," said Da, but he had tears in his eyes.

Chapter 11 - Harry Weir

On Monday morning I was up bright and early. I had dressed casually but smartly. I had my story well rehearsed, and I was fairly confident. David Armstrong knocked the door dead on eight o'clock. We made small talk as he drove his MGB expertly along the road to Londonderry. As we approached Ebrington Barracks, headquarters of the 5th Battalion, he said, "I just want to call in here for a moment."

The guard at the gate seemed to recognise Captain Armstrong and his car even though he was in civvies like me. We parked on the parade ground, and Armstrong asked me to accompany him into an office. I was surprised when Captain Leslie came in to join us.

"Relax Charlie," said Armstrong. "We're just going to go over your story and then give you a couple of tips. Let's all sit down and you tell us what happened, in your own words, from start to finish."

I told them my version of events without interruption while they both took the occasional note.

"Well done," said Blair Leslie. "Now let me cover a few points. You will be interrogated by Superintendent Machonachie of the RUC. Now he's a fair-minded man but he is under pressure from people who aren't exactly fans of the UDR, especially now that we have this Labour government. He will be out to catch you out if you didn't follow procedures. The other chap is Lieutenant-Colonel Baring from the Army Legal Corps. Now he is a qualified barrister, and his job is partly to look after your interests, also to find out if you have committed a civilian crime but also whether you have breached army discipline."

He looked over at David Armstrong, "Anything to add, David, before we get down to specifics?" Captain Armstrong shook his head.

"OK," said Leslie. "The shooting of Breen and Conroy is not a problem. Private Patton has confirmed that you shouted a warning. and then you were fired upon first before returning fire. Forensics have shown that the teenager, Christopher Toner, had helped to fire the M-60. You had already been injured in the head by a pistol shot from the other machine-gunner when you thought that Toner was pulling a pistol on you, which was a reasonable assumption. The fact that it turned out to be the bolt from the M-60 is just too bad for him."

Armstrong broke in, "We now know that the shot which you fired hit him on his hip-bone and then richocheted up tumbling through his internal organs."

Leslie went on, "Now we turn to the guy in the van. You admitted that you fired four shots into the van, which is against standing orders. On the other hand, it was being driven by a man who had already wounded you, who had probably served the M-60 that had killed and injured seven others. For all you knew, he still had his pistol and was liable to fire back at you at anytime."

David Armstrong took over, "Do you see what we are getting at? For both of the machine-gunners you had reasonable belief that your life was in danger. That's how you tell it."

Captain Leslie shook my hand and wished me well. Armstrong and I went out to the MG, and ten minutes later we drove into the compound of the RUC base in the Strand Road.

Eventually, we were ushered into an interrogation room. An RUC superintendent and an officer wearing the crown and pip of a lieutenant colonel were seated behind a table. I was invited to sit down facing them, and I was told that Captain Armstrong could remain in the room as my 'friend' but he was not to be allowed to speak. I was cautioned and told that I had not been charged at this stage.

The superintendent led me through my version of events while the army officer scribbled furiously onto a pad. Then the RUC man got stuck in.

"It turns out that Christopher Toner was unarmed, yet a bullet from your rifle was found in his body. How do you explain that?"

I told them, "I expect that you have found out by now, from forensics, that Toner helped to fire that machine-gun." They turned and exchanged glances.

I went on, "I could have told you that I shot Toner when he was serving the machine-gun but instead I told you the truth. I had already been injured by his mate when Toner turned to me and pulled a black object from his pocket. I was scared that it was a pistol, so I shot him first."

"Be that as it may," said the superintendent. "However, you couldn't see the occupant of the van when you fired four rounds into it. His wife and children might have been in there."

I couldn't help laughing. "Are you seriously suggesting that is what you'll say in a court of law? An IRA active service unit takes their wife and children along for an ambush and a picnic?"

"Private Cunningham!" shouted Captain Armstrong.

"You would do well to treat this affair seriously, Private Cunningham," said the colonel.

"I reasonably assumed that the four terrorists and the machine-gun and their weapons had travelled to the ambush in the little Morris. It never crossed my mind that there could be others in the van. I knew that the machine-gunner had got into the van – I saw him. I knew very well that he was armed and prepared to use it." I reached up and rubbed the scar under my chin, for effect.

"I thought that I could see his outline through the windows in the rear doors when I fired the first two rounds. When he turned, I could clearly recognise the driver, who I knew to be armed, so I fired two more rounds. I was wounded, there was blood running into my right eye, and the rifle was damaged, so unfortunately I missed."

"Oh, did you?" remarked the colonel. "Is there anything else that you want to tell us?"

"No, sir," I replied.

"OK, could you go outside and wait in the refreshment room. Captain Armstrong, could you stay behind to help us with a couple of points," ordered the superintendent.

I went down the corridor and found a refreshment room where I poured myself a mug of coffee from an urn. I nodded at an RUC constable as he was leaving the room.

A few seconds later, a very big man in his forties came into the room. He was well over six feet and must have weighed twenty stone. He looked like a farmer. He wore massive brown corduroy trousers and a lumberjack shirt. He carried a Walther PPK in a holster under his left armpit.

"Are you young Cunningham from Maddenstown?" he asked as he stuck out his massive right-hand.

"Yes," I said as I put my hand in his.

"That was a fucking good job you done at Ballylisson. Not many of us get a chance to kill three of the bastards."

"No, I killed two of them, my mate killed the other one."

"Ah, you haven't heard then. I'm Detective Sergeant Harry Weir. We traced your Morris van to a farm near Nixon's Corner. It was hidden in a barn and no wonder. The driver's seat and floor was like an abbatoir.

Somebody lost a lot of blood. We brought it in and found Dominic McGann's bloody prints all over it."

"What about McGann?" I asked.

"Well his mother told us that he had emigrated to America but I could show you where he's buried. Dominic must have lost too much blood before they got their doctor to him. They got a tame priest to bury him in a corner of their spud field. He had it coming to him. We reckon that he was involved in the murder of at least eight members of the security forces but we could never get to him. Fucking good job son. Are they giving you a hard time in there?"

I shrugged and he patted me on the shoulder. "Stick to your story and you'll be alright."

As he left I wondered how he knew what my story was.

Five minutes later David Armstrong came into the room. "They just asked me about your background and your service record. I gave you a glowing reference. They're talking things over. If it's not long, it will be good news."

We waited for another twenty minutes before a police sergeant told us that we should go back in. When we entered the room, the colonel told me that I should stand to attention.

"Well, Private Cunningham. On the first matter we feel that, under the circumstances, you were entitled to think that Toner was about to do you harm, and there will be no further action on that count. On the second matter we feel that, although you were reckless in firing so many rounds at the van, because we have no proof that anyone was actually injured by those shots, we will recommend that your Officer Commanding admonishes you before you return to your duties." He smiled and said, "Captain Armstrong, thank you for your contribution. March him out."

As we drove back over the Craigavon Bridge, David Armstrong turned to me and remarked, "That was a good result."

I didn't think so. I felt that I was guiltless but on the other hand it was nice to know about McGann.

"Did they mention the blood in the van, sir?"

"Yes, they know about that but they take the view that you might have injured the machine-gunner when you fired at them when they were still at the gun. The fact that you pointed out to them that you could have said the same about Toner made you a credible witness."

"Do you know that McGann actually died from his wounds?"

"No," he replied, "Who's McGann?"

I told him about my conversation with Harry Weir. He was almost struck dumb.

"The superintendent doesn't know about this. They don't even have a name for the fourth man."

"I got the impression that Sergeant Weir was a bit of a maverick," I replied.

"Well let's keep quiet about this. We don't want it all opened up again. Let's call into Limavady for a drink."

We had a very nice lunch with lots of beer at a hotel just outside of Limavady. David, as I now called my newfound friend, didn't seem to give a toss about the possibility of being breathalysed as we drove towards Maddenstown.

"Are you alright to drive?" I asked him. "We could leave the car and get a taxi."

"No need," he replied, "they're not going to breathalyse me."

"Oh yeah," I replied. "I got the impression that they're out to get us."

"Believe me," he laughed. "There is no Maddenstown RUC man that'll bother me. I've got too much on them. Who's shagging whose wife? Who's selling stories to the UVF? I'm an intelligence officer for fuck's sake."

We made it back to number nine without incident.

On Saturday morning I was marched in to face Major Crawford. He read out the charge that contrary to UDR standing orders I had fired into a vehicle. I pleaded guilty and then the major announced, "You are admonished. March him out Corporal Irvine."

I was on base guard for the rest of the day and a couple of hours later the major sought me out in the rest room. I stood to attention but he stuck out his hand to shake mine.

"Sorry about that, you did a good job, let's forget it now."

But I didn't forget it. My relationship with the army had changed.

Chapter 12 - Tricia Corcoran

One of the greatest loves of my life was cricket. I was picked more for my enthusiasm than my talent. I rarely scored runs but I took the odd wicket because I bowled straight, and at the level where I played this usually got most batsmen out sooner or later. I was also worth my place for throwing myself around when we fielded. I played for the second eleven of Maddenstown Rugby Club which paradoxically had a lovely little cricket pitch behind the main stand. Jim Toy, who was the Head of Maths at the Tech, was the captain of the second eleven, and the Tech provided two other players.

On a beautiful Friday evening in May, we left the school at four o'clock and piled into Jim's old Landrover. We had a twenty overs game at the Rugby club starting at 4:30. In those days a twenty overs game was what it says; a normal game of cricket restricted to twenty overs for each side. We elected to bat and knocked up 93 runs before I was clean-bowled first ball to end the innings in the 18th over. The opposition were a staff team from a posh college in Derry. They were fit and took it seriously so they easily knocked up 94 for four in 16 overs. The game finished just after seven o'clock, so after a shower we were in the bar at half seven to make an early start.

In one corner of the lounge, three large leather sofas had been scattered around a very large coffee table. Half a dozen of us arranged ourselves around the table and got stuck in. I drank pints of Tennents with an occasional Bushmills chaser in those days. After an hour or so I was feeling rightly, and we were all in good form swapping jokes and outrageous stories.

I paid a visit to the men's room and when I returned, I noticed that the sofa opposite me was now occupied by three young women. I noticed one of them looking me over. She looked vaguely familiar but it was her friend, a willowy brunette with big blue eyes that grabbed my full attention. In fact, when she caught my eye, I felt like I had been hit in the face with a frying pan just like Tom and Jerry. It had been a long time since a woman had made such a first impression on me.

It was my round, so I staggered to the bar. By the time I had got served and persuaded a bar stewardess to carry my tray of drinks to the table, I found that I had lost my place on the sofa as the clubhouse started to fill up. I grabbed a spare chair and found a place on the outside of the table next to the woman who looked familiar. She was a blonde of about my age, not bad looking but starting to put on the beef, casually but well dressed with expensive accessories.

She leaned over and said "I know you, I went to school with you at the tech – must be ten years ago".

"Madeleine" I slurred. "Sorry, I can't remember your surname".

"No wonder with the amount of drink you've taken" she laughed. "How long have you lot been in here, it's still early? And the name's O'Hagan or rather it was, it's now Hart".

I looked down at the ring finger of her left hand for confirmation.

"Oh, dear. There's another one that I've let slip through my fingers" I joked.

"Piss off, you were never interested in me." Maddy, as I used to know her, told me that she had married a local solicitor and now had two little boys. She went on to tell me that the three girls all worked at the Hibernian Bank and that they had come to the Rugby club to see a folk group.

"Who's your friend at the end?" I asked, discreetly indicating the willowy brunette.

"That's Tricia Corcoran," she replied. "But you're wasting your time. She's from over the border, and she doesn't go out with prods. Her father is the new manager from Athlone. She's come north with him and the rest of the family. She's working at the bank with us."

"How do you know she doesn't go out with prods?" I asked.

"Ah, she was brought up to believe they've got tails and they fry slices of Catholic babies for breakfast," Madeleine retorted with a twinkle in her eye. "Do you want to meet her? I'll swap places with her – I'll make an excuse."

Maddy got up and spoke to Tricia who looked at me with startled eyes. She shuffled past Maddy and sat on the sofa, to my left. Now I know that I'm not God's gift to woman, but there has been the occasional woman in my life that didn't find me totally repulsive as they say in the play. I can't remember which. I had been out with better looking girls, so I rated my chances.

"Hello, where have you been all my life?" She gave me the standard answer, "For the first ten years I wasn't even born."

"But I'm a long way from thirty, and you're drinking so that can't be true," I replied. "My name's Charlie – what's yours?"

"Tricia, short for Patricia," and this led us into an interlude of pleasant banter. On later reflection, I probably wasn't as witty as I thought I was.

I bought her a drink and got a bottle of Tuborg to top up my pint – I was starting to feel it. Then the folk group struck up. Jim and two of my teammates said that they were off, and I told them that I would stay a while.

The problem with Irish folk music is that either you love it or you loathe it. I was in the latter group. For me the problem is that too many of the artists try to disguise their lack of talent by playing too loud and shouting. They usually end up playing Republican songs but this lot knew better than to do that at the Rugby Club.

After half an hour I gave up trying to talk to Tricia. I told her that I was moving on, and I said, "I don't have my car with me, or I would offer to take you home."

She looked at me incredulously. "Fuck off. I wouldn't get into a car with you in that state."

"What a charming turn of phrase from such an attractive young lady," I retorted.

She had the grace to blush. "Ask me sometime when you're sober, then I'll know that you mean it."

"Well, can I have your phone number?" I asked humbly.

"Yes, but it's my home number. If my mam or Dad answers say that you want to talk to me about my Rugby Club membership." She took out a diary and carefully wrote a number on a torn out note page.

I thanked her and made my way to the locker room. I picked up my cricket bag and the old Gladstone bag, which I carried my schoolbooks in. I went to the office and got the steward to ring me a taxi.

When I went home, I went straight to bed, early for me on a Friday night. I tossed and turned for hours. I mentally kicked myself for being so pissed just when I met a girl that I was really struck on. I made a point of not going out with Catholics. I wasn't bigoted but I wanted to avoid future complications. Tricia was not only a Catholic but a southerner too, possibly a Republican. I mocked myself, you hardly know her, you haven't spoken 100 words to her and already you are worrying about where the wedding will be. Get a grip. You're on duty at eight o'clock, you've got six hours of 'up and downers' in Derry ahead of you. Get some sleep.

I checked in at HQ at eight o'clock and drew my rifle and flak jacket. Eight of my platoon had turned up, which was good for a Saturday. Sergeant

George McMullan from 35 Platoon was in charge and we set off in two Landrovers. We checked in at the Masonic Hall in Derry, which had been taken over by the army. We were joined by a corporal from 26 Locating Regiment of the Royal Artillery who led us out of the base and took us down the few hundred yards to the sangar outside of the city gate in the Guildhall square.

We took over from a section of artillerymen and divided up the duties. One guy stood in the middle of the square and checked vehicles wanting to enter the city through the gate, which was part of the ancient walls of Derry. Another soldier stood behind a wall of sandbags at the entrance to the sangar to cover him. Two others were unarmed and stood at the pedestrian gate where a large queue was waiting to enter the city. I drew this duty, which I hated. 'Up and downers' suggests what it says. We were supposed to search the men up and down patting their legs and arms and feeling their jackets supposedly for weapons. Like all UDR duties, it was just a gesture but it was damned hard work. After half an hour my knees were knackered, and I was sweating like a pig under my flak jacket. There was sometimes a member of the Womens' Royal Army Corps to search the women but not today so we had to let them through unchecked.

Most of the pedestrians were good natured and appreciated what we were doing but there was a sizable number of young Catholics who muttered expressions such as, "Does your dole clerk know that you're working today," and "Spud gathering must have finished around Coleraine - are you hard up for money?" Worse things were also whispered but we were under strict instructions to ignore them. Sometimes we found that we had been spat on when we were searching the bottom of their trousers.

After an hour of this, I was relieved and was entitled to an hour's rest in the sangar where tea and coffee was available. Jim Toy, my cricket captain, was also a member of the UDR. He was a lance corporal in my section. and he was on duty in Derry that day.

"You were a bit keen on that young woman last night," he remarked. "Did you get anywhere?"

"I got her phone number and a half promise," I replied.

"Well, you want to be careful. You do know she's a Fenian, and you never know what she will lure you into," he responded with concern.

"I doubt that she's an old Irish US soldier but yes, she is a Catholic and yes, I will keep my wits about me," I came back defensively.

"You were pissed out of your tiny mind last night, and you would have gone wherever she wanted to lead you. Were you carrying?" Jim asked.

"I never carry when I'm going out drinking, and besides she was a really nice girl."

"Well, you be careful," he said kindly.

After our hour's rest, a section of the UDR's city company turned up and took over from us. We were to do a "bomb patrol" through the streets. This entailed the eight of us, four on each side of the street, walking the streets to show the flag and to discourage bombers.

We set off down Shipquay Street between the city walls and the river Foyle. After half an hour we entered the city through another gate. We were back in the shopping area and the crowds were heavy by now. As we made our way along, I noticed a television crew shadowing us. There was a cameraman, a guy wired for sound carrying a mike, and a woman who seemed to be the reporter or director. As they overtook me, I heard them speaking in French, and I noticed the ORTF insignia on their equipment. They moved in front of us then turned around to point the camera at Sergeant George McMullan, in fact they stuck it into his face.

George was a gruff, no nonsense garage owner in Maddenstown. I heard him telling the crew to back off but they persisted. Finally George shouted, "Fuck off!" The director shouted, "Oh that's good! We have got that on tape." The cameraman stuck the camera so that it was almost touching George's nose. George grabbed the lens with his free hand and pushed backwards. The cameraman must have been off balance because he fell backwards and dropped the camera, which smashed. To their credit, most of the crowd cheered but the director went spare.

"This is brutality! This is what the Catholics of Ireland are up against! I will make a formal complaint," she raved.

We carried on and then finished off at the Masonic Hall where we unloaded our weapons and went in to eat our lunch. We all had a good laugh over George's mishap but we all agreed that he had been justified. As we finished our lunch, a young lieutenant in the Royal Artillery came over and asked George to accompany him upstairs. George got up and followed the officer out to the stairs. We looked at each other.

"Surely he's not in trouble," said Jim.

George returned ten minutes later. His face was the colour of tomato soup.

"Right, saddle up!" barked George. "We're out of here. No more bomb patrols. No up and downers. We are ordered to move out of the city and set up a checkpoint at Eglinton."

We filed outside, loaded our weapons and piled into the Landrovers. Twenty minutes later we set up a checkpoint on the main road a few miles outside of the city. I jumped over a low wall to cover the guy who was flagging down the traffic coming west.

During a lull I shouted to him "Bobby, did George say anything?" They had been in the first Landrover; I was in the second.

"He got a right bollocking from some major, and we were ordered out of the city. I don't think he's been formally charged but he's properly pissed off."

We gave it a couple of hours then headed back to base. We checked in and then some of us went to the bar to wind down. Members of other sections quizzed us – word seemed to have got around.

"I don't know about you lot but I've had enough," I said. "I've been bollocked for arresting an obvious player. I've been formally investigated for shooting someone who has killed four of my mates and then shot at me. Today's the final straw. I'm putting my papers in."

"Me, too" said Malcolm Glover, a quiet insurance clerk who had been with us in Derry. "It's obvious that we were only created to quell the backlash when they disbanded the 'B' Specials. They don't want us to come into contact with Fenians because they're worried about the English so-called liberal press and criticism from American Democrats. They want to sell us out to the south, we are an embarrassment to them." Malcolm usually didn't say much but his vehemence shocked us.

"The south will rue the day they ever have to take us over. This will look like a garden party," said Bobby Nash. The expression on his face scared me.

We broke up after a couple of pints. The RUC were not keen to check for drink drivers outside of the town but they often pulled over UDR men driving out of the base. I went home and changed out of my uniform. There was still time to sink a few drinks, so I wandered up to Brennan's at the end of my road. Like most bars in Maddenstown, it was owned by a Catholic family but the clientele was mainly prod. I ordered a pint and looked around me. My young cousin, John McClelland, gave me a wave. I went over to him and asked him about the afternoon's football results. He was able to give me chapter and verse.

"Are you coming up to Aunt Sadie's for some supper?" John suggested. We had a couple more pints and then made our way over the river and up to Thiepval Park.

Sadie was glad to see us, and she soon rattled up snacks on toast and broke out a bottle of Bushmills. When we had finished eating and were sitting back clutching hot whiskeys, Sadie leaned over conspirationally and said, "Tell me all about that nonsense in Derry today."

"How is it that you know everything that's going on inside the company before the day is out?" I spluttered in amazement.

She put her finger beside her nose and laughed, "I have my sources – go on, tell me your version."

I relayed the events as I had seen them up to where we set up the roadblock.

"Aye, but what happened in the bar afterwards? I heard that there was almost a mutiny."

"No, that's an exaggeration. Some of us are a bit disillusioned about a series of events which have happened recently," I replied.

"Well what are you going to do about it? You lot are not the only company that has had enough. The same thing is happening in Belfast and Newry."

"How do you know these things?" I asked.

"I have contacts all over the north!" she snapped.

"Who are you working for? Does Carson know what you are up to?"

"He keeps his head down, besides he's got other fish to fry from the trade union end," she stated.

"Well, I am putting in my papers next week. I've had enough," I told her.

"Now, don't be hasty. Come for tea on Thursday night. There's somebody I want you to meet." She turned to John and said, "Now you keep your mouth shut about anything you hear in this house. These are dangerous times."

John croaked, "Don't worry. I know nothing. I don't talk to anybody. Can I come on Thursday night?"

"No, you bloody well can't!" she shouted. "We want you to keep clean for the time being."

"OK, OK," conceded John. At that point Carson came in. We made our goodbyes and left them to it.

"What was that all about?" asked John.

"Don't ask. Keep out of it for now," I told him.

I spent all day on Sunday marking books, preparing lessons and updating pupil records. My thoughts kept going back to Tricia. I prayed that I hadn't ruined my chances. What would Sadie think if she knew that I was involved with a Catholic girl? But you're not involved, I chastised myself.

My last task on Sunday evening was to write a formal letter resigning from the UDR.

Chapter 13 – Dinner at the Sperrins

On Tuesday evening I got ready to do a duty. I waited until seven o'clock, then I rang Tricia's number. My heart was hammering. She answered the phone, which I took as a good sign. I apologised for being out of order at the Rugby Club. She didn't say much.

"Look, I know it's a bit conventional, but would you like to go to the pictures with me tomorrow night? There's a romantic comedy which you might like."

"No, I don't want to spend two hours with you in a dark room looking at a screen," she replied. "I'd like to go somewhere where we can see each other face to face and get to know each other."

"Well, would you like to go out for a meal?" I asked nervously.

"That would be nice. Where do you suggest – I don't know this town."

"I'll try to get a table in the Sperrins Hotel. It's the best food in Maddenstown. How about eight o'clock?" I suggested.

"Sounds good to me," she replied.

"If I can't get a table, I'll get back to you. What if I pick you up at half seven?"

"Better not" she replied. "I'll meet you in the car park at a quarter to eight."

"Thank you – I'm really looking forward to it."

"OK," she said, and she put the phone down.

I rang the Sperrins and managed to get a table for two.

As I drove to HQ I went over and over her words in my mind. Was she just being polite before she let me down gently? She hadn't exactly been keen.

I drew my weapon and got ready for a night's duty guarding HQ. Before I started my stag I called in at the company office and gave my letter for the CO to the company clerk, Corporal Irvine.

I spent the next two hours patrolling the boundary of HQ with Tommy Mulholland who was in another platoon but was doing an extra duty. When we got to the furthest point of the rear wall away from the main block Tommy broke the silence.

"What was all that about on Saturday?"

I outlined the events including what had been said in the bar afterwards.

"We won't do duties in Derry," said Tommy. "34 platoon decided a long time ago that it's not worth the bother. The regulars only want us there on Saturdays so that they can have time off but they don't want us to do anything that upsets the local Fenians. You won't get any support from the officers of the regular battalion."

"Well, I won't be going again. I put my papers in this evening. I've had enough," I said.

"Well, good on you. I only do it because I need the money," replied Tommy.

When we got back to the guardhouse, Corporal Irvine shouted, "Cunningham. Smarten yourself up. The CO wants to see you straightaway."

I followed Irvine up the stairs to the CO's office. He knocked, and then marched me in formally. I saluted the Major as we did indoors in the UDR.

"Stand easy, Cunningham" ordered the Major. He held up my letter and said,"What's all this about?"

"I have decided to resign, sir. I've done two years, and now I want to concentrate on my teaching career – it's time I looked for promotion."

"Are you sure there isn't more to this?" he barked. "You were in Derry on Saturday. Has that got anything to do with this?" He waved the letter again.

"Well, sir, events like that make you wonder whether the UDR is appreciated by the powers that be. In the two years I have served, this battalion has lost 23 men to Republican action, and what do we get for it?"

"You don't have to lecture me about the price we have paid!" he shouted. "I've personally lost nine men and one child from my company. I know that you have had a couple of knock-backs from actions where you thought you had done the right thing. If it's any consolation, I have always supported you. You're a good soldier, an intelligent man, the type we need. You should have applied for a commission but that's all dried up now."

He stood up and came around the desk to get closer to me. "We are under scrutiny. We can't get anything right. Loyalists condemn us for not doing enough. British MPs are suspicious of us. Politicians all over the world despise us. They have this romantic notion about the brave Irish patriots. They don't realise that they are criminal scum supported by Marxist regimes.

The IRA are funded by Russia through Libya; they train with the Palestinians yet American Democrat politicians see them as the good guys."

He calmed down and returned to his desk. "I want you to think hard about this. Give me another three weeks of your time, then come to see me again." He pressed a button on his desk and Corporal Irvine came in to march me out.

I returned to the rest room and had my supper. I spent an hour on an armchair wrestling with my own thoughts. Then it was my turn to do a two-hour stag in the sangar at the main gate. For the first hour it was my duty to cover Tommy who was on the gate checking cars in and out. We swapped duties for the second hour and then returned to the rest room for a hot drink. At four o'clock in the morning we checked in our weapons and made our way to our cars to drive home.

I got home and crawled straight to bed hoping that I might snatch two hour's sleep before getting up for a day's teaching.

I managed to snatch another two-hour's sleep when I came home from school. Then I had half an hour in a scalding bath before getting ready for the dinner date. I shaved again and opened the body splash, which I had been given for Christmas. Not too much. I dressed smartly but not formally though I did wear a tie. After all, it was the Sperrins Hotel. Should I bring a present, flowers? I thought not. This was a first date, and, after all, I would be paying for the meal.

I left in good time to be in the Sperrins' car park at twenty to eight. I got out and stood nervously by my car. Two minutes later a Volkswagen Beetle with southern plates spluttered into the car park. I wandered towards it. It was a couple of minutes before Tricia got out. She was a vision to behold. Her hair was pinned back from her face on one side. She wore a white silk blouse under a dark blue trouser suit. Pity, I still hadn't seen her legs. Christ! She was taller than me. I looked down and was relieved to see that she was wearing very high heels.

"Don't worry," she said in that soft southern accent. "I don't drive in them. I've just changed from my driving shoes."

I reached over and grabbed her right hand, which I raised to my lips.

"Thanks for coming," I managed to get out.

She looked surprised. "Get you, did you have a holiday in Italy – so gallant."

It broke the ice perfectly, and we both burst into laughter.

We went in to reception and confirmed that a table for Cunningham had been booked. The teenage waitress who led us to our table for two near the window addressed me as 'Charlie' when she invited us to sit down. Tricia looked at me with an enquiring look as I pulled out her chair for her.

"I didn't take you for a baby-snatcher," she said nervously.

"Don't worry. That's Sally, I used to teach her maths, or rather, she was in the same room as me as I struggled to teach 30 teenagers basic maths."

Sally came back with the menus and said, "What would you like to drink, Charlie?"

Tricia ordered a glass of white wine, and I said that I would stick to water.

We started to exchange life stories over a starter of melon slices with ginger, which was very avant-garde in 1970s Ulster. Tricia was twenty-three, and she had graduated from college in Galway with a diploma in accounting.

Tricia then went for the full roast chicken dish and nearly fell off her seat when I was served with a Spanish omelette, peas and French-fries.

"What are you eating?" she asked.

I explained to her that I didn't eat meat of any description for reasons that I wouldn't go into.

"But don't you eat fish?"

"No, I don't eat creatures which were once living," I informed her.

"Are you a vegetarian?"

"Not in the sense that vegetarians think it is wrong to deprive animals of their lives just to satisfy our hunger - I couldn't give a monkey's. No, I just don't like the thought of eating animals."

"Well, what do you eat – you seem to be very healthy?"

"I eat lots of fruit, vegetables, cheese, nuts and pulses with the occasional egg, but I'm thinking of giving eggs up."

"Jesus. You're full of surprises," she exclaimed.

After that we got on like a house on fire. We compared musical tastes, movies we liked, books we had read, and places we had been to. She seemed surprised that I was a big reader and about the cultural activities that I had experienced.

"My first impression of you was that you were a drunken boor, a typical jock-strap," she confessed.

"Just cos you met me in a rugby club, and I'd had a few drinks. Why did you agree to go out with me then?"

"You can thank Maddy for that. She is my guru."

"What did Maddy say about me?" I asked innocently.

"Oh, that you were a nice guy, intelligent and not bigoted."

"Did she tell you that I am a prod?"

"I knew that the moment I first saw you," she said derisively.

"But you still agreed to go out with me?"

"Well, I guess that I was intrigued," she came back defensively.

"Yeah sure, I have intrigued a lot of women in my time but they don't always want to go out with me," I said with a wry smile.

"Besides, I'm not really a prod. I call myself a scientific rationalist." I immediately realised that I sounded pompous.

"You're so full of shit," she said laughing.

I explained to her that I had been raised a prod but had lost my faith when I studied Darwin and Sagan at Manchester University.

"You are so deep. What else goes on behind those big brown eyes?" she mocked me.

"Enough, here comes the fruit salad."

When we finished, I went up and paid the bill. I came back and helped Tricia out of her chair. As we left the table I became aware of another couple waiting to take the table.

"Nice meal, Charlie?" commented the woman. I looked up and stared into the beaming faces of Jim Toy and his wife.

I made some pleasant remarks and joined up with Tricia at the exit.

"Does everybody know you?" she laughed.

"Just an old work-mate. I was born and raised in this town." I escorted her to her car.

She turned to thank me and I leaned over and kissed her on the cheek.

"Are you all right about getting home? You know that the centre of the town is barricaded off for security reasons? Where do you live?"

"Bristol Gardens," she replied.

"Is that the new posh development to the west of town?" I enquired.

"It's not posh," she laughed.

"Well you're going to have to go round the one-way system. That means you have to go down Limavady Street, which is a bit staunch. They might notice your registration plates."

"Would that be a problem?" she asked with concern in her tone.

"Don't worry. I'll drive along behind you."

I got into the woodie. It had thick padded leather seats. I had cut a slit in the front of the driver's seat where I kept my .38. I reached down between my legs and pulled the butt out so that it stuck out for easy reach.

Tricia set off around the one-way system and I followed. To say that Limavady Street was 'staunch' was an understatement. It was coming up to the 'marching season' and the kerbstones were painted red, white, and blue. Every house displayed a union jack or an Ulster flag. Outside of the Orange Hall a garland had been erected across the street. It portrayed the British crown, King Billy on his white horse, the burning bush, and references to 1690 and the Somme.

There were a gang of youths hanging about outside of an off-licence. There was a lone call of "Fenian bastard" but no real trouble.

We branched off to a part of town, which I hardly knew, and eventually entered Bristol Gardens. Tricia pulled up to the kerb outside of a large mock Tudor family house. I noticed a Mercedes in the driveway. I stopped and waited until Tricia reached the front door. She turned and blew me a kiss before entering the house.

I was surprised at how much the gesture affected me.

I took a short cut that I knew and soon reached Union Street. I put the .38 into my jacket pocket and went in. I went to bed and kept the .38 beside my feet, not under the pillow.

As usual, I had trouble sleeping. Could this be the one? I personally didn't give a toss that she was a Catholic. What would my father and Aunt Sadie say? Forget it, I rebuked myself. Tricia will not want to have anything to do with you if she finds out that you are a UDR man. But that wasn't a problem any longer. I had put my papers in. I resolved that I wasn't going to let her get away.

Chapter 14 - Marcus Macrory

When I got home from school on Thursday evening, I sat down with a mug of tea, and I agonised about what to do next. I wanted to see Tricia again; I couldn't get her out of my thoughts. Would I go to Sadie's for tea? In Ulster 'tea' was the main meal of the evening in working-class homes. I reckoned that Sadie would expect me about six o'clock.

At a quarter past five I figured that Tricia would be home by now. I rang her and she answered. She seemed pleased to hear from me. I thanked her for her company the previous evening, and she told me how much she had enjoyed the evening.

"There's another romantic comedy on at the Playhouse. Are you ready to spend two hours in a dark room with me on Saturday night?"

She chuckled and said, "Yes, I would like that. I think we talked ourselves out last night."

We arranged to meet in the car park ten minutes before the show. Then I got ready for my meeting at Sadie's.

I decided not to carry, so I stashed my piece away in the usual place.

I drove up to Thiepval Park and left the woodie two streets away from my aunt's house.

I went down the alley at the back of her house and knocked on the back door. Sadie invited me in and pointed to the rocking chair in her kitchen. She poured me a mug of tea with which you could have varnished the hull of a speedboat. She carried on preparing the meal and said, "How's your nice wee southern lassie?"

I exploded. "I swear to Christ, is there anything that you don't know?"

"I know that she's clean. We've checked the family. There's no Republican connection."

"Who is this 'we' you keep referring to? Where do you get all of this information?"

She put her finger to her lips and pointed to the door to the lounge from where I could hear her children playing. "There's someone I want you to meet. He will explain everything."

A few minutes later Sadie's husband, Carson Boyd, came in through the back door. He was still wearing his overalls; he worked as a fitter in one of the town's shirt factories. We exchanged pleasantries and after a mug of tea Carson went upstairs to wash and change.

It was a council house, so there was no dining room. We gathered round the kitchen table to eat. We were joined by Sadie's two daughters Victoria and Elizabeth. I made polite enquiries about their progress at school. Kids of that age were used to it. It was the only topic that adults could talk about with kids unless they wanted to make a fool of themselves talking about pop-music and TV programmes. Sadie knew that I did not eat meat so she served me a cheese omelette with my chips instead of bacon. When we were done, the girls asked if they could visit their friend down the road, and Carson made his excuses and went upstairs. I helped Sadie to wash the dishes and then sat down expectantly with another large mug of strong tea.

Suddenly the back door opened and a tall, rugged man in his fifties strode confidently into the kitchen. He nodded at Sadie and then looked me over as he took off his Macintosh and scarf. He sat down at the table opposite me and took a mug of tea from Sadie.

"Charlie, I want you to meet Marcus Macrory. He's been a friend of this family for a long, long time, and his father served in the trenches with your grandfather on the Somme." Macrory stuck out a large boney hand, which I shook with trepidation.

"Let me tell you my story," began Macrory. "I hardly got to know my father. When he came home from the war he joined the newly formed RUC in the twenties. When I was six, he was murdered by Republican scum near Strabane. He was off duty and was visiting his old mother when they burst in and shot him down in front of her. I served in the RAF for the last two years of the war. No, I didn't fly; I was an armourer. I serviced machine guns for Lancasters, and I loaded bombs onto them. When the war was over, I got a job driving bowsers at RAF Ballykelly. I joined the 'B' Specials, and I was mobilised in the 1950's campaign. I worked my way up to District Commandant."

He paused to polish off his tea. "When the 'B's were disbanded, I applied to join the UDR but they turned me down. No explanation. Funny enough, I was never an Orangeman. I was never political. Somehow my face didn't fit. But they did tell me to watch out because they had found my name on a death-list when the RUC raided a Provo house in Limavady. My family has given a lot to Britain and Northern Ireland but they didn't want me anymore. You know, they let a lot of ex-B men keep their firearms but not me. I had to hand it in."

He took a swig of tea and then went on, "I considered my options. I could keep my head down and wait for the Provos to come and get me. I could rely on the RUC and UDR to protect me. I decided that I wanted something more pro-active. I considered the UDA. They do a reasonable job reminding Republicans not to come back to this town but they don't carry the fight to the Provos. I could join the UVF but my only contact with them was a man I didn't like. After a few weeks I was approached by a man who I had known in the 'B's, someone I trusted and respected. He invited me to join the Northern Volunteer Force, the NVF. You won't have heard of us. We make no claims or threats. We just pick off known Republican terrorists when we can without risk. We have no quarrel with the security forces, we don't target innocent Catholics, we don't get involved with drugs or crime, and we just do our bit quietly."

He paused to look me straight in the eye. "We are always on the lookout for intelligent men who are not afraid of using a gun. Who can keep their mouths shut. Who want to get at the Provos. Interested?"

"I might be," I answered. "Why me?"

"You're an intelligent lad, a graduate, from a proven loyalist background but not a religious nutter. You owe the Provos for the scars you bear. I hear that you have been let down by the UDR. I don't blame them. They are only there to put on a show and to keep forty thousand Loyalists under control. Their hands are tied. Their political masters have to get the OK from Dublin and Washington. Have you ever done a patrol in Dungiven? Ever set up a VCP there? No, we don't want to upset the locals, do we. If you want to take the fight to the Provos, then join us."

I was stunned at this brazen proposal. I turned to look at aunt Sadie.

"Where do you fit in to all of this? Is Carson involved?"

"I'll grant you that I'm not an active member but I do my bit. No, Carson is not an active member but we use him to bounce ideas off. Think about it, Charlie. We don't need your answer tonight, but promise us that if you turn us down that it doesn't go any further."

I told them that I would think about it, and I promised them that I wasn't a grass.

"OK, off you go. Marcus and I have got things to discuss," she said wearily. I wondered how deeply she was involved and what price she was paying for it.

I wandered back to Union Street and watched a movie. I couldn't concentrate on the plot. Was this the opportunity that I had been waiting for? But what were the risks, what was the moral position?

A couple of days later, a note came through my letterbox. It was from Aunt Sadie inviting me to call round on Saturday evening. I made my way over the river and took the usual precautions before entering Sadie's house by the back door. She reached me a mug of steaming tea and told me to sit down at the kitchen table. We made small talk about the family until Marcus Macrory threw open the back door. Sadie took his coat and he sat down clasping a mug of tea.

"Well, young fellow. I've been making discrete enquiries about you. You seem to be a reliable type, and you have certainly done your bit for the UDR. You're intelligent and you're clean. You don't shoot your mouth off in bars even when you are full of drink."

He looked over to Sadie who was nodding approvingly.

He went on, "We want to start you off with a very important task which requires brains and good organisational skills but don't be disappointed because it doesn't involve you in an operation."

I was intrigued. "Go on," I said.

"I want you to buy old typewriters," he replied.

"Typewriters! Did you say typewriters?"

"Yes, portables, actually. I want you to look at newspaper ads, ads in shop windows, Exchange and Mart, and even junk shops for portable typewriters. I want you to make sure that they are not traceable back to you, so when you buy them pay cash, use a cover story. You are a student at the university in Coleraine who needs it to write a thesis. Got the idea?"

He reached into his pocket and gave me a roll of notes. "That should buy five or six, which will be enough to get started with."

"Sure, no problem," I replied. "But what for? How will this help to take the war to the Provos?"

He laughed, "Wait and see. Misinformation. Haven't you ever heard of psy ops. Psychological operations? The pen is mightier than the sword and all that?"

Sadie broke in, "All will be revealed when you bring back some portables."

Marcus got up and grabbed his coat. He bid us goodnight and vanished out of the back door.

"What the hell was that all about?" I asked.

"Wait and see but make sure that you get it right. This is a test. Now run along. Aren't you going out with your wee girl tonight?"

I was so confused that I left by the front door but all of the cars in the street were friendlies.

Chapter 15 - Cormac Dillon

On Thursday I called in at the mini-market and bought two weekly Coleraine newspapers, the Belfast Telegraph and a copy of Exchange and Mart. Before walking home, I studied the notices in the shop window but no one was selling a typewriter. When I got home I scanned the small ads of my papers and found an advert in the Chronicle from a lady in Ballymoney who was selling a portable Olympia Splendid. I wandered up to the town square and gave her a ring from the public telephone. She was eager to sell and agreed that I could call round that evening.

I dressed scruffily in an old parka and jeans and drove over to Ballymoney. I parked two streets away from the lady's road, and I went up and rung the bell. A lady in her forties invited me in and introduced me to her husband. I told her that I was a post-grad student at the New University of Ulster in Coleraine and that I needed a typewriter for a dissertation that I had to submit. I didn't quibble when she asked for ten pounds for the machine that seemed to be in good condition and came with half-a-dozen spare reels of ribbon. I had one dodgy moment when her husband re-appeared in a police uniform. He asked me if I was travelling by bus and offered to drive me into Coleraine, but I managed to convince him that there was no need because I had a return ticket.

Over the next week I bought a Remington from a junk shop in Causeway Street in Portrush and a Smith Corona from a student in Portstewart.

I took Tricia to the movies in Limavady on Wednesday night to see a Carry On comedy. She had no idea what I was talking about when I told her that Kenneth Williams and Charles Hawtrey were gay. I was too embarrassed to tell her what gay guys got up to and it left me thinking that she really was pretty innocent. Homosexual activities were a serious crime in both parts of Ireland at that time. The topic was not discussed in polite company, and I guess that Tricia was just like Queen Victoria who did not believe that such activities existed when she was asked to sign the bill outlawing them. Tricia had to go Belfast the next morning for a training course, so I dropped her at the mini-market where she had parked her car. A quick snog and she was on her way. I shadowed her around the town but she didn't run into any trouble.

I delivered the three portables to Aunt Sadie's on Thursday evening but I left them in the back of the woodie on the next street. Marcus was pleased with my purchases and told me to keep the change to try to buy two more. He pulled his old Landrover pick-up behind my car, and I transferred the typewriters into the back of it. He told me how to find his smallholding near Macosquin, and we made a date for ten o'clock on Sunday morning.

On Saturday night I took Tricia out for a Chinese meal in Coleraine but she drove. Maddenstown didn't run to the exotic. Luckily they served vegetable biriani on chips, so I was able to pass myself without gagging. Tricia got stuck into the full works; she started with spring rolls and then proceeded to spicy garlic chicken with rice. She finished off with Chinese sponge cake with ginger ice cream. I don't know where she put it all and still kept her beautiful figure, and she nearly went for a plate of chips on top until I persuaded her to take half of mine.

On the drive home we tried to agree on our next date but I had to keep in mind my UDR duties and my commitment to Marcus.

"What do you do in your spare time?" asked Tricia. "You seem to be doing something every night. I want to see more of you."

I made feeble noises about marking exams, playing poker, visiting my father but I knew that I sounded unconvincing. We stopped at the end of Tricia's road and she turned to me and offered her lips. I almost threw up at the taste of Chinese. We arranged to meet at the Sperrins on Tuesday night.

I walked home. There were no UDA barricades. I worried about my weight. I had never eaten out so regularly as I was doing now. I broke into a jog but then I caught myself on.

On Sunday I got up bright and early and retrieved my piece from the outside toilets. Macosquin was a very staunch village but Marcus had told me that he was on a Provo hit list. As I drove over I tried to figure Marcus out. He had no visible means of support yet he was not short of cash. Perhaps his farm made enough to keep him. I easily found the place that turned out to really be a smallholding with a couple of run-down greenhouses and a few old sheds behind a small family house. Again, I wondered about from where he got his money. I rang the doorbell and Marcus ushered me through to the back door.

He led me down to a chicken shed at the bottom of his garden and took me through long grass and brambles to its rear. He showed me a disguised door that led into a concealed compartment about nine feet by six. The stench of chicken shit was overbearing. The room was wired for electric light because there were no windows. It had a bench along one of the longer walls and a filing cabinet at one end. The three typewriters that I had bought were spaced along the bench, and there were boxes of typing paper and carbons. He motioned to me to take the only chair and then he unlocked the filing cabinet. He brought out a wallet folder from which he pulled a list of names, addresses, and personal information about Republican prisoners.

"Here's what I want you to do. Let's take Cormac Dillon from Derry. He's in Long Kesh doing five years for possession of a firearm and resisting arrest. He's thirty-seven and his wife Celine is a good ten years younger. They have three children. She is well known for attending Republican fund-raising functions, dances and concerts; she's a fun-loving girl behind a cloak of Republican activism."

Marcus put the list beside one of the portables.

"I want you to send Dillon an anonymous letter warning him that his wife was taken home from a dance by a young man – name unknown. She has also been seen letting this young man buy her drinks at a folk concert. Suggest that he puts one of his goons onto her case. At the least, this will help to demoralise him. At best it will spread dissent. It might even get out and weaken his authority. Maybe, he'll order drastic action like giving Celine a hammering. Perhaps, he might even try to break out."

I broke in, "Is it likely that an informer from the Bogside would use a typewriter?"

"True, but I want to protect your handwriting. I've got other people writing the occasional letter by hand but I need you for a long term project."

"Fair enough, but where did you get all of this information about Celine?"

He laughed, "It's all made up. Now, I want you to make the occasional typo and spelling mistake."

He reached into the folder again, "Now here's another one I want you to have a go at."

He pointed to the details of Sean Dolan who was an internee from Claudy.

"Use a different typewriter but I don't want to flood the market. It would soon get around if lots of prisoners were getting these letters and I expect that Five are doing something similar."

"Five?" I asked.

"MI5, they devote a lot of time, money and effort to psy-ops."

He reached me a bundle of new wallet folders. "I want you to keep a separate file for each target. Use the carbons and make a copy of all letters for filing. We'll also put newspaper clippings about the target into the file.

Any rubbish which you create must go into this bin for burning." He kicked a plastic bucket under the bench.

"Are you happy with this?"

"No problem," I answered, "but won't they catch onto us? They're not that stupid, are they?"

"No, never make the mistake of thinking that they're all stupid. Some of the minor players are incredibly stupid; that's why the Provo leadership exploits them but they are all humans with human weaknesses. They've also had the best of advice to be on their guard against psychological warfare. Some of them have been trained by Soviets in Palestine and Libya; others have had training from the CIA. But you never know, and of course we'll never know how successful we've been unless something drastic happens."

He gave me a spare key for the filing cabinet and showed me the second drawer where he kept a variety of envelopes, typewriter ribbons and a box of rubber medical gloves.

"Type the address on the envelopes, put out-going mail into this red folder, and we'll make sure that they get posted. We'll post them from Republican areas and some from over the border in Buncrana and Letterkenny."

Then he pulled two other lists from out of his folder.

"This list is for key players and post holders in the Provos, some of them locked up, and this one has names and details of minor Republican players and their useful idiots."

He passed me both lists. "I want you to send letters to the key men naming some minor players as grasses and paid informers for the RUC. Say that you are a sleeping sympathiser working for the police and that this type of intelligence crosses your desk regularly."

He took the dust cover off a full-size Olivetti typewriter at the end of the bench.

"This one was surplus to requirement when they closed the RUC station in Listober so it fits the bill. Do me three of these. You pick the targets and the victims but keep meticulous records about everything you do. I've labelled all of the typewriters A, B, C and so on. You should make a note on the carbon copy of which machine you used. Remember, all of these letters will be read by the authorities before they deliver them to the prisoners, so we don't want any mix ups. Use the rubber gloves when handling the stationery and don't lick the envelopes. Use this swab and dip it in this ash-tray full of water."

"Fine," I told him, "I'm looking forward to it."

"Good, now next Sunday I've got a much more interesting project for you. OK. I'll leave you to it. Lock everything away. I'll lock the door when I see you leaving." Then he was gone.

I spent the next two hours composing and drafting five letters that I typed eventually on the corresponding typewriter. The stench and the noise from the birds were distracting but I relished the intellectual challenge of pitching the language in the letters to suit the supposed sender. Finally, I put the sealed envelopes into the red folder and filed the copies and clippings into the individual case folders. I locked the filing cabinet, closed the outer door, and went out to my woodie. Marcus waved to me as I passed the kitchen window, and I gave him the thumbs up. I got the impression that there were two other men in the kitchen. Young, fit with close haircuts.

As I sped along the road to Maddenstown, I said to myself, "They also serve who only sit and type."

Chapter 16 – The EVF

A week later I reported to Marcus early on Sunday morning, and we made our way down to the chicken shed. I had brought another Remington that had been advertised in the Northern Constitution, a weekly Coleraine paper, by a teacher from Portrush. This time Marcus produced a list of English journalists and Labour and Liberal politicians who had been critical of the British presence in Northern Ireland. They made up the rent-a-mouth squad, which the BBC always called on for a quick quote whenever an operation by the security forces had gone wrong.

"I want you to pose as a Catholic living in Derry or Dungiven or Swatragh. The spin that I want you to take is that you are a Republican sympathiser but that you are being oppressed by IRA thugs who demand contributions. Say that you suspect that most of the money goes on drink and that these IRA yobs have beaten up young Catholic teenagers for stepping out of line."

"I get the drift," I replied, "but once again, would such a person have access to a typewriter?"

"No, this time you are going to write them. Some in your normal hand, some with your left hand, and some after you have taped two of your fingers together. It doesn't matter if it's a scrawl, we are talking about poorly educated people here. Write them anonymously. Keep records about which hand, which pen, which type of paper you have used for different people."

"OK, no problem," I responded.

"OK, then I want you to write to these three Republican prisoners spinning them the line about their kids stepping out of line. This sheet has details about their children. Spin the line about daughters playing free and easy with young men and about sons getting into drink, drugs, and petty crime. I know that you can do it. I've looked at the copies of your previous letters, and I like your style. Now when you have finished come up to the house because I want to talk about a much bigger project."

It only took me two hours to produce nine letters because I was getting into the swing of things. I filed them and locked up. I knocked on Marcus' back door, and he invited me in. We sat at his kitchen table, and we shared a saucepan of tomato soup and a large doughy loaf.

"You know that the Westminster government is getting ready to sell us out?" he remarked.

"They don't rate our politicians because they don't think that they can find common ground. They don't think that they can defeat Republican terrorism without taking measures, which will alienate misguided Yanks and European politicians. The families of British soldiers are at the point where they won't accept any more casualties, recruitment is low and desertion is high. And finally the government is shit-scared that the Provos will widen their bombing campaign in England ruining tourism and international commerce."

"I agree with your analysis, so what do we do?" I commented.

"The government thinks that we're a soft touch. Your average Labour politician is incapable of understanding the psyche of Ulster loyalists. They see us as spongers and religious bigots."

"We've got to convince them that we are stronger than they think by upscaling our operations against Republicans and by taking the war over the border. However, the project that I have in mind for you is to convince them that we have hard-line support in England from people who are prepared to fight to keep Ulster British. Obviously we have massive support in Scotland and other units are taking measures to strengthen paramilitary groups in Glasgow and the south-west Scotland."

He paused to dip a chunk of bread in his soup and then champed on it noisily. Meanwhile, it crossed my mind that Marcus was part of a much larger concern than I had been led to believe.

He went on. "My next task for you is to set up a phantom paramilitary organisation in north-west England. Now, you went to Manchester University so you must know the area well,and you are familiar with common surnames in that region and the idioms that the locals use. I want you to use the big typewriter to create a series of official looking forms for the English Volunteer Force. We will duplicate them and fill them in with strength returns, intelligence reports, arms rolls and so on. We will bundle them together and send them to the Guardian or the BBC with a cover letter stating that they were found in a briefcase left on a train. Hopefully, the information, sorry disinformation, will reach the British authorities."

"Where do you get all of these ideas from?" I asked.

Marcus laughed and continued, "Of course, they've got to be convincing. Think you can do it?"

"No problem," I replied. "I can't wait to start."

"So why don't you start coming around here in the evenings then, how about tomorrow night?"

I reminded him that I would soon be leaving the UDR and would have more time to devote to these activities.

"Now, you're going to be busy because I want you to carry on sending the letters to Provos."

"Don't worry, I'm up for it. I want to feel that I'm doing something pro-active rather than guarding a drinking club or annoying lawful citizens by searching their cars."

He laughed. "Do this job right, and then I'll move you on to something much more pro-active."

I drove home with all sorts of plans in my head but there was also the nagging feeling that I was becoming part of a much larger machine than I had first thought.

When I came home from the Tech on Monday evening, I did a bit of marking and waited until I thought that Tricia would be at home. I rang but it was a middle-aged lady with a southern accent who answered. I asked politely if I could speak to Tricia but she just hung up. About twenty minutes later Tricia rang me, and she sounded upset.

"I've just had an almighty row with my mother. She says that you are not to ring here anymore, and you know that I can't take personal calls at the bank," she sobbed.

"Don't worry, sweetheart. I'll meet you at the Sperrins on Wednesday night, usual time, and we'll sort something out."

"I can't wait until then to see you. Could we make it tomorrow night?"

I agreed and calmed her down. I rang the Sperrins and booked a table for eight o'clock. My life is getting just a bit complicated now, I thought to myself. Between my job, the UDR, Tricia, and Marcus I couldn't remember the last time that I had spent an evening with my model railway.

I finished my marking, got my piece from down the garden and headed off to Macosquin. Marcus welcomed me and led me down to the shed.

"Let me show you our latest toy," he said.

On the bench was a duplicating machine. He showed me how to remove the ink ribbon from the big Olivetti and how to insert a skin for the duplicating machine. He demonstrated that as you typed the hammers cut the typeface into the skin. When the skin was removed it was inserted into the duplicating machine. He showed me how to feed it with ink and paper and then he started to wind the handle. The paper fed through and picked up the

116

ink from the typeface so that the machine rolled out multiple copies of the typed document.

"If you're careful you can run off fifty, maybe one hundred decent copies," he explained.

Then he showed me how to score lines on the skin with a stylus so that we could produce forms. I was broadly familiar with the whole operation because the office staff at college used a similar system.

"I want you to design a monthly strength return for the EVF. Call it EVF Form 216 and design it for a company strength unit broken down into platoons with cells for the number of personnel for each rank for each of four or five weeks. Bring it up to me before we start filling some in. Understand?"

I assured him that I knew exactly what he wanted. Marcus left and I got down to drafting the form on a blank sheet of paper. Down the left hand column I created rows for the various ranks that would be found in a company strength unit and then I made columns for company HQ and six platoons. I decided to call the privates 'volunteers' just like the IRA.

I took the skin out of the typewriter and threaded it into the duplicator. I tentatively rotated the handle, and I was delighted when it fed out a crisp, clean copy of the form. I ran off twenty more copies then removed the original and hung it up on a hook to dry.

I took the forms up to the house, and Marcus let me into the kitchen. We sat down at the table, and Marcus scrutinised the form carefully.

"I like it. Just what I wanted," he exclaimed. "Now, let's look at this." He produced a roadmap of northwest England.

"Let's fill in one of these forms for 'A' Company of the 3rd Battalion of the EVF based in Burnley." He took two of the forms and inserted a carbon between them. He started to fill in the details with a Biro pen. He had a white sticky label wrapped around the shank of the pen. He showed me the label, which was marked '3/A Burnley'.

"Got to be consistent. I have a dozen different pens, all labelled, different shades of blue and black."

He proceeded to fill in the details for the company HQ.

"One captain, one CSM, one corporal, and so on," he droned. "Now, a company in the British Army has an establishment of about 110 but the paramilitaries grossly inflate the importance of their units. A typical UVF company has about twenty members. We'll make our units bigger than that so make the platoons between six and twelve and the whole company about sixty."

He completed the form and signed the bottom with the name 'J. Windham'.

"Now, take these pens and fill in sheets for companies from Accrington, Nelson, Colne, and so on. Here's the map, you know what to do."

I spent the next two hours creating a brigade-sized organisation for the northwest of England. I created battalions and companies. I made up names of company commanders and battalion officers. I concentrated hard on disguising my hand for the different forms. It was made easier because I was mainly filling in figures. Occasionally I thought, "What the fuck am I doing here?" It was surreal but I really got into it.

When I had finished Marcus reached me a mug of steaming tea. He had also been busy filling in forms for a mythical Cumbrian brigade.

"Good stuff. Now, next time I want you to create an intelligence report form and run some off. That's enough for tonight."

He reached into a cupboard and produced a shotgun. "I'll escort you to your car. You never know who's about."

He accompanied me out and waved me goodbye.

My head was spinning as I drove home to Maddenstown. What had I let myself into? Was it cost effective? Maybe I should be out setting up VCPs.

Tricia came around to number nine on Tuesday evening to cook a meal. We spent the remainder of the evening on the sofa listening to Simon and Garfunkel. As we walked down to our cars I suggested to Tricia that we might go to see the latest James Bond movie on Saturday evening.

"Forget it, sonny boy. We're going to a party on Saturday at Maddy's. I want to show you off to the people that I work with. I want you scrubbed up and in your best gear and on your best behaviour. We'll go to the movies on Friday night."

As I followed her around the town I began to realise that Tricia was gradually taking over our relationship, and I had to admit to myself that I didn't mind one little bit.

Chapter 17 – Maddy's Party

Saturday, the day of the party soon came around. I used the morning to finish off my school preparation and to catch up with my cleaning and laundry. I figured that I might not be in a fit state on Sunday to do much. On the other hand, I mentally cautioned myself, I didn't want to get too pissed and do anything that would embarrass Tricia in front of her colleagues.

I went out and bought a bottle of good quality wine, which I personally never touched, and a specially made up bunch of flowers for Maddy. I also bought a six-can pack of Australian lager. From experience I knew that middle-class people usually brought nothing but wine to a party and then the husbands got stuck into some other poor sucker's beer. I never got time to put a bet on and probably saved the price of the drink and the flowers. I watched the football round up and then had a shower. Tricia had asked me to dress smartly. She had suggested that the men would be wearing suits. I hated my only suit, which I kept for weddings and funerals, so I went for black trousers and a smart grey jacket with a discreet pattern. I put on a crisp white shirt and carefully knotted a black tie with small white dots. I thought that I looked smart.

I grabbed the bag of drink and the flowers and quickly rejected the idea of carrying my piece. At half past seven I strolled down towards the unbarricaded end of my street that joined Church Street. It was a clear, dry summer's evening. A couple of people gave me a second glance; men didn't often carry flowers in public in Ulster. Then I met a group of girls from the Tech dressed up to go out for the evening.

"Going somewhere nice, sir?"

"Who's the lucky girl, sir?"

I laughed and quipped, "Don't get too drunk, girls, we're doing simultaneous equations on Monday morning."

I reached the junction and stood beside the telephone kiosk. A few minutes later I heard the deep throated chug of Tricia's VW. She saw me and pulled over to the kerb. I got into the passenger's side.

"Mmm, don't you look smart, and nice flowers too?" she observed quizzically.

"Relax sweetheart, they're not for you, they're for Maddy. Play your cards right, and you'll get lots of flowers."

She was wearing a camel jacket over a black frock, and for the first time I got a glimpse of her delicious knees as she changed gear.

"My, you smell nice," I said. "Do you know where you're going?"

"Like the back of my hand, sugar," she replied confidently. "I go over to Maddy's quite regularly. Don't worry, I always know where I am going." She looked over at me coyly.

We skirted the Sconce Hill and came down the Glebe. Tricia turned left at Hazlett's Corner, and half a mile later she pulled into a very large, recently built family house overlooking Castlerock. There was plenty of parking space for the dozen cars which were already drawn up. These people aren't teachers, I thought. There were Mercs, Audis, and even a couple of foreign sports cars. The only British car was an 'E' Type Jag. So much for the poor, oppressed Catholics of Ulster, I thought.

"Just give me a minute to change my shoes, Charlie."

Maddy met us at the door and embraced Tricia. Then it was my turn. I kissed her cheek and offered her the flowers.

"Didn't I tell you that he's the perfect gentleman," she squealed at Tricia. "When he's not drunk." She grabbed my arm and introduced me to her husband Eugene who was balding and developing a corporation. I knew that he was a successful solicitor in the housing sector but that he didn't touch criminal law.

I carried in the bag of drink and found my way to the kitchen. Sure enough, they had a breakfast-bar, which was covered with bottles of wine and a large bowl of some kind of punch. There was no sign of any beer. I nodded at a trio of well-dressed strangers who had obviously been at the wine for a while. I found a pint glass in a cupboard and cracked open one of my cans.

"Thank Christ, somebody had the wit to bring beer," said one of the trio. "Do you mind if I take one?" I nodded my assent and reached him a can, thinking, here we go.

Maddy had taken Tricia's coat and shown her into the lounge. I poured Tricia a soft drink and headed out to the corridor where I ran into Maddy.

"Come on, let me introduce you to the gang." She took Tricia's drink and grabbed my free hand. She led me into a massive lounge and declared, "This is the famous Charlie who Tricia has been bending our ears about."

The men gave me a perfunctory glance and then resumed their conversations. I noticed that some of the women looked me up and down and then leant towards their friends, presumably, to talk about me. I was pretty sure that I was the only prod in the room.

I looked around and took in that one wall was completely shelved full of books. The opposite wall contained a massive picture window. I stepped over to it and could see the hills of Donegal to the west, fields sweeping down to Castlerock in front, and I could make out Portstewart and Portrush to the east. Then I went over to the bookshelves. There were hundreds of books on Law, Irish History, and Philosophy. I had always considered that you could make a pretty fair appraisal of someone by the books they read, so I raised my estimation of Eugene when I found that he had an extensive collection of books by and about Flann O'Brien including some first editions.

I noticed a large leather armchair that was unoccupied, and I settled down in it with my pint. I scanned the partygoers. They were all in their late twenties, thirties, or early forties, expensively dressed and the women bejewelled; nothing like the Catholics portrayed in the TV newsreels from the Falls Road and the Bogside. An expensive, German hi-fi system was playing traditional Irish harp music, which was one type of Irish music that I really appreciated but surely not at a party. I looked over and saw that Tricia was surrounded by a group of men who she was obviously at ease with. Their tongues were almost hanging out as they vied with each other to impress her. She was lapping it up, throwing her hair back as she laughed and swaying on her high heels. I experienced an incredible pang of jealousy such as I had never felt before. I had not really recognised that she was such a stunner.

"Move over, Charlie," said Maddy bringing me back to reality as she sat on the arm of my chair. "Isn't she popular? I hope that you know how lucky you are. Now, I want you to treat her right, she's a bit innocent, you know, and she has really fallen for you."

"Don't worry, I know when I have backed a winner, and I don't intend to lose her."

"But do you know where you are going?"

"We still hardly know each other but I won't let her down."

"Thank you for coming, by the way. I know that this is not your usual thing. Go and get another drink. We're going to start dancing soon, and I want you to circulate."

I made my way to the kitchen and was miffed but not surprised to find that all of my lager had gone. The boozing trio were still there arguing about Gaelic football. I poured myself a liberal shot of Bushmills Black Label and added some ginger ale. I took a big swallow before going back into the party. Maddy and Eugene had just finished rolling back the carpet to expose the natural wooden floor, and they had used the new-fashioned dimmers on their lights. Maddy changed the record to Bill Haley, and soon the floor was full of couples jiving.

I finished my whiskey and thought that I had better get in there and fight for my woman but as I walked towards Tricia, I noticed that she had kicked off her shoes and was being led onto the floor by a tall, suave good-looking bastard. I felt another intense pang of jealousy. I went back to the kitchen and poured myself another stiff belt of whiskey. The guy who had asked for a can of lager stuck his hand out.

"Hello, you're Charlie, aren't you? I'm Dennis O'Kane. I share an office with Tricia. You're a very lucky man."

He introduced me to the other two drinkers. We tried to make small talk but I knew nothing about banking and business. These people really were different. They looked different, they spoke different, they had attended different schools, they followed Gaelic sports, and they drove foreign cars not even to mention religion and politics. Christ! I thought, how are we all ever to live on this island. I was starting to feel the drink but I wasn't stupid enough to think that all Catholics supported Republican terrorists. Even a cursory analysis of election results and demographics revealed that many of them secretly voted for Unionist politicians. They knew which side their bread was buttered.

Tricia burst into the kitchen and grabbed my hand. "There you are. I might have known that you would be where the drink is. Come on, they're playing a slow one."

I let her lead me to the floor where she flung her arms around my neck. My arms automatically encircled her waist. They were playing 'Crying Time' by Skeeter Davis, so dancing skills were not required. We shuffled around the floor cheek to cheek. When we got to the darkest corner of the room Tricia kissed me long and deeply. The music changed to Patsy Cline wailing 'Sweet Dreams of You'. I pulled Tricia even closer and dropped my hands to her flanks.

Just then Maddy burst between us. "Excuse me Tricia. This is my dance, I do believe." Tricia didn't have time to object because the tall handsome bastard had seized his opportunity and swept her into his arms.

I put my arms around Maddy at shoulder height and kept a respectable distance between us. "I've been waiting for ten years for you to put your arms around me," she mocked.

"You seem to be very happy with Eugene," I countered. "Where are the kids?"

"They are being spoiled rotten by their grannie, I expect. They couldn't wait to be dropped off."

The music stopped, the lights were turned up, and Maddy announced that it was time to eat. This was the part that I dreaded. I would face the inevitable barrage of questions about my eating habits and then the usual problem with handling a drink, a plate, and a fork simultaneously.

"Charlie! I've made you some vegetarian sausage rolls," announced Maddy.

"Isn't that an oxymoron?" proclaimed a weedy guy sitting in the corner.

There was general laughter, and people started to look at me quizzically. We made our way into the kitchen where Maddy reached me a plastic plate piled with cheese, salad, and 'sausage' rolls. I went back to the lounge where I was lucky to get my favourite armchair.

Tricia came over and sat on the arm. She had a plate piled with chicken drumsticks, salad, and a baked potato. She had no problem cutting her food into chunks with the side of her fork. I had never seen her look so happy; she was in her element.

"Do you want a top-up?" she asked. "There's masses of food."

"No thanks, I'm going in for another drink. Can I get you a coke or something?" She declined and looked at me anxiously.

"Take it easy with the booze, Charlie."

"Do you think I can't handle it?" I responded.

"No, I'm just worried that there are some drunken ass-holes here and they might provoke you into saying something which would embarrass Maddy."

"OK, I'll just have a coke myself then." I did, but I laced it with a shot of Bacardi.

"Right, let's get back to dancing!" shouted Maddy as she dimmed the lights. Before I could get back to Tricia, the handsome bastard had pulled her to her feet. Country and Western music was big with both communities in Ireland. This time it was Skeeter murdering 'The End of the World' but it seemed to work for the dancers.

As Maddy swayed past me, and she shouted, "Go and give Dimmie a dance." She pointed to a studious looking blonde standing on her own by the picture window. She didn't look like much but she had a sensational figure. I went over and asked her to dance.

When we had got into an easy rhythm I said, "Go on, why do they call you Dimmie? You don't look stupid."

She laughed attractively and answered, "It's short for Dymphna, and it's a play on words. They think that I am very bright, actually."

"Are you?"

"Well, I got a scholarship to Cambridge, and then I did my MBA at Harvard, but I don't consider myself particularly intelligent. For instance, I ran out of petrol last week, miles from a garage."

"But why Dymphna? I've never heard that one before."

She laughed, revealing a mouthful of perfect white teeth. "Dymphna was a seventh century Irish saint. If my parents had only known her real story, I don't think that they would have chosen that name."

"What's the story?" I asked, intrigued. She swayed against me, and I was made aware that she was certainly well endowed.

"It would take too long, look it up. Tell me about yourself. You have certainly made a big impression on Tricia."

I started to tell her my life story but the music stopped, and I was aware of Tricia at my side.

"Sorry, Dimmie, I haven't really had a chance to dance with my man."

We stayed together for the next half hour. Tricia told me that I was honoured to have been given a dance with Dimmie who, it appeared, considered most men to be some sort of pond-life. I started to ask her to explain when Maddy bellowed, "Now for some Irish dancing!"

I was coerced into taking part in a six-hand reel but I didn't really catch on to the complexities of it. Besides, the music was didley-dee that I had never got my head around. I dropped out to the kitchen after the first set, and I was back in my favourite armchair when they started the Irish rebel songs. I drew the line at dancing to those, so I let Tricia share her favours with her coterie of admirers. I don't know where she got the energy, and I thought that she genuinely thought that it was just playground fun and was unaware of the sexual longings of her partners. Wasn't it Oscar Wilde who had observed that 'dancing was for people who couldn't go to bed together'?"

At about one o'clock there was a lull in the music. The handsome bastard announced that his group were heading off.

"Watch out for the Gestapo if you've had a drink," someone warned.

"No, you don't need to worry about the police," retorted my rival. "They go back to their barracks at midnight just like Cinderella. It's the SS bastards in green berets you have to worry about. They don't breathalyse you; they just shoot you."

There was a general peel of laughter but Dimmie piped up, "But didn't Cinderella stay out after midnight?" This provoked another peel of laughter.

"Not if she had lived in this fucking country!" commented a big red-haired loud mouth.

By now Tricia had come to my side and had taken my hand. "Who are the SS?" she asked innocently.

"The fucking UDR," answered the loud mouth. "They are just low-life Protestant scum."

I noticed Maddy looking at me with concern as she ushered loud mouth out to get his coat. The party was fast breaking up, so I helped Tricia to find her shoes. Maddy came back with Tricia's coat.

"You don't want to listen to those big gob-shites," she said. "Most thinking Catholics recognise that the security forces are there for their protection, not just for the prods."

I thanked Maddy and Eugene sincerely as they showed us out of the door.

"Well, I know one little girl who had a really good time, and she didn't even have a single drink," said Maddy as she kissed Tricia on the cheek. "Take care, safe home and I'll see you on Monday, Trish. Here, Charlie, these are for you." She reached me a brown bag, and when I looked inside I saw that it was stuffed with 'sausage' rolls.

Tricia changed into her driving shoes, and then she pulled out of the forecourt and turned left.

"I don't fancy driving back over the mountain; there's a bit of a mist," she explained. We set off down the Lions' Brae into Downhill and headed off along the coast road.

"What were you and Dimmie talking about?" she asked.

"Oh, just why she's called that. She seems to be very bright."

"Yes, she certainly is. She's got all sorts of ideas for expanding the bank's business. She's going to teach me about business development."

"Is she a Lesbian?" I asked, but Tricia hadn't a clue what I was talking about.

"Does she ever go out with men?"

"Occasionally, but they have to meet up to her standards," replied Tricia. "Why, do you fancy her?"

I laughed. "She's not in the same league as you. You're all the woman that I can handle." She looked over at me with a self-congratulatory smirk.

"Shite!" she exclaimed. "It's a roadblock. I hope that it's not the UDA."

I could see a swinging red light to our front with figures around it.

"Relax, it's just an army check point, probably the UDR. Switch off your main lights and wind down your window. Approach the guy with the torch very slowly."

Tricia stopped by the soldier who looked in and said, "Good evening, Miss, where are you coming from at this time of night?" It was Jim Toy.

I leaned forward so that he could see me. "It's OK, Jim. We're just coming back from a party. I guarantee you that she hasn't had a drink."

He laughed. "Well I can see that you made up for it. Take care, Charlie. OK, drive on through slowly, Miss."

"Hello, Charlie!" It was Noel Gibson beaming through the window. The stupid bastard straightened up and shouted, "Member coming through!"

We drove on for a mile. The frosty silence was broken when Tricia spoke.

"How come those soldiers know you, Charlie?"

"That's the UDR, they're a locally recruited regiment. I was brought up around here. These guys know me. The soldier with the torch teaches with me at the Tech. We met him the first night that I took you to the Sperrins."

"Well, I don't want you mixing with people like that."

"What do you mean 'people like that'? They are just ordinary citizens who give up their spare time, so that it's safe for people like you to drive about at this time of the morning. Some of them are Catholics. They are not all like those loud mouthed friends of yours at the party."

She never spoke another word until she stopped at the corner of her road. She turned her head away when I tried to kiss her cheek. I got the picture.

"Good night Tricia. Don't try to pick my friends, and I won't pick yours."

She gave me a glare and then drove off. I staggered off through the short cut onto Church Road but it was quiet. I never saw another soul until I arrived at Number Nine.

Chapter 18 - Sammy Cameron

I rang Tricia on Sunday evening and thanked her again for taking me to the party. I suggested that we went for our usual dinner on Wednesday evening but she surprised me when she said that she wanted to see me sooner than that. She suggested that she came round to my house and cooked a meal for us on Tuesday. We agreed that she would show up about half past seven, and I asked her if I needed to get anything in.

"Just clean your kitchen; I know what you men are like," she said.

I got away from the Tech as fast as I could on Tuesday evening, and I got stuck into cleaning the whole house. I paid special attention to the kitchen and the utensils, and then I made an unusual effort in the bedroom and bathroom. I even changed the sheets and pillowcases. Oh yeah Charlie, I thought, you've got high hopes. Then I made an effort with my personal hygiene.

Tricia arrived on time carrying bags of groceries. It was the first time that I had ever seen her casually dressed. She was wearing jeans and a tight fitting sweater that reminded me that she didn't just have great legs.

I poured her a glass of wine. She reckoned that she could risk one, and then she banished me to the lounge where I put on some music and tried to read a book while I sipped a beer. It was no good; I couldn't concentrate. I went into the kitchen but Tricia kicked me out again. She compromised and said that I could sit in the dining room where I could see her and we could talk.

She moved expertly around the kitchen occasionally bending over to get something out of a bottom drawer and giving me the benefit of her beautifully sculpted backside. Eventually she closed the oven door with a bang, took off her apron, and turned to give me her full attention.

"We've got forty minutes," she said. "Let's go into the lounge."

We went into the front room and sat side-by-side on the sofa. We were soon in a passionate clinch. When we came up for air she pulled away and spoke.

"I was talking to Maddy today. She's got a lot of time for you. She says that you helped her out once and that you're a nice guy for a prod."

"What did she say?" I asked warily.

"She said that a gang of Protestant shites gave her a hard time at the Tech when she was wearing a cross on her forehead on Ash Wednesday. She said that you stepped in and sorted them out."

"I remember, in those days all sorts of people went to the Tech, all religions, all levels of ability. The girls did commerce or pre-nursing, the boys did mainly technical subjects but there was a small group of us who had passed the 11-plus but had chosen not to go to the grammar school. I was in that group and we followed a mainly academic curriculum. Some of the lads who did motor maintenance and building were a bit rough. There was a small group that couldn't hack that, I don't know how they got in, they spent their time picking on others."

"Well, she thinks that the sun shines out of your arse. Was there ever anything between you pair?" she asked with apprehension in her eyes.

"No, don't be silly. She's a really nice girl but she was not my type at all. And another thing, I'm going to have to turn you into a lady. Your language is foul. I've noticed that with southern women."

"Oh come on! I only occasionally use 'shit' and 'arse'. You've never heard me use the F-word. And just how many southern women have you known?" she asked mischievously.

"None, to be honest. In fact, you are the first Catholic that I've ever been out with," I replied.

"Are we going out?" she enquired.

"Is that what we're doing? I think we're beyond that. We're staying in tonight," she said with a glint in her eyes. "Come on, let's eat."

She ordered me to sit down at the dining-room table. I poured myself a beer and asked her if she wanted to risk another glass of wine. She assured me that she could handle it along with a big meal.

She brought me a plate of lasagna accompanied by potato wedges that I'd never seen before. She placed two bowls of various salads on the table then she sat down opposite me.

"Don't worry, it's vegetarian lasagna, and I want to see you eating lots of salad. I want you to keep that beautiful brown hair and those lovely eye-lashes," she said.

"Is that how you keep your beautiful figure and perfect skin?" I asked her with a smile.

"Yes, I like to look after myself."

We filled each other in about the gaps in our lives that we didn't know already. She was very keen to find out about my previous love life. There wasn't much to tell.

"But what about those lovely English girls you met at university?" she asked.

"In those days, lovely English girls didn't want to have anything to do with men who looked like Irish terrorists. I had long hair and a big moustache. The only girls who were interested were Marxists and Trotskyists. You know the type, champagne socialists with the dead lice dropping from them. You know me, I only go out with smart looking girls who take a bit of effort with themselves."

"Like me?" she simpered.

"I've never met a girl before that looks like you," I said seriously.

"Ah, you're so full of …"

"Don't say it, young lady. Your trouble is that you can't take a compliment. But it's not a compliment. I mean it. You're the most attractive woman that I've ever met."

She blushed, then stood up and grabbed our empty plates.

"Now for fruit salad," she announced. "But it's not that out of the tin crap that we got at the Sperrins Hotel. I made this myself."

She returned with two bowls and a large glass bowl of fruit-salad, which she proceeded to ladle out.

"You'll want lots of this because you are not getting anything with it. No cream, no ice cream. It's my turn to think about your figure," she laughed.

It was delicious. My thoughts strayed to imagining what it would be like to come home to this treatment every night. When we finished, Tricia disappeared to make coffee.

"Don't worry about washing up," I called to her in the kitchen. "I'll do them tomorrow."

"Away and raffle your arse!" she shouted through. "I have no intention of washing up. You're going to do it tonight, before you go to bed. I'm going to take you in hand, young man. I don't go out with slobs."

We took our coffees into the lounge and put on some more music.

"It's your turn to tell me more about your romantic past. You've told me that you don't go out with slobs. Who did you go out with? Bank managers?" I asked.

"I was boarding in a convent school until I was eighteen," she said. "Then I boarded with my aunt in Galway for three years when I went to college. I've been out with lots of guys on dates but this is the first time that I've been alone in a house with a man."

"Don't worry, you're safe with me," I told her.

"That's all right then," she said as she put her cup on the floor. Then she moved towards me and held her arms out. I moved naturally into a clinch. We kissed each other hungrily. I couldn't help moving my hands up from her waist to cup her fantastic breasts.

"They're all mine," she whispered huskily.

We were soon in my favourite position with me lying along the sofa with Tricia on top. I raised my right knee between her legs and she squeezed it with her thighs. I was fully aroused.

Suddenly the music stopped, and I eased her off me. I took the excuse to get up to change the record. Tricia was looking at me enquiringly. I just didn't know what to do. I grabbed the cups and took them into the kitchen.

Tricia followed me and grabbed me after I had put the cups into the sink. We kissed long and deeply. When we broke off I said, "Maddy asked me where are we going to."

"And?" she enquired.

"I told her that we hardly knew each other. I'm getting to know you better than anyone that I have ever met."

"But?"

"There are all sorts of difficulties," I told her.

"Yeah, I'm a Catholic, you're a prod. I'm from the south, you're from the north," she said bitterly.

"Oh there's much more to it than that," I replied emotionally.

"What else could there be?"

"Oh, things. I can't explain it," I responded.

"You're not married are you?"

I laughed with relief. "No, nothing like that. Let's see how things work out. You know that your parents are never going to accept me?"

"I love them, but I'm not going to let that stop me being happy. I'm going to control my own destiny," she said.

"Look, let's see where thing's take us. And remember, whatever happens always remember that I love you. I mean that."

We gathered her bits and pieces together, and I helped her into her coat. I walked Tricia down to her car that was parked outside the mini-market.

"Do you want me to escort you home?" I offered.

"No, I'll be alright, besides you're over the limit," she replied despondently.

"I could come with you and walk home," I suggested.

"But its three miles!"

"I'll take the short-cut home across the old railway bridge and down Magilligan road. I'll be home in thirty minutes."

"Would you do that for me?" she asked.

"You know that I would do anything for you. I mean it."

She slid into my arms and gave me the full works with her lips. We got into the VW and chugged off.

"Why don't you trade in this heap and get something more modern with northern plates?" I asked Tricia.

"But I'm attached to it. It was my first car. Would you come with me to find another one?"

Of course I agreed. We reached her road and I got out at the corner. I went round to her open window and kissed her goodnight.

"Don't worry, things are going to work out," I assured her. I thought that I saw tears in her eyes.

She drove off, and I turned around to walk back into town. Twenty minutes later I reached Church Street. As I walked up the road, I noticed a makeshift barricade opposite the Presbyterian Church. I approached it without anxiety. I was well known in the town, and I didn't expect any trouble.

When I got to the barricade, I saw that it was manned by members of the Ulster Defence Association, the UDA, but there were lots of younger hangers on. The UDA members were dressed in the same olive green smocks that the UDR wore. You could buy them in any army-surplus shop. They were also wearing Afrika Korps style baseball caps. Many of them hid their faces with camouflage scarves. The hangers on wore tartan scarves tied around their wrist. Some of the UDA men brandished baseball bats, and I was in no doubt that some of them were carrying hidden pistols.

"You're out late, Charlie," said Bobby Gibson, Noel's older brother. "Have you been out courting?"

There was a round of laughter and I nodded. I made my way past the side of the barricade and made to continue on my way. I was confronted by Sammy Cameron, a yob of about eighteen, who had been expelled from the Tech during my first year teaching there.

"How's your wee Fenian girlfriend, Charlie?" he asked.

I ignored him and walked on. As I moved away from the barricade another voice commented, "Well, if you can't fuck the pope, fuck his people."

This provoked a raucous round of laughter. I clenched my fists and bit my lower lip. There were too many of them. But the cat was out of the bag; they obviously knew about Tricia. I resolved to tighten our security. The VW would have to go, for a start.

Then I became aware that Cameron had run after me. I turned around but was relieved to see that he had stopped a few yards away from me.

"Make sure you know which side you're on, Charlie!" he shouted at me.

I walked on and turned up Union Street. I did wash the pots and pans before I went to bed. As usual, I couldn't sleep. I was leading a double life. I really did have to leave the UDR. How far could I go with Tricia? I wanted her but I didn't want to offend her by moving too fast. 'Love them and leave them' was the philosophy of most of my mates or more likely 'fuck them and forget them.' But that only applied to scrubbers, and Tricia was certainly no scrubber.

What is she then, Charlie, I asked myself. How could we ever settle down together in Ireland? She would expect me to turn to be a Roman Catholic. I could do that, I could put on a show, but I couldn't stay in this country if I did. Maddy might accept me but to the people at her party I would always be a prod. Sammy Cameron and his friends would automatically become my enemies. Would Tricia move to England with me? Hold on Charlie, there you go again getting way ahead of yourself.

Chapter 19 - Rosalind Hunter

I signed in for my last duty on the Thursday night. The base was very busy as many members had come in for the two-hour training session but my platoon were doing the eight-hour duty. My section was detailed for base guard, my least favourite duty. I did an hour's stag on the main gate and then joined the trainees for an hour on the .22 range. I loved competitive shooting.

Then it was my turn to do perimeter guard with Arnold Dempsey, an old hand from another platoon. We wandered around the perimeter, and every time we came past the Other Ranks' bar we could hear the guys, who had finished training, getting stuck into some beers. Then it was time for refreshments. We went into the rest room and joined half-a-dozen other guys. They seemed to know that this was my last night. Many of them sympathised. Morale was low; three UDR members from other battalions across the province had been killed in the past week. We rarely heard reports about PIRA members being taken on or even arrested.

Then it was back out to the sangar for another hour. Arnold was kept busy letting the guys out who had been training. He gave them all the benefit of his mantra.

"Watch out, son, the crows are out tonight." He was referring to the RUC who wore a dark-green almost black uniform. They knew that the UDR bar was busy on Thursday nights.

Then back to the rest room for an hour. The others spent the time looking through folders containing details of known and suspected terrorists. There was no point in me doing it. Then it was time to go out on perimeter patrol with Arnold for another hour. It was a beautiful night but my heart was heavy. When I came back to the rest room for the final hour Roddy joined us.

"Well, Charlie, this is it. You've been a valuable member. You've done more than your share of duties but I understand your reasons for leaving."

He shook me by the hand and said, "There's no point in you hanging about for an hour. Come on, let's sign in your rifle and ammunition, and then you can go home. If you could call in on Saturday morning with your uniform and your kit."

I waved the guys goodbye and accompanied Roddy to the armoury. I kissed my faithful SLR and handed it in. I shook Roddy by the hand again and made my way to the car with tears in my eyes. I drove out and never looked back.

On Saturday morning I was up bright and early. I folded my uniforms and packed them away in my kitbag. I was feeling good. I was cutting my ties with the UDR, and I was looking forward to a new phase in my relationship with Tricia starting that night. I drove over to the base and carried my kit to the storeroom. I had my stuff signed for, and as I went to leave, the civvy storeman reminded me to hand over my ID card. That was it. I drove away. My platoon had gone to Derry. I didn't know the guys on gate duty. I headed into town to start a new life.

I cleaned the house, went out and got a paper, picked a few horses and headed down to the bookie's. I didn't have a care in the world. I put on my Yankee and went into Brennan's for a pie and a pint.

I didn't stay because I was driving that evening. I went back to the house and marked a few exercise books. Then I watched my horses. No, they didn't all win but three of them did, one at a good price. This gave me a treble and three doubles; I had also backed them singly so I had a right few quid to lift. I went down to the bookie's and handed over my docket.

"Christ, Charlie! Are you trying to put me out of business?" said the bookie.

"That's what I try every Saturday, just think of all those bets that went down the drain," I rejoined. "I see that you're still driving a Merc."

He laughed and reached me my wedge. "See you next Saturday, Charlie!" he bid me.

I walked back up to the house, I felt on top of the world. I decided to walk past the house, went through the barricade nodding to the reserve RUC constables and turned into Main Street. There was a jeweller's halfway down the street. I let myself be frisked by the security guard. I went in but didn't waste my time at the display of rings. I went over and picked a beautiful, silver, Celtic cross on a chain. I handed it to the assistant who happened to be Aunt Sadie's neighbour.

"Has some wee girl finally stolen your heart, Charlie?" she asked with a smile.

"Well, Roberta, I'm hardly going to wear it myself," I responded

"Do we know her?" she asked hopefully.

"Not yet, but you might soon. I'll tell you this, it will be a surprise."

"Do you want it gift wrapped?"

"Oh yes, please."

I handed over a good chunk of my wedge and took the package. I wished Roberta goodbye knowing that the information would have been passed to Aunt Sadie by nightfall.

I went home and had a quick bite. I started my usual routine before meeting Tricia. Shower, shave, shampoo. I dressed casually but smartly. It was soon time to meet Tricia in the cinema car park. I collected my piece from the toilet in the yard and put it into a brown paper shopping bag along with the gift. I strolled down to my car, instinctively gave it a quick check, got in and stuffed my .38 under the seat and then drove off to the cinema.

I parked behind the cinema and got out to wait for Tricia. She was late but I was not unduly worried. Ten minutes later I became annoyed that we were going to miss the start of the movie. I gave it another ten minutes and was just about to get back into my car when the old VW pulled up on the other side of the car park.

I walked over expectantly to greet Tricia. I was surprised when she got out dressed like a scruff with a scowl on her face.

"You bastard, Charlie!" she screamed. "You fucking liar! What was all that crap about 'I'm not a bigot'?" She was sobbing now.

"You lied to me, you said that you weren't in the UDR. No wonder those soldiers knew you the other night. We're finished, you lying bastard!"

"Hold on," I protested. "I never said I wasn't in the UDR."

"Fuck off out of my life!" she screamed and stomped back to her car.

I ran after her and stopped her from closing the driver's door.

"Listen to my side," I pleaded. "Whenever you criticise someone for joining the UDR you should ask them two questions. One, why did they join? In my case there was a bomb in this town, you might have heard about it. My aunt was blown to bits."

Tricia looked concerned but made no response.

"Two, ask them what they would have joined if there was no UDR. Do you want to know the funny thing? I'm not in the UDR any longer. I handed in my uniform this morning. I did it for you. Ah well, I'm well rid of you, you hysterical bitch. Back to fucking stamp-collecting!"

She made as if to speak but I slammed the door in her face. I stamped back to my car and drove off without a backwards look.

I was going to go to Brennan's but I changed my mind and drove out to the Rugby Club. I went up to the bar and ordered a pint of Tennent's Extra and a double whiskey. I lowered them in pretty short time and asked the bar stewardess for the same again.

"Christ's sake, slow down, Charlie, have you had your tea?" But I was in no mood for conversation.

I lowered half of the second pint then poured the remains of the whiskey into the beer glass to make a depth charge. I had just put it to my mouth when someone grabbed my arm. I looked round and recognised her face. I would have known her big blue eyes anywhere.

"Ros, what are you doing here?" Rosalind Hunter or Rosalind Doherty that was. We had gone out for a few months before I went off to university. I knew that she had since married a successful painter and decorator and had two kids.

"Aren't you going to buy me a drink, Charlie? Bacardi and coke please."

I ordered her drink and another double whiskey for me.

I studied Ros. The eight years and two kids hadn't been bad to her. She was a very attractive woman but there was a hard edge to her eyes.

The drinks came, and I asked her "What are you doing here?"

"My husband Hugh is a member here; we usually come here on a Saturday night."

"Where's Hugh?" I asked, looking around nervously. He was a big bloke.

"He's next door playing in a snooker tournament. He won't be back for hours," she said wistfully. "I'm sitting with the other snooker widows."

"How's life treating you?" I asked. "You look very prosperous." She was wearing a classy red dress, which just permitted a peek of her ample cleavage. She wore expensive jewellery, and she looked as if she went to the hairdresser every week with her beautiful blonde hair.

"I can't complain. Hugh's business is doing very well." She paused.

"But?" I prompted.

"But I'm very unhappy. I should have gone to university. I did have the 'A' levels but I never used them. My life is a cultural desert," she mused.

"Look, Charlie, have you got your car here?" she asked.

"Yes, but I'm in no fit state to drive. I'm going to get a taxi when I'm finished here."

"I just want to talk to you somewhere in private," she said.

"OK, it's the old green Morris estate with the wooden trim. Wait a couple of minutes before you come out, make sure that nobody sees you getting in."

I made my way out through the throng and got into my car. She slipped into the passenger seat a few minutes later. The courtesy light did not come on because I had removed the bulb. Old UDR habits die-hard.

Ros was wearing an expensive dark-brown suede coat with a fur collar. Her expensive perfume stirred feelings in me, which I wanted to deny. Everything about Ros was expensive.

"Awe, Charlie. We should never have split up. You were the love of my life," she murmured.

"You should have told me," I spluttered. "I thought that we were just passing time. It was all very innocent."

"Yeah, we should have got it together. You know that I married Hugh on the rebound."

"I didn't even know that you were married until I came back from university. I spent most of my vacations travelling and working abroad," I told her.

"If I had gone to uni we could have travelled together to romantic places. Hugh's idea of a foreign holiday is a week in Scotland. He's only interested in beer, rugby, and snooker."

"Awe, come on, life can't be bad for you. I heard that you had a big house and two lovely kids."

"Charlie, it's not enough. Hugh's not interested in me, we never go anywhere, and he doesn't want to talk about cultural ideas. You know, I see you sometimes at the mini-market but you never notice me. I lie awake at night wondering how life would have worked out if we had got married."

"Ros, get real. We were never anywhere near that stage," I protested.

"You never did get married, did you, Charlie?" she asked. "Do you still fancy me?"

"Look, Ros, you are one of the most attractive women that I've ever met, and you know it. There's just one problem." I grabbed her left hand and brought it up to her eyes. "It's this big golden ring."

"You don't have to worry about that." Suddenly she slipped into my arms and we were kissing passionately. I look back, and I blame the amount of drink I had taken. I didn't push her away but the thought crossed my mind that I was two-timing Tricia. Don't be fucking stupid, Charlie, I thought. You and Tricia are finished. Enjoy the moment.

I pulled away and said hoarsely, "I don't go out with married women, Ros."

"Pretend that I'm not married. I'm not really. Hugh hasn't had anything to do with me for months. Let's just take up where we left off, only more seriously now."

"I don't do it in the back of cars. I think it's so demeaning for the woman," I told her pompously.

"Well then, let's meet somewhere. I heard that you have a house in Union Street, just up from the mini-market. What's the number?"

I told her, reluctantly. "I'll put a note through your letter-box. We'll work something out."

"What excuse did you make to your friends?" I asked.

"I told them that I had left my lipstick in the car."

"Well, you'd better run-along; they will be getting suspicious," I warned her.

"Just let me give you something to remember me by, lover boy," she murmured huskily in my ear. Then she gave me the full works on my mouth. She grabbed my right hand and cupped it under her breast. Believe me, they were real. Then she was gone.

I waited until I had cooled down, then I went back into the bar. I tried not to let my eyes wander to where Ros was sitting with her friends. I ordered a pint of Tennent's ordinary, and then I studied Ros in the mirror. She caught my eyes and smiled. I let my eyes wander down to her figure. She was sitting with her legs crossed. Her dress had ridden up above her beautiful slim legs. I was a leg connoisseur in those days. Her slim figure belied her ample breasts but I now knew that they were real.

It's sitting there on a plate waiting for you, I thought, but not tonight.

I finished my beer and walked out. I shouldn't have done it but I drove down to Union Street. I left the car, and my piece, and went into Brennan's. I sank pint after pint while watching the football highlights.

At closing time I staggered out of the bar and set off up Union Street. I can remember leaning over the wall of the little bridge and spewing my guts into the stream. I meandered on home and collapsed on the sofa.

That's where I woke up at four o'clock with a blinding headache and vomit down the front of my shirt. I crawled upstairs and chucked all of my clothes into the laundry basket. I cleaned myself up and drank a pint of water.

Christ, I thought. My piece and the cross are still in the car. I was taking a terrible risk but I dressed in my jeans and a sweater and went out into the night. I looked up to the barricade but could not see any police officers. I walked quietly down to the car and looked around for watchers. There was nobody around. I opened the car and slipped the gun into the brown paper bag with Tricia's present. I wondered whether Ros would soon be wearing the cross but it would have to have been gold for her.

I locked the car and scurried back to the house. I changed for bed and took the piece with me. I didn't make the mistake that Hollywood amateurs make of placing the gun under my pillow. I put it down between my ankles.

I was soon fast asleep but I was troubled with dreams. I was having a great time in bed with a woman. She smelled like Ros but when I went to kiss her she had the face of Tricia. I woke up with a start. Where the hell do I go from here, I wondered. I should get out more, I thought, and meet some nice little unmarried Protestant girl. But I knew what I really wanted. I wanted to take Ros to bed with no complications but I wanted most of all to get back with Tricia to spend the rest of my life with her.

I awoke near ten o'clock with another splitting headache. I got up and made some breakfast, which I forced down. I went down the garden and hid my piece. I decided to go for a run along the beach at Downhill. I pulled on my jeans and a sweatshirt. I covered them with a driving coat and headed off to Downhill. I parked in front of the Downhill Hotel, and I shed my coat.

I ambled across the road under the railway to the beach. I ran west for about two miles. I was breathing hard and sweating the booze out. I resolved to do this every Sunday. I ran back to the bridge and thought twice about my resolution. I almost threw up again but I rationalised that it must have been doing me good.

I called into the hotel and bought six bottles of Guinness for my father. I drove into Coleraine and parked outside of the ex-servicemens' bungalows. I knocked on my da's door and he let me in. He seemed overjoyed to see me. I had been neglecting him recently.

We sat in front of the fire, and he poured two bottles of beer into glasses.

"You stink of booze," he said.

"I had a few last night, and I've been running on Downhill strand."

"When are you going to settle down with some nice wee girl and give me some grandchildren, like your sister?" he asked light-heartedly.

"All in good time. I'm working on it," I replied.

"Well, you'd better hurry up. I'm not going to be around forever."

"You've got years ahead of you yet, da," I replied.

We emptied our glasses and I opened two more bottles and poured them.

"Da," I said hesitantly. "Did you ever go out with a Roman Catholic girl?"

"No," he replied. "We were brought up very differently in those days. Different schools, different dances, different jobs. Of course, as we got older we met them more and more but never socially. If it had come to anything like marriage, the couple would have had to skip off to England. You know your mother's brother Ian married a Catholic. He met her in England, mind you, but they could never come back here."

We both took a swallow, and then he looked at me strangely.

"Have you got something to tell me, Charlie? Are you going out with a Catholic?"

"Not now. She dumped me yesterday," I answered.

"Did you have feelings for her?" he asked.

"Yeah, but I've only realised how much today."

"Well, take my advice. If you love her, go after her. Don't let me stop you. You know that I only brought you up in our church to please your mother. I never believed it, and I know that you don't. One thing that I learned in the RAF is that it's all bollocks."

We both laughed. I became serious. "Now, da, it's your birthday next Saturday. What do you want?"

He reached over and caught my knee. "I don't need anything. I've got all that I want. I would just like you to come round and share a meal with me."

"Don't worry, da. I'll be here, I promise."

"And you can bring that wee Catholic girl with you," he joked.

"Well, I can't promise that."

I stayed to watch the football highlights with him then bid him Goodnight. I vowed to myself that no matter what, I would be there for his birthday.

Chapter 20 - Tricia or Ros

It was the following Saturday. I had gone through my cleaning routine, and I had been to the bookies. I was just settling down in front of the TV for my first race at two o'clock, when there was a banging at my front door.

Shit! I thought. Who's that? I opened the door and there was Maddy.

"Charlie, you've broken that wee girl's heart," she accused me.

"Come in." I closed the door.

"It was her that dumped me, she actually told me to 'fuck off'!" I said defensively.

We went into the lounge and she sat down on the sofa. I took the armchair.

"Why didn't you come clean with her earlier on? Everybody knows that you are in the UDR; we just assumed that she did. She had a business meeting last Saturday morning with one of the guys from the party, and he happened to mention it. It came as a proper shock to her."

"But I'm not in the UDR anymore. I resigned because of Tricia. I handed in all of my gear last Saturday."

"I know. She told me. She doesn't care one way or the other. She just wants to get back with you," said Maddy.

"Well, I can't meet her tonight. I've got to go somewhere."

"You haven't got a date with Ros Hunter, have you?"

"Don't be daft," I replied. "She's a married woman. They don't go out on dates."

"Well, I watched you at the Rugby Club last Saturday night. You seemed to be very close," said Maddy.

"Nonsense, she's just an old girl-friend from way back. I bought her a drink. If you must know, it's my father's birthday, and I can't let him down. He's got nobody else."

"I'm sure that Tricia will understand," said Maddy. "When can you meet up?"

"Tell her that I go running across Downhill strand every Sunday afternoon. I'll be parked outside of the Downhill Hotel at two o'clock."

"I'll tell her. I'm sure that she will want to meet you there. Be gentle with her, Charlie, she's a bit fragile."

"Listen to me, don't tell anybody else what I'm going to say. I would do anything for that girl. She's the centre of my life. I can't tell you what sort of week I've had."

"Good, I believe you. I'll let her know where you will be and that she has nothing to worry about. Thank you, Charlie." She got up to leave and, I ushered her out of the front door.

So she doesn't care whether or not I'm in the UDR, I mused. I wonder what she would think of me joining the NVF. Christ, what a mess. If only I had waited.

After I had watched my last race and thrown my betting slip in the bin, I popped out to the off-licence and bought some cans and a bottle of Bushmills for my father. I called into the mini-market and bought a birthday card. There was no point in buying a cake; my father wouldn't have thanked me for it. I bought him a couple of packets of ginger biscuits, his favourite. When I was queueing up to pay, I noticed a powder blue Mercedes-Benz convertible pulling into the car park. Christ! It was Rosalind. She was a stunner. She had her blonde hair drawn back in a ponytail, and she was wearing a yellow sweater over tight fitting faded blue jeans. I ducked down to re-arrange the items in my basket as she walked down the other side of a display case. I paid as quickly as I could and strode off up to number nine.

That was a close call, I thought, then mocked myself. Hiding from a very attractive woman who had made it clear that she wanted me, what was that all about? Sure, I was meeting Tricia the next day but it didn't follow that we would take up again. You have always been spineless when it comes to women. I put thoughts of Ros out of my mind and concentrated on getting ready to meet Dad.

I drove over to Coleraine and parked in front of my father's bungalow. He came out to meet me grinning from ear to ear. We went in, and I gave him his presents. He proudly showed me the electric blanket, which my sister Kathy had sent over from Scotland. We discussed the state of the Irish League for a while, then I popped out to get fish and chips. I had left my .38 in the car but I didn't need to get it. Coleraine was predominantly Loyalist so I had no fears as I walked to the chippie. The twelve ex-servicemens' bungalows formed a crescent. The council had been criticised by Nationalists for 'wasting' money on them because most ex-servicemen were Protestants but I knew that one of them was occupied by a Catholic who had served in the RAF during the war. Perhaps it was nominalism. I bought a packet of cod and chips and a separate bag of chips for myself. It

143

annoyed me that the chips were fried in the same fryer as the fish but I put up with it.

We scoffed our food and washed it down with cans of Tennents. I tidied up and then made two hot whiskies. As usual, my Dad enquired about my marital status. I asked him tentatively what he would think if I married a Catholic. My father had never been bigoted. Sure, he came from an Orange background but I had never heard him utter a negative comment about Catholics. He hated Republicans and Nationalists, and I shared his views on them.

"You know that your uncle Ian married a Catholic," he said. "We never saw much of him after that."

My mother's brother had met a girl from Newry when he served in England with the RAF. He had converted to Roman Catholicism and returned after the war to live in England before coming back to Newry. He rarely returned to the north coast, and I had met him only once. My mother's father had resigned from the Orange Order but the rest of the family seemed to accept it. It was Ian's choice to keep away from the family.

"I know, but it's not like that nowadays," I replied.

"Have you got someone in mind?" he asked. "As long as she's not a Republican."

"There's no danger of that," I replied. "In any case we are nowhere near that stage."

I made him another hot whiskey but I took a cup of tea. I didn't want to be stopped by the RUC with an illegal weapon in the car. We watched Match of the Day, then I hugged him and bade him goodnight. My head was spinning as I drove past the Sconce Hill. Ros? Tricia? Was I really considering marrying a Catholic?

Sunday morning came, and I woke up feeling as if a lump of lead had been removed from my heart. I couldn't wait to see Tricia. What would I say?

I had a light breakfast, then I spent the morning planning lessons for the return to teaching on Monday. I packed away my notes, and then I cleaned myself up. I got into a clean sweatshirt, jeans, and socks. I put on my car coat and walked down to the woodie. I didn't bring my piece.

I drove down the Glebe and turned left past the Lions' Gates down into Downhill. I parked outside of the hotel with ten minutes to spare.

Would she turn up? My heart pounded like a teenager's on a first date. Five minutes later the old VW chugged down the brae and pulled into the car park. Tricia got out and ran towards me. She was crying but she was smiling.

"Charlie, Charlie, I'm so sorry," she sobbed.

I grabbed her and covered her face with kisses.

"Hush, girl, you've got nothing to be sorry about. It was all my fault," I told her.

"Oh Charlie, the things I said to you, I'm so ashamed."

"It's me that has to apologise for my foul language. Come on, let's go for a walk on the beach away from all of these people."

A small crowd were hanging about their cars pretending not to listen but not making any haste to get in out of the cold. We locked our cars, and I led her by the hand to the little wooden bridge under the railway line.

"Where does this take us?" she asked.

"Wait and see." We came out onto the beach, and she stared in astonishment at the miles of golden sand. The only problem was that there was an icy gale blowing in straight from the Arctic.

We jogged along together for half a mile, then Tricia stopped me. She flung her arms around my neck and kissed me full on the mouth. Her cheeks were freezing.

"Let's go back to your house, Charlie. You can make me some hot soup. I skipped my Sunday dinner to come here. My parents just can't figure out what's going on."

"No Sunday dinner? Now I know that you care about me." We both laughed.

We jogged gently back to the bridge. Her eyes widened when a train came out of the tunnel in the cliffs and roared past above our heads.

"Where did that come from?" she stuttered.

"Castlerock," I replied. "There's two tunnels through the cliffs before you get to Castlerock. I'll show you someday. Come on. Race you to the cars."

We headed off to Maddenstown in convoy. Finding parking space in Union Street was easy on a Sunday afternoon. I guided Tricia to my home. I didn't care who saw us; I was proud of her.

We went straight to the kitchen and Tricia said, "I need to get something hot inside of me."

I wish, I thought. I opened a large can of vegetable soup and soon had it bubbling. Tricia cut a fresh loaf into chunks, and we sat down at the dining-room table. She soon looked more like herself.

"I've got something for you," I said. "Actually, I was going to give it to you last Saturday night."

"What is it?" she asked excitedly.

When I reached her the gift-wrapped jeweller's box her eyes were like saucers. She ripped away the paper and opened the box but I thought that I detected a glint of disappointment when she saw the contents.

Shit! I thought. Surely she wasn't expecting a ring. We still hardly knew each other.

"It's beautiful," she gushed. "Can I put it on now?"

"Of course you can." I rose and stood behind her chair. She put the chain around her neck and offered me the two ends. I fastened the catch, and then I kissed her on the nape of her neck. She half turned and offered me her lips. I greedily devoured her.

"Let's move into the sofa," she suggested.

We went into the lounge, and I put on some romantic music, the Carpenters. We were soon in a clinch on the sofa. I had never known such fervour from Tricia before. I was soon aroused, and I slid my hands down around Tricia's backside and pressed her to me. I rubbed up and down against her then I pulled away.

She looked straight into my eyes. "Charlie, why do you always pull back? Why do you never try it on with me?" she asked.

"I'll tell you," I began, huskily. "I respect you far too much, maybe, I even love you. I know where you are coming from, and I don't want to offend you."

I rushed on, "Believe me, I'm not gay. I'm a full red-blooded male, and I lust for you. You would not believe the things I dream about that I want to do to you. But not yet, I don't want to force you into anything."

"Wow!" she said. "I know I'm not meant to say it, but I feel the same about you." She paused, "Did you say that you loved me?"

"I think I do. I've never loved anyone before. I think about you, worry about you, all of the time."

"Why do you worry about me?" she asked.

"Well, you know, your safety. This country is becoming a dangerous place to live in," I replied.

"Charlie," she began, hesitantly. "Have you got a big bed up there?"

I laughed, "You'd better believe it."

We got up and ascended the stairs. Thank Christ, I thought, I had changed the sheets and pillowcases yesterday. They were still relatively fresh.

She sat on the edge of the bed and looked at me shyly. "Charlie, I don't know what to do, just be gentle."

"Relax honey, leave it all to me." I went over and closed the curtains. Then I returned to her and took off her driving shoes.

I knelt on the bed beside her and kissed her deeply. I pulled her up and helped her to remove her sweater. She was wearing a black, lacy bra that pulled up and presented her cleavage to perfection.

I unfastened her belt and stood at the side of the bed to pull off her jeans. She wasn't wearing any tights, just walking socks that I soon pulled off. Her black, lacy panties matched her bra. I knelt beside her and kissed her all over her lovely stomach.

"Get into bed" I grunted. "And take off your ear-rings." She did.

I removed my own boots and socks and took off my sweatshirt.

I congratulated myself for regularly going to the UDR gym on Thursday nights after training. I wasn't looking too bad. All that jumping in and out of Landrovers had helped, too. I undid my belt and rolled off my jeans. Tricia was sitting up in the bed studying me. An enormous erection forced my boxers out in the front.

Our eyes met and she smiled nervously. Yes, I thought, this is going to be all yours, Tricia.

I slid into bed and grabbed her. I kissed her deeply while I struggled to unfasten her bra.

"Let me help you," she said. "Are you out of practice?" She giggled.

The bra came free, and I flung it to the floor.

Her nipples were standing out proudly. She was a stunner.

"Magnificent!" I said. I leaned over and put my lips around her left nipple and sucked it and massaged it with my tongue. She was moaning and squirming.

I kissed her again on the mouth; my tongue almost reached her tonsils. I put my hands down and slipped off her panties. You can imagine what happened next but just before I entered her I asked, "Is it safe?"

Tricia murmured in my ear, "It's OK, I'm fixed. I saw a doctor."

When it was over we lay side-by-side gasping.

"Charlie, where's your toilet?" she asked. I told her that the bathroom was en-suite to the rear bedroom, and she jumped out giving me the benefit of her delicious bottom.

When she returned, she was laughing. "You weren't kidding when you told me about your train-set and your soldiers and dinky toys."

"It's not a train-set," I replied huffily, "It's a model railway lay-out."

"Well there sure as hell isn't any room for a bed," she responded.

"Get in," I ordered. "I'm not playing trains today."

Two hours later I had run out of ideas for positions. To be honest, I had run out of steam.

"Charlie, have many girls seen your train-set?" Tricia asked anxiously.

"None," I replied. "You are the first woman to come upstairs in this house, ever!" I said emphatically.

"Well, have you had many girls?" Tricia asked wistfully.

"Surprisingly few," I lied. In fact, even that was an exaggeration. I had never had trouble attracting woman; it was just that I didn't know what to do with them and how to get them as far as bed.

"But I've read loads of manuals," I continued. "I've wasted far too much time playing with my train-set, but it was worth the wait."

I grabbed her and surprised myself when I came up with another erection. An hour later, just as we came out of the front door touching and laughing, I spotted Ros gaping at us from the far side of the street. She was clutching a white envelope but she was too late. I had already made up my mind.

Chapter 21 - Joe Neilly

The biggest mistake that Joe had ever made in his life was to share his grandparents with Malachy Toner. Toner was the second in command of the PIRA Derry Brigade. He was sprung from a prison van on his way to his appeal in the High Court in an ambush, which left one prison warden dead and a young RUC officer paralysed from the neck down.

The Maddenstown platoon of the NVF had been searching for Toner for three months since the prison van ambush. They owed him because the murdered prison warden was the younger brother of Andy Creith, a sergeant in the platoon. We had dickers covering Toner's home in Dungiven and at his grandmother's house near Derry. We even had a team who kept an eye on Toner's favourite fishing pitch but there had been no sign of him. The manpower cost was too high so we needed a different approach.

The platoon HQ group had met to consider the case and reckoned that Toner had gone to ground in the Republic. They were reluctant to hit Toner's wife or grandmother but had sanctioned a hit on his cousin Joe Neilly. There was no direct evidence that Neilly was a player or even a supporter, but Toner and Neilly had been bosom pals in their teens, and the HQ group considered that a hit on Neilly would hurt Toner and send a message to local Republicans.

Marcus informed us that the policy had come down from the NVF supreme command. For years Republicans had hit members of the security forces and Unionist politicians without regard to the presence of members of their families. Brian Montgomery, the UDR training staff sergeant, was a typical example. The terrorists, who blew up his car, must have known that Brian drove his eight-year old daughter to school every morning but they went ahead with their operation. A prominent Republican politician was confronted with this and replied, "You can't make an omelette without breaking eggs."

A directive from NVF headquarters stated that the families of Republican players were now legitimate targets. We couldn't get at the terrorists directly because they hid in the Republic or were shielded by the police and army in the north. By hitting their family members we would hurt them land spread the belief that PIRA and INLA could not defend them, which, we hoped, would hit their morale.

Andy Creith and Walter Jamieson were selected for the hit, and I was chosen as the getaway driver. This would be my first active operation against the terrorists. I wondered what Tricia would think of me but I was too far in to get out. Besides, I had vowed to get back at the terrorists because of the Station Street bomb, Brian Montgomery, and the scars that I bore. The hit was scheduled for the following Thursday to get maximum media coverage.

Early in the morning of D-Day a helper parked a freshly stolen black Ford Cortina at the end of my street. I dressed in black, nylon golfing gear and leather gloves, made sure that I had a long piss, taped my Webley .38 to my lower right leg and picked up the keys and a Polaroid picture of the Cortina, which had been dropped through my letterbox.

I opened the front door and checked that nobody was watching. I found the car, and I drove off down the Listober road.

About a mile outside of Listober I pulled in behind a white Vauxhall Viva that was parked in a lay-by at the side of the road. Creith and Jamieson immediately got out of the Viva and slipped into the back seat of the four-door Cortina. A third man gunned the Viva, did a U-turn and headed back to Maddenstown.

"All set?" I asked the boys, who grunted affirmation. I pulled out and carried on at a sensible speed to Listober.

Joe Neilly worked in a hardware store on Donegal Street. He could usually be found in the yard mending lawnmowers and bicycles. I did a U-turn and approached the front of the store. A youth wearing a donkey jacket stood outside of the store eating an apple. As we approached, he threw the core into the gutter and walked off. We now knew that Neilly was actually in the yard. I parked outside the yard gate but kept the engine ticking.

Creith and Jamieson got out and entered the yard. I found out later that they approached a man who was knelt down testing a bicycle tube in a basin of water.

"Joe Neilly?" asked Creith.

Joe looked up and nodded. Creith pulled out a Star .22 automatic and Jamieson reached for his old Belgian rim-fire revolver. They pointed their weapons at Neilly and began to fire. At least Creith did, he put three rounds into Neilly's upper body but Jamieson's Belgian piece of shit misfired repeatedly. The .22 rounds from the Star didn't cause much damage to Neilly who fell back flat on the ground tipping the basin of water.

He spluttered, "Why… I'm not… " Then Creith tapped him twice in the head.

A young fellow came out of a shed at the back of the yard with his mouth hanging open, and a middle-aged woman came out of the back of the shop and started to scream. Creith and Jamieson ran out of the yard shouting, "That's for George Creith! That's for George Creith!"

They jumped into the Cortina, and I gave it the full wellie and roared off down the Maddenstown road. Creith and Jamieson were screaming, "We got the bastard!"

About two miles out of town I pulled into a lay-by behind the white Viva. The boys jumped out and clambered into it. The Viva sped off but I drove soberly towards Maddenstown. Another mile along I met a police Cortina but it sped past me on the way to Listober.

I drove the Cortina into the supermarket car park in Maddenstown. There was no need to burn it. There was nowhere I could have done so without attracting attention. We had left no prints or fibres. We had all had a close haircut the previous day. I had washed my hair twice since then. It was unlikely that we had dropped any hairs. There was no DNA testing in those days. I was pretty sure that the car could not be traced to us. I waited until there was nobody around and then got out. I left the keys in her hoping that some yobs would steal it.

I walked home quietly and hid my .38 in its usual place. I changed and then wandered down to spend the afternoon in the bookies behind Brennan's but I didn't have a drink, yet. Like most bookies in Northern Ireland at the time, it had a door leading directly into the back of the pub. At 5:35, after the last race at Newmarket, I went into the pub and ordered a hot pie and a pint of Tennent's.

The TV was on and the local news soon fired up. It confirmed that Neilly was dead, and it speculated that the deed had been carried out by protestant paramilitaries, the UDA or Red Hand commandoes or by the UVF or LVF or what the fuck VF.

A series of Neilly's friends and relatives came on and dutifully stressed that Joe had no connection with terrorism. None of them mentioned the connection to Malachy Toner. The BBC commentator reiterated that this was the work of Protestant paramilitaries although they never described the PIRA or INLA as Roman Catholics.

I stayed until near seven o'clock lingering over two or three pints. Nobody engaged me in conversation but I nodded in recognition to some former classmates and pupils I had taught in the past. It was a mixed bar, usually quiet mid-week, as clients wound down after work before making their way home.

When I left I wandered across town to Aunt Sadie's. I was interested to see that the black Cortina had disappeared from the supermarket car park.

I was pretty sure that the police knew that Sadie was some sort of sympathiser if not a low-level player but they didn't have the manpower to watch all the suspected players from half-a-dozen organisations from both sides of the divide. I casually checked the cars in her street; I knew most of them and none of the others were suspicious looking. As usual, I went through an entry a few doors away from her home then I stepped over the low fences to get to her back garden. Nobody challenged me; her neighbours could be trusted and they all knew me. I opened the back door and stepped straight into her kitchen.

Sadie was cooking at her range and showed no surprise when she turned around to check me. I went into the lounge, and Sadie joined me to watch a comedy show. I heard someone flushing the upstairs toilet and then descending the stairs. It was Walter Jamieson. We assured each other that everything was OK. He told me that Andy Creith was well on his way back to Scotland in a fishing boat to continue his family holiday near Ayr. There was no way that the police could place Andy in NI on the day of the shooting. He would be number one suspect but they would not be able to pin it on him.

After the programme we went into the kitchen for tea as the main meal was called. We were joined by Sadie's husband Carson who had been working in his bedroom. As we sat down, Marcus Macrory, the platoon commander, came through the back door and took a seat. Sadie's twin daughters were eating at a friend's house so that we could hold the debrief in Sadie's home.

"Well, talk me through it" said Marcus. Walter and I retraced the events of the day. Walter was disgusted that the Belgian piece had let him down. When he had checked it later, he found that it was loaded with centrefire ammunition but the gun was for 1920s rimfire.

"Get rid of it" said Marcus. "We haven't a hope of getting any rimfire ammo. It's 8mm, for God's sake. Who makes ammunition of that calibre nowadays?"

We kicked around the perennial bitch that we couldn't lay our hands on decent hardware. Unlike the PIRA, who had regular shipments of modern weapons, explosives and radios from sympathisers in the USA and Marxists in Libya, the Loyalist paramilitaries relied on old weapons from collectors and the occasional piece, like my Webley .38, stolen from the army.

"That problem is being addressed," stated Marcus. "The same boat that brought Andy from Scotland has also brought a consignment of arms and explosives, which we will get our share of soon."

He went on to question Walter in detail about how Andy had been collected from Ballintoy harbour and returned there after the operation. Satisfied that everything seemed to be in order, he turned to Carson who acted as our conscience.

"Are you ready to sign off on this operation?" he asked.

"No, I am not. This was an innocent workingman. He had a wife and four young children to support. This was a damned foul deed!"

We were all shocked by his tone. "I don't want to hear of this sort of operation being planned in my house again."

"Or what?" asked Marcus.

"Or you won't be holding your meetings in my home anymore. I suggest that you leave this sort of cowardly action to the IRA scum and concentrate on taking out some real players. We are above this sort of action."

"Are you a member of this organisation or not?" snapped Marcus.

"I was never a member of your organisation as you well know. I see myself as the voice of reason," said Carson as he stamped off upstairs.

Sadie looked shocked. "I suggest that you all go home and let things cool down," she said.

We left at ten-minute intervals through the back door. I walked home and went to bed. I didn't get much sleep. I was ashamed of myself but at the same time I tried to justify our operation. I wondered what Tricia would make of my part in the day's proceedings but I couldn't bear to imagine it.

Chapter 22 - Marty Darby

About two weeks later, I was called to a planning meeting unusually on a Tuesday evening at Aunt Sadie's. I made my way there in the usual way and was soon settled around the kitchen table with fried eggs and chips in front of me. Just as I started to tuck in, Marcus Macrory slipped in through the back door. He sat down at the place, which had been prepared for him.

"We're just waiting for Robin Hume to join us. Where's Carson and the girls?" Marcus asked.

"Don't worry. They've all gone to Carson's mother for their tea. They won't be back until late," replied Sadie. At that moment a skinny young man entered the house and looked at us nervously.

"Come on in, Robin, and sit yourself down. You don't know my nephew Charlie," she said, pointing at me. Robin nodded but did not look me in the eye.

Sadie served large mugs of hot, sweet tea as was the custom in Ulster, and the planning meeting began.

"I want to tell you a story," began Marcus mysteriously. "My sister lives in a little bungalow in a council housing estate in Magheraderg, about two miles west of here."

We looked on in anticipation. "These houses were built in the 1950s but they've never had central heating. Maddenstown Urban District Council has started to rectify this, and they have had a company installing boilers and radiators for the past few weeks."

He paused and took a swig of tea. "Now the Magheraderg estate is one hundred per cent Protestant but the council, in their wisdom, has given the contract to Donnelly's Plumbing and Heating from Derry, and all of their workers are Catholics. The council probably got a government grant, and one of the conditions was that the job went to Fenians. All very commendable, and I am sure it will help to deflect criticism about sectarianism."

We all laughed cynically and I asked, "So?"

"So. There is a team of three workers, and it has been reported to me that two of them are asking young weans in the houses strange questions."

"What are they asking these young children?" I asked.

"Oh, questions such as, 'Does your Daddy ever go out at night dressed up as a soldier?' and 'Does your big brother ever wear a policeman's hat?' Those type of questions."

"Do we know anything about these Derry men?" I asked. "Are they players?"

At this point Robin Hume spoke for the first time. "The leader of the team is Marty Darby from the Bogside. We don't know anything directly about him but his brother Seamus is doing eight years for possession of weapons, circuits, and detonators. The other one that asks questions is a teenager called Corrie but that's all we know. The third one is an old boy, a real tradesman who doesn't say much."

Sadie broke in and addressed me. "Robin's mother also lives on the Magheraderg estate. Her mother was killed in the Station Street bombing two years ago."

"That was my grannie" said Robin bitterly. "I hate the bastards!"

Marcus retook control of the meeting. "It is obvious that these guys are involved. They are passing on intelligence. Who knows where that will lead? They need to be taken out and incidentally, Maddenstown Council and the government need to be given a message."

"I agree" I replied. "What do you propose?"

"We have acquired a few Sten guns from the Ayr fishing boat that took Andy Creith off."

He brought out a piece of paper and began to make a sketch.

"Charlie, you will be given a Cortina as usual. You will drive out the Limavady road to where Robin and I will be waiting behind the wall of a lay-by. You can't miss it because there is a telephone box half-way down the lay-by."

"Timing?" I asked.

"This Thursday. Time it so that you pick us up at five minutes to one. The workers sit in their van between one o'clock and half one to have their lunch. We will wait for a phone call to confirm that they are working that day and that they are sitting in the van. If so, it will take us ten minutes to get to Magheraderg – here's the plan."

He drew a road with another coming off at a right angle. "This is the main Limavady road. The road coming off leads down to the housing estate. They park their van here – it's a red Bedford pick-up. All three of them will be sitting in the cab. Charlie, you will drive past it slowly and then pull in at an angle in front of it. I will sit in the front passenger seat and Robin in the

155

left-hand rear seat. We will both have Sten guns. We will spray the cab with full magazines and then you will do a U-turn and come back to the lay-by."

"What if a Sten gun jams?" I asked. "They're notorious for it."

"That's why we've got two. If they both jam, then you and me, Charlie, will jump out and use our handguns. You will go to the driver's side."

"How are you going to be recovered?" I asked.

"You drop us at the lay-by and drive on back to Maddenstown to dispose of the Cortina as usual. Don't worry about the police looking for the Cortina. Nobody from the estate is going to make a 999 call." We all laughed.

"Any questions?"

"What if the phone call tells us that the targets aren't there?"

"Then all you have to do is go back to Maddenstown to get rid of the Cortina. We'll be picked up. We'll have another go as soon as we can."

We broke up and went our separate ways.

I spent all day on Wednesday cleaning the house and doing minor repairs. I cleaned up and had a shower all ready to welcome Tricia who was cooking for me as usual. We had a lovely evening on the sofa in front of the television but I was starting to feel frustration about the lack of progress on the physical side.

I drove escort vehicle for her as had become our habit. When we stopped outside of her home she came and kissed me passionately through the car window.

"Do you fancy going for a picnic on Saturday afternoon?" she asked nervously.

"Fantastic idea," I enthused.

"Well, I'll ring you on Friday evening to sort out details, goodnight lover," and she was gone.

Yeah, lover, I wish. I got to bed quickly. But I couldn't sleep. What I intended to do tomorrow was criminal. But was it? These guys looked as if they were players. The intelligence, which they passed on, would make some UDR man or a reserve RUC man a target. Nobody seemed to be looking after the interests of the part-time security personnel. Their hands were tied by the government. At the worst the big sell-out was coming, at least it was a policy of appeasement.

I got up early and did a few chores. Then it was time to get ready. I had a shower making sure that I washed my hair well. I put on my nylon golfing gear and basketball boots. I laid out my baseball hat and gloves. I went down the garden, climbed up on the toilet seat and reached through to retrieve my piece wrapped in my balaclava. I took them into the kitchen and laid the .38 out on an old newspaper. I removed the six cartridges, lightly oiled them and rubbed them down with an old flannel cloth. I cleaned the revolver, oiled it and checked the action. I reloaded it and weighed it in my hand. I had an ominous feeling that today was the day when I might have to use it in earnest.

Just after twelve I heard my letterbox banging shut. I went out to the hall and picked up the Polaroid and keys. I studied the Polaroid, it showed a green Cortina, and I memorised the registration. I put a match to the Polaroid and then stuffed my piece and the balaclava into a supermarket bag. I wandered down the street and spotted the dark-green Cortina parked near the bridge. I had a quick look around but the few people in sight seemed to be getting on with their own business. I opened the door and slipped in.

The engine started readily, and I pulled away smoothly. Out onto the Listober road and then turned off to get onto the Limavady Road. I travelled through the little capsule of orangism and sped up when I left the town. A mile later I pulled in beyond the telephone box in a lay-by. Marcus and Hume jumped over the wall and got into the left-hand seats. They both carried Sten guns.

Marcus ordered young Hume to roll down his window and did the same himself. He looked at his watch and rasped, "Any minute now." Sure enough, the phone in the box began to ring. Marcus jumped out, went into the box and answered the phone. He was back in the car in seconds.

"OK! We're on," he said calmly. "Drive on."

A mile later I came to a junction signposting Magheraderg to the right. I turned and then pulled over. Without a word we slipped on our balaclavas, and the two shooters inserted a magazine into their Stens and pulled back the cocking-handle.

"Got your piece ready, Charlie?" asked Marcus. I pointed to the butt protruding between my legs. "OK, let's do it."

I drove down into the housing estate and sure enough there was the red Bedford parked on the left. I passed it slowly then pulled in at an angle to give the shooters room to work with.

Marcus and Hume opened up immediately. There were no stoppages. The sound was deafening and the smell of the burnt propellant was acrid in my nose and throat. Through the smoke I saw that the cab had been well and truly peppered. Three bodies were slumped back on their seats.

"Let's go, let's go!" shouted Marcus. Robin Hume was screaming with joy, "We got the fuckers, we got them."

I did a U-turn and sped back up to the junction. People were coming out of their doors with their mouths agape. Some of them were cheering. I turned left at the junction and drove soberly to the lay-by. It was deserted.

"Bye, Charlie," said Marcus as he and Hume jumped out. They ran behind the car and dove over the wall. I took off my balaclava and pulled away and headed for the supermarket in Maddenstown.

I pulled to a halt in the car park, well away from the supermarket entrance. I stuffed my piece and the balaclava into the bag. Christ, I noticed that there were spent cartridges from the Stens lying in the passenger's footwell. I looked behind and saw more shells scattered in the back. I got out and went round to the far side and collected all I could see from front and back.

I put them all into the bag. I left the car open with the keys in the ignition as before. I walked nonchalantly away and was soon back at number nine. I went into the kitchen and emptied the contents of the bag onto the newspaper. I counted 17 empty shells. I hoped that the other 13 were lying on the road at Magheraderg. I wrapped my piece inside the balaclava and went down the garden to hide it away.

I returned to the kitchen. What to do with the cartridges? They were a direct forensic link to the murders, no, the executions. I had to dump them as quickly as possible. I wrapped them in the supermarket bag, and then I changed into my running gear. I threw my nylon golfing gear into the bath with warm soapy water.

I went out and got into the woodie. I drove off carefully towards Portstewart. I parked on the beach and stuffed the rolled up bag inside my jeans pocket. I locked the woodie and headed off towards the barmouth. The beach was deserted. When I reached the pier I stopped and had a good look around. Nobody was out on the beach on a cold Thursday afternoon. I scrambled up onto the pier and looked over towards Castlerock on the other side of the Bann.

I walked halfway out the massive stone pier then stopped again to do my checks. I pulled the spent cases out one-by-one and chucked them far out into the Bann. There was absolutely no probability of anyone finding them by chance.

I jogged back to the car. I felt good. No second thoughts about the operation. Hopefully we had saved lives. In any case, we had sent a clear message to the Provos. Keep your guys out of our territory. We will catch them and we will kill them.

I went home and switched on the TV. The early evening news would be on soon. It even made the top-story on the main BBC news. Three Catholic workers had been murdered by Protestant paramilitaries in a drive-by shooting. The usual parade of Nationalist politicians, Catholic priests and family members were put up. Their stories were broadly similar, three innocent Catholics with no connections to terrorism butchered by Protestant gunmen probably in collusion with the security forces.

I smiled, at least it was confirmed that they were all dead. Then a BBC sympathiser gave an RUC inspector a hard time. Why hadn't the area been cordoned off as soon as possible? Why hadn't the police been able to find witnesses? They didn't even have a description of the car.

I slept soundly that night and then had a quiet chuckle when the BBC radio news, next morning, had to report that the Irish News contained death notices for 'Lieutenant' Martin Darby and 'Volunteer' Thomas Corrie. There was also an interview with one of the council house residents who said that she had refused to let the heating engineers into her house because they were asking personal questions and had been suspected of looking through paperwork in residents' houses. This put a new slant on things. There were no priests or politicians making accusations this morning but there was an analyst from one of the more responsible mainland newspapers who seemed to be very well informed. He argued with the BBC presenter that the three so-called Catholic workmen had in fact been an 'active service unit'.

I was disturbed that the third man, sixty-three year-old Seamus Ross, did appear to be another of Ulster's innocents who just happened to be 'in the wrong place at the wrong time'. Another egg for the omelette.

Tricia rang me on Friday evening and confirmed that the weather forecast was good, and we would go for a picnic on Saturday afternoon. She finished work at mid-day on Saturdays, so she expected to call with me at about two o'clock. We arranged for me to buy the food and a bottle of wine, while she would bring a rug and the picnic basket. She wanted to know where we were going to go but I told her that it was a surprise.

I got up bright and early on Saturday morning and did my usual chores. I nipped down to the bookies and did my usual Yankee with singles. Then I drove to the supermarket where I was relieved to see that the Cortina was no longer in the car park. I picked up rolls, ham, cheese, and some goodies because I knew by now that Tricia had a sweet tooth. I went home and stashed the food and then strolled over to the off-licence on Station Street to pick up a bottle of wine. I could never get over the changes to the head of Station Street since the bomb. New commercial units had been built where the Laundromat used to be and the windows of all the old premises had been replaced.

Tricia arrived at number nine carrying an old-fashioned wicker picnic basket with a tartan rug folded over her arm. I led her into the dining room where we transferred the wine and food into the basket, which was fitted out with cups, glasses, and utensils. She was a picture. She was wearing a tight fitting yellow sweater and figure hugging jeans. Optimistically she had sunglasses perched on top of her hair. I pulled her towards me and kissed her hungrily. She waited a minute before pulling away.

"Cool down, lover boy," she said. "Let's get moving. Is it far away?"

"Wait and see, sugar-pie," I responded.

We walked down to the woodie. I didn't bring my piece. Soon we were speeding down the Glebe. I turned left towards Downhill but I pulled in at the Lions' Gates to Downhill Castle. We parked near the castle and gathered up the basket, rug and our coats. We walked past the ruined castle and took the path down to the Mussenden Temple, which was perched precariously at the edge of the cliffs. We had to push our way past the hundreds of sheep being very careful about where we put our feet. We could see Donegal in the distance off to our left and could just see Portstewart to our right.

"What's that land out there on the horizon?" asked Tricia.

"That's Scotland, or rather, the Isle of Islay, which is Scottish," I replied.

We found a patch in the gorse, which was not contaminated with sheep shit and spread out our rug.

Tricia took control. She arranged the plates and was soon splitting and buttering rolls. I pulled the cork and poured us both a glass of wine, which I usually avoided. She reached me a cheese roll and got stuck into the ham herself. When she had polished off the goodies we stretched out head to head.

"I love it here when the weather is fine," she murmured.

"That's not often," I responded. "You know what they say about Islay?"

"What's that?"

"If you can't see it, it must be raining; if you can see it then it's going to rain."

"I never knew that places like this existed in Northern Ireland. All we ever saw on the television were the mean streets of Belfast and Derry with riots and soldiers. What are British soldiers doing here anyway?"

My hackles rose. "Well it is part of Britain or the United Kingdom anyway. What do you think it would be like if there were no British soldiers?"

"I'm sure that we could sort it out amongst ourselves," she replied wistfully.

"Don't assume that all Protestants or Loyalists are like me, some of them scare me."

"Well let's not fall out over it. I just think that this would be a lovely place to bring up children if there were no troubles."

Oh yeah, I thought. I told her about my childhood and how my sister and I had explored the castle and the temple when we were children. I told her about the Earl of Bristol who had been the Bishop of Londonderry and how the temple, his library, was a replica of the Temple of Vesta in Rome.

"Now you know why your street is called Bristol Gardens, and if you go to the continent you will find hotels all over Europe called the Bristol or the Londonderry after the bishop who spent a lot of his time on the grand tour."

"Will you take me there someday?" she asked. "Or would you like to come down to Galway and I'll show you the sights. You'd love the Galway Races."

That'll be the day, I thought.

"This sounds as if we are getting serious," I told her.

"Oh yes, I'd love to spend the rest of my life with you," she replied earnestly.

I grabbed her and kissed her deeply but then rolled apart. There were scores of sightseers now on the path. Why hadn't I taken her over the sandhills at Castlerock? On the other hand Tricia was unlikely to do it al fresco.

"Come on, let's get back to the car. I want to take you somewhere secluded."

"My, that sounds inviting," she chuckled as she folded the rug.

Chapter 23 - Vinty Costello

I was called to a Friday night planning group at my aunt Sadie's. I was surprised at how many members were present and amazed to see that they had set up a slide projector. After tea had been served Marcus Macrory called the meeting to order.

"We are here to discuss and plan an operation against Vinty Costello." There was a ripple of murmuring as members gave each other inquisitive glances. He switched on the projector that displayed a photograph of a short and wiry man in his thirties. Marcus continued, "Costello is an active member of the INLA. We have intelligence that suggests that his group planted the bomb that killed Brian Montgomery and his daughter. We intend to eliminate him."

He switched to the next slide, which displayed a view of a farm taken from a nearby hill. "This is Costello's dairy farm a few miles east of Dungiven. Costello lives there with his wife and four children. There are also about three farmhands but we are especially interested in these two characters who we will call Groucho and Harpo for obvious reasons."

He flipped to a slide which showed two well built men in their thirties. One was dark with a large moustache and the other had a shock of blonde hair. "These two guys don't seem to have a role around the farm, and one or both of them accompanies Costello where ever he goes. You should consider that these guys are players and that they are armed and dangerous. Do not have any compunction about taking them out if you get an opportunity.

As always, only take extreme measures against family members or farmhands if they attempt to stop you in your actions."

"I don't have a date yet, but it will be on a day when we are sure that Costello is on the farm. He normally drives a grey Opel Kadet estate wagon but he also has access to a grey mini-van and a red pick-up truck." Marcus displayed three slides that showed the three vehicles in question.

"I will lead the team, and I will carry a Sten gun. Wesley is second-in-command, and he will have the jungle carbine. Howard will carry the sawn-off and Charlie, you will carry your usual Webley .38. I know that we will be outgunned with our museum collection against their AK-47s and Makarovs, but we will have surprise. May I remind you to grab any weapons that you can during the raid?"

"We will approach from the hill to the east early in the morning at milking time. We will run into the two main buildings – the house and the milking shed taking targets as we meet them. Howard and I will take the house, and Wesley and Charlie will take the shed. Retire back over the hill when you hear my whistle. We will park our car in a lay-by on the Dungiven road. Any questions?"

Howard was a very large countryman but he was no fool. "What if the doors to the house are barricaded?"

"Good point," said Marcus. "I will carry a Czech grenade to blow the door off its hinges."

I was nervous but I had to ask, "Shouldn't we cut the telephone line before we attack?"

"No need," replied Marcus. "Who are they going to ring – the police? Besides, if they pick up a dead line it would alert them that something is up."

"Right lads, you will be contacted very early on the morning of the day. Usual dress. Check your weapons. Transport will be at the end of your road thirty minutes after you have been contacted. Wesley, bring the fishing gear, that's our cover if we are stopped. If the police or army attempt to search the car then the game is up, go quietly, no shooting, mouths shut, you will get legal support as soon as possible, do your time, you will get out quickly because a settlement is going to come. And remember, if you are interrogated, do not believe anything, which they say about any of the rest of us coughing up. Whatever you say, say nothing!"

We slipped out of the back door at ten-minute intervals. I walked back over the bridge to my side of the town. I considered calling into a bar for a few drinks but reason prevailed. I had been called up by the first team to play in their last game of the season the next day. It was their last league game so it was a 40-over game starting at ten o'clock to make best use of the late summer light. The pressure was on me so I would need a good night's rest and a clear head.

I got up early and had a full breakfast. In one way I felt great. I was looking forward to the game and I was taking Tricia to the Rugby Club disco in the evening. On the other hand, the upcoming operation against Vinty Costello weighed heavily on my mind. I wanted to get revenge on Costello for Brian Montgomery and his daughter but I didn't want to jeopordise my future with Tricia. The operation was dangerous never mind criminal. We would be tackling well-armed, ruthless men who could kill or wound us or we could end up in gaol. I had looked forward for two years to get a chance to injure the terrorists but now when I had the opportunity I couldn't face it. I had to accept it, I wanted to spend the rest of my life with Tricia, and that would probably mean walking away from NI and its problems.

I packed my sports bag and tried to put the operation out of my mind. I drove out to the Rugby Club and made my way into the changing room. I was greeted by Jim Toy who had also been called up to the first team. The pre-match banter soon lifted my thoughts away from Tricia and the operation. The captain went out to the toss and then came back to tell us that the other side were batting first.

We ran out onto the ground and started to throw balls to each other to get used to the light. It was a typical, fresh Ulster morning. Overcast but no sign of any rain clouds. We took up our fielding positions and awaited the opposition openers. Our captain didn't know me so I did not expect to get a chance to bowl early on, he directed me to field at long off. The two batsmen came out and we clapped them on politely. I noticed that they were young, fit and immaculately turned out.

Our captain tossed the ball to a tall, athletic looking chap who I recognised as Andy Messenger, a PE teacher at the local grammar school. He took a very long run up and delivered a ball at blistering pace. The young batsman disdainfully hooked it and just failed to put it over the boundary but it bounced over for a four. Christ! What have I let myself in for, I thought. The batsman blocked the next two balls and then stepped out to hit the next ball over the bowler's head for another four. He survived an LBW appeal to the next ball and then prodded a single to amble down to the other end.

The captain then gave the ball to Jim Toy. Jim fancied himself as a fast-medium swing bowler. He had a nightmare. The young batsman took fifteen off the over and finished up back at the other end. I had never seen anyone bowl so fast as Andy, in real life, but the batsman wasn't fazed. He hooked, he drove, he glanced; he even ran a risky two before judging a safe single to take fifteen off the over and to hog the batting. Jim had another nightmare giving the young fellow his fifty but did manage to strand him. Our captain's face was a picture. I saw him looking around in desperation until his eyes rested on me. Oh Christ, I thought as he tossed the ball to me.

"Well, Cunningham, any ideas?"

It was my chance to bowl at the other batsman who hadn't faced a ball. How would he play it, I wondered. Would he be content to hold up an end while his partner made all of the runs or would he be eager to show what he could do? He looked about seventeen but confident with it. I bowled two looseners to Jim, and then I made my conventional field placings. I didn't really know much about it. As long as they were well spread out that was good enough for me.

I took my usual shortish run up and delivered a medium paced straight ball. The teenager stepped out to knock me over the boundary, missed and then looked back in horror to see that he was missing middle-stump. My captain ran up and patted me on the back.

"Well done, Cunningham. Charlie, isn't it? Well done, Charlie, we needed that."

The new batsman treated me with respect. He blocked my straight balls and ignored any that were missing the wickets. My team and the dozen or so spectators clapped me as I resumed my fielding position. The captain put our spinner on at the other end but the fifty maker knocked him all over the ground. Six overs gone and the opposition were 73 for one.

It was my turn to bowl again, and this time I faced the run maker. I ambled up and gave him a slow Yorker, which he blocked at the last second. I bowled two more dot balls and was congratulating myself for working him out when he pulled one for four. He took one off my next ball leaving the new batsman to face my last ball. I put a bit of effort into it and I was delighted when he played on to his leg stump. The captain was all over me and I got another smattering of applause from the crowd.

The morning went on like that. Their best batsman was too good for any of our bowlers and he soon passed his century. I half hoped that he would retire as players usually did at my level of cricket but this was a league game and he carried on. I bowled two more overs during which their star took two fours off me but their other man got nothing. Our captain changed our bowlers again and I found myself fielding at mid off. Rodney came steaming in and delivered a very fast ball which the star batsman knocked in my direction. It shot to my right at head high and I dived and got my hand to it. It fell and Jim Toy rushed in to throw it at the stumps that had been deserted by the batsman who was halfway down the wicket screaming at his static partner. He had no chance of getting back in time as the stumps were destroyed. Jim and the captain were dancing around me in joy but I had other things to think about. The ball had hit me on the thumb, which was now sending excruciating signals to me. I stood up to examine my hand. The thumb was swelling up before my eyes and it stuck out at an unnatural angle. Jim and the captain stopped their cavorting and came over to stare at my hand.

"Great stop, Charlie, but it doesn't look good. You'll have to go off and get it looked at."

I went off, and Jim Toy's wife Mary drove me to Coleraine Hospital. As we waited for my X-ray she gave me the third degree.

"Are you still seeing that lovely girl we saw you with at the Sperrins?"

I told her that I was but that there were problems.

"She's a Catholic you know, from the south."

"We all know that but what's that got to do with it?" she said.

"If we married, I would have to turn, and we couldn't live here."

"If you love her, marry her and follow her to the ends of the earth."

I was called in and an hour later the picture confirmed that the thumb was broken. It was taped, and I was given a sling and a bottle of strong painkillers.

Mary drove me back to the match. They were taking lunch when I entered the dining room. My teammates gave me a cheer and the opposing captain came up and made polite enquiries about my thumb. They had made 247 for six from their forty overs, an unheard of score in my experience. I sat in the pavilion and watched us being bowled out for 128. I went into the changing room but I needed help to pack my gear away and to buckle the straps. I made my way out to the car park and stowed my bag in the rear of the woodie. I was OK to drive but I was gradually becoming aware that I couldn't fire a pistol. I drove over to Thiepval Park and called in with Aunt Sadie. I showed her my thumb and told her to contact Marcus. I was in no fit state to go on the operation.

As I drove back to number nine I realised that a weight had been removed from my shoulders. In fact, I was elated. I resolved to cut my ties with the NVF. When I parked in Union Street I surreptitiously transferred the .38 into the side pocket of my sports bag. I went in and hid the .38 behind my cistern in Mrs Warke's outdoor toilet. I wouldn't be needing it for a while. I rang Tricia and told her my tale of woe. She would have to drive over and pick me up to go to the disco. I took two more painkillers and went to bed. I was in pain but I felt good. I thought that I had done well in the game, which was probably going to be my last. I felt that I was done with the NVF, and I was looking forward to spending my life with Tricia.

Chapter 24 - The Raid

I was in my front room listening to The Moody Blues and marking a set of books that I had taken in that afternoon. It would soon be time to make a light bite and then get ready to take Tricia to our usual Wednesday night visit to the movies. I was having trouble making ticks and crosses with my left hand. Writing comments was out of the question. I was interrupted by a quiet double-tap to my front door. I went to open it and was pushed aside by Robin Hume.

"Sorry, Charlie, I didn't want anybody to see me calling on you," he gasped.

"What's the problem?" I asked. I hadn't seen him since the operation at Magheraderg when we had sorted out the heating engineers.

"The raid on Costello's farm is either tomorrow or Friday. I have been picked to take your part. The only problem is that we're short of hardware, and I have come to borrow your .38."

"What happened to your Sten?" I asked.

"The fuckin' thing is useless. The magazine locking catch broke off when I took the magazine out after Magheraderg."

"Sure, just let me get it from out in the garden but remember, I've only got six rounds."

I retrieved the .38 from Mrs Warke's toilet and took it into Robin.

"Let me put it into a shopping bag so that you can carry it."

"Thanks, Charlie. I hope that I don't have to use it but I will use it if I have to," he stuttered.

He bade me goodbye, and I wished him good luck as he left me. I couldn't understand it. Marcus seemed to have wads of money to spend on typewriters and stationery and he had lots of contacts, how come he couldn't get his hands on some decent weapons? There were plenty about. A number of UDR armouries had been raided by 'Loyalists' in the past year and boats were coming in from Scotland every week. I turned my thoughts to Tricia and packed up the exercise books.

I met her in the cinema car park, and we spent two hours in the company of Jaws. Tricia would not believe me when I told her that bigger sharks than that could be found a few hundred yards off the beaches of Castlerock, Downhill, and Portstewart. Of course I didn't tell her that they were basking sharks, which are harmless to humans. She didn't come back to number nine that night because she told me that she had a heavy load of visits to businesses over the next few days. We arranged to go for another Chinese meal on Saturday evening. I just couldn't figure where she put it all away.

When I got home on Friday evening I could not believe my ears when I switched on the radio. There had been a gun battle at a farm near Dungiven. Vinty Costello, the notorious INLA leader, had been killed in an explosion. Three farm workers had been shot dead and two other people had been injured in the explosion. A spokesperson for the Irish Republican Socialist Party eulogised the part that Costello had played in the struggle for Irish freedom and blamed a plain-clothes unit of the SAS for the 'murders'. A journalist from one of the Nationalist newspapers stated that it was more likely to be the work of the UVF but he did not rule out that it was another chapter in INLA's feud with the Provos.

I walked over the bridge and turned up into Thiepval Park. I passed by the road where Aunt Sadie lived and went on up to Wiltshire Drive where I could look down onto her house. I could not spot any strange cars nor any strangers, so I walked down the steps then jumped over the fence into her back garden and entered the house by the back door.

Sadie was standing over Marcus Macrory who sprawled back on a chair. His face was a mess of small cuts, which Sadie was treating with TCP. Marcus was in good spirits and he raised a glass of whiskey to me.

"Ah, you missed it, son. Clockwork, bloody clockwork. Well, almost," he chuckled.

He related the morning's events to me. The four of them had parked the car in the lay-by on the Dungiven road. They had approached the farm as planned, over the wooded hill and then lay up to reconnoitre the target.

"It was more or less what we had expected," he went on. "There were four vehicles parked in the yard, the Opel Kadet, the pick-up truck, and the mini-van, so we reckoned that they were all in. There was also a car with southern plates so we were hoping that Costello had a visitor from the south, maybe a bonus target."

He offered his glass to Sadie for a refill and then went on.

"We could hear the milking machines in the shed, so I detailed Wesley and Robin to circle around and approach it from the rear. I gave them a couple of minutes, then me and Howard made our way down to the house. Just as we got there, Groucho and a young woman came from around the side of the house carrying trays of eggs. As soon as he saw us Groucho dropped

168

his eggs and started to reach inside his jacket. Howard gave him both barrels. Christ, what a mess. The young lass was down on her knees pleading, so I told her to fuck away off. Then we turned to the front door. I could hear somebody trying to open it from the inside, so I pulled the pin of an RG-4 and tossed it inside the wooden porch and ducked down outside."

Marcus started laughing hysterically. I thought that he was in shock but he took another swallow and then composed himself.

"We had never tested the RG-4. I had no idea how it would perform. It had a fragmentation sleeve. It blew the porch, the front door, and the whole shooting match to matchwood. That's how I got my face. We went through the door. It was carnage. Three people were lying on the floor writhing in agony. There was Costello and a smartly dressed couple. Kids came running into the room screaming. I checked them out. Costello was still living, so I aimed the Sten to give him a burst but would you fucking believe it? It jammed."

"Well, did you finish him off?" I burst in.

"Howard reloaded the shotgun and literally blew his head off. You can't beat the old shotgun. A young woman in the green suit was screaming but something stopped me from finishing her off. The other smartly dressed young woman had multiple injuries but something stopped me from killing her. I ordered Howard to get out. We stopped to relieve Groucho of his Walther P38, and then we ran over to the shed."

"What about Robin?" I almost screamed.

"We met Robin coming out, he was off his head. He told us later that when they entered the milking shed one of the farm workers had run up to Wesley and tried to pull the jungle carbine from out of his hands, so Robin double tapped him in the head with your .38. It seems that at that point Harpo came out of a little office with an AK-47. He gave Wesley a burst and almost cut him in half. Now, according to Robin, isn't he an icy little bastard, he emptied the .38 into Harpo's chest."

"What happened to Wesley?" I begged.

"When we entered the shed milk-maids were running out screaming. Harpo was stone dead and Wesley was a mess, no hope. I checked the other guy out but couldn't identify him. He was dressed like a farm worker. We grabbed the AK-47 and Wesley's carbine. We found a tarpaulin and put the remains of Wesley into it. I checked the vehicles and, sure enough, the mini-van had the keys in it. We put poor Wesley into the back, and I drove it away to the lay-by. Robin and Howard ran back over the hill to the lay-by where we met up. We put Wesley into the boot of the Cortina, and we drove back to my place."

"Was that wise?" I asked.

"What could we do? We buried Wesley in my cabbage patch and hid the Cortina in one of my sheds. It was a great do. We killed three INLA players. I don't know who the others were. We picked up an AK-47 and the Walther. Sorry, we lost your .38."

"Aren't people going to miss Wesley? Aren't the police going to be looking for him?"

"No, no. Wesley was a loner. He never married; his folks are long dead. He's got a sister living in Articlave. I'll see her but she'll keep her mouth shut. She's very staunch. Wesley worked as a casual labourer for various farmers. Nobody is going to miss him straightaway."

We finished off the bottle of Bush while Marcus elaborated on his story. We reckoned that there were no loose ends. He told me that Robin was over the moon but he was a secretive little bastard. He would be already looking forward to the next operation.

I got up to go when Marcus grabbed my arm.

"I've got a bonus for you, son. Remember Celine Dillon? Cormac's wife? Well, last night they found her tied to a lamppost in the Bogside. Her hair had been shaved off, and she had been painted with creosote. She had broken fingers on both hands. There was a placard tied around her neck. It said, 'Be true to our Republican heroes – or else.' How about that?"

I walked back over the bridge to my side of town. Questions, questions. Could I have done what Robin did? Had I just missed being cut in half with an AK-47? Could the .38 be traced back to me? Who were the other people that got killed or injured? More eggs for the omelette? What about Celine? Had she been innocent? How would this affect Cormac Dillon and the other Republican prisoners? What a fucking country. How are these people ever going to live together in harmony?

I couldn't wait to see Tricia on Saturday night. I resolved to start putting out feelers. I wouldn't propose outright but I needed to know if we could have a future together. I accepted that I would have to turn to the Roman Catholic faith but that didn't bother me. I wondered about emigrating. Canada, too cold. Australia, maybe.

I turned into Union Street and entered number nine. I crawled into my pit but I was missing something that I couldn't put my finger on. Then it hit me. No .38. I was defenceless. I got up and went down to the kitchen. My knife drawer contained a vicious steak knife that I had no use for. This time I did decide to keep it under the pillow rather than between my legs. Too close to my bollocks!

Chapter 25 – Aftermath

I was woken early the next morning by a battering on my front door. Shit, I thought, it's the police. I went down in my dressing gown and opened the door to find Maddy.

"Charlie, you haven't been to see Tricia, and she's crying out for you!" accused Maddy.

"What are you on about?" I asked. "Where's Tricia?"

"Tricia's in Coleraine hospital, in a bad way, and she needs you!"

"What has happened to her?" I squawked.

"She got caught up in that bomb yesterday and was rushed to Coleraine hospital."

"Christ! How is she? Is she hurt?" I begged.

"I'm afraid that her face is scarred for life, and she has a broken arm. But it's the baby we are most concerned about," said Maddy.

"Baby? What baby?" I asked incredulously.

"Are you fucking stupid? Tricia's baby, your baby. Tricia is two months pregnant. Didn't you know? Or are you just so fucking self-centred. It can only be yours!"

I almost collapsed. "She never told me. Oh, Jesus Christ!"

Maddy pushed her way in. "Get dressed. You're coming with me, now!"

I ran upstairs and threw on some clothes. I didn't stop to wash or shave. What bomb? I thought about yesterday's events. It couldn't be.

I ran out with Maddy to her car and we got in. "What bomb?" I asked, but I knew the answer.

"At a farm out near Dungiven," said Maddy. "People were killed, some of them were shot. It wasn't just a bomb, it was an attack."

"What the hell was she doing out there?" I asked. "Those guys were terrorists! Why was she visiting them? Christ! What has she got herself into?"

"Sometimes I think that you are really fucking stupid. That girl worships you. She's not involved in anything. Tricia and Dimmie were visiting the farm to work out a loan deal. Dimmie is the development manager; they just got caught up in it. Wrong place at the wrong time. You know how it is in this god-forsaken country. Besides, how do you know that they were terrorists?"

"I saw the news last night. It said who owned the farm. Remember, I was in the UDR, I know about all of the local terrorists."

"Well, Tricia couldn't have known that."

We pulled into the car park at Coleraine Hospital. Maddy ushered me through Reception and took me up to Intensive Care.

"Jesus! She's not that bad is she?" I asked in desperation.

"She'll live, but it's the baby that they're worried about." We spoke to the nurse outside of the ward. She seemed reluctant to let me in. Just then a tall, middle-aged man in a smart suit along with a plump middle-aged woman came out. The woman was crying. The man looked at me with contempt.

Maddy went over to speak to them. The nurse turned to me. "You can go in now," she said. "Don't upset her and don't be long."

I went through the swing doors and saw Tricia propped up in one of the six beds. There was only one other patient lying in the corner with her back to us. Tricia smiled bravely at me then burst into tears.

"Charlie, I'm so sorry. I should have told you, and now I'm going to lose our baby!" she wailed.

I grabbed her good hand and kissed it. "You have nothing to be sorry about, and you're not going to lose the baby. You are a very strong girl, and these injuries are superficial," I lied.

She seemed to perk up and went on to explain what had happened at the farm. She told me that Dimmie had to have shrapnel removed from her legs but was otherwise OK.

"That's her sleeping in the corner. The nurses are letting her sleep on because she got no sleep last night," she whispered.

I kissed her on the side of her brow that was not bandaged. "What did your parents say?" I asked.

"They're shocked but relieved that I am not seriously hurt. I'm sure that they are disappointed about the baby but they said nothing. My mother has always been planning for a big white wedding."

"Well, you will have a white wedding just as soon as I can arrange it, and we are going to get out of this bloody country as soon as possible."

Tricia seemed to have perked up but I saw her face cloud over just as I heard the swing doors opening. I turned and saw the nurse leading in the

RUC inspector who had interviewed me a couple of years previously accompanied by a uniformed sergeant. It crossed my mind that they had come for me but I quickly dismissed the thought. They had come to interview Tricia. I kissed Tricia again and promised her that I would soon be back. I nodded to the police officers as I left the ward. I dreaded meeting Tricia's parents but they had gone.

Maddy approached me. "I hope that you're going to do the right thing by that girl."

"I will, I will," I retorted. "I'm going to sell up and resign from my job and then get to hell out of this country as soon as I can."

"What about those of us who have to stay here?" she asked.

"It's different for you. Me and Tricia are never going to be accepted by either community."

"Don't be fucking stupid. There's lots of cross-religious marriages. I know that you are not going to turn but you can still get married here."

"Yes, but we're different. Her parents probably hate me, and there's other issues. No, I'm leaving this country. I want to get away from it all," I rejoined.

"What other issues? What are you not telling me? Tricia told me that you said that your father was easy about you marrying a Catholic. What's stopping you living here?"

"It wouldn't work, believe me. Leave it. Not all of my friends think like me. Most of them are pretty bigoted. Besides, not all of her work colleagues are like you. Remember? I have met them. They are very nice on the surface but when the drink is flowing it all comes out."

"Just because a few dinosaurs spouted about the RUC and the army it doesn't mean that they'd reject Tricia just because she married a prod."

"I'm not a prod, but that's neither here nor there. Give me a lift over to the centre of Maddenstown. I've got things to do."

We left the discussion at that, and Maddy set me down near the main square. I made my way up to Aunt Sadie'. I didn't bother to sneak in the back way. Sadie let me in with obvious concern in her eyes.

"How is she? Have you seen her? We are all terribly sorry. This isn't what we wanted," she said.

"I know, wrong place – wrong time. She will pull through but she'll bear the scars for life but there's another complication. She's pregnant, two months, how the shock will affect the baby we don't know."

"My God!" She lifted the falls of her apron to cover her face. "What are you going to do?"

"I'm going to find a priest who will marry me and Tricia without me turning, and I don't think that I'll find one around here. We are going to have to move to England where priests are more liberal." I paused for breath. "That means that I'm going to sell the house and give up my job. I am pretty sure that I'll have no trouble getting a job in England. There's a desperate shortage of Physics and Maths teachers. My only problem is with Marcus."

"That won't be a problem. He's coming round tomorrow night, and I'm expecting good news. Come and meet him."

"What good news can come out of all this?" I begged.

Sadie put her finger to her nose. "Wait and see. Listen to the BBC tomorrow morning. I'll say no more."

Sadie made me lunch but would say no more. I walked back into the town and got a quick meeting with the solicitor who had acted for me when I bought the house. He assured me that a quick sale was very likely because there were always young professional couples looking for a modernised first house near the centre of town. He promised to get things rolling with his brother who was an estate agent.

I went home and managed to contact my boss by telephone. I explained the situation and the need for me to resign. He asked me to give him a month of the new term so that he could find a replacement. More good news, he actually had someone in mind. I went upstairs and started to dismantle my train set, sorry, model railway layout as best as I could with my thumb still in plaster.

I dreaded a knock at the door. If the police connected the NVF to the raid then it wouldn't be long before they got my name out of one of the members. I knew that I could count on Marcus to keep his mouth shut but I had always thought that Robin Hume was flakey. I consoled myself that I had not actually taken part in the raid nor had I ever fired a shot in any of our operations but I knew that I faced ten years for simply acting as driver at Listober and Magheraderg.

I bought a bunch of flowers and some expensive chocolates before the shops closed. I cleaned myself up and drove over to Coleraine for evening visiting hours. Once again I had to wait outside the ward until Tricia's parents came out. Her father strode past me but her mother stopped to speak.

"Are you Charlie?" I nodded. "This is terrible, are you going to do the right thing by my Tricia?"

"Don't worry, Mrs. Corcoran, I am making arrangements to marry Tricia as soon as possible. The wedding may have to be in England but it will happen."

"Thank God. Tricia tells me that you're a good man. It's just that I had always dreamed that she would be married at home. Wherever it is, I'll be there but I can't speak for Emmett. He's very concerned about Tricia but he's very disappointed."

She left me and I went in. Tricia had bucked up tremendously. I kissed her and gave her the flowers and chocolate. She told me that her blood pressure was back to near normal and that the medical team felt that things were looking much better for the baby. I told her about the sale of my house and my resignation from the Tech. She started to cry.

"You've given up so much for me," she moaned. I assured her that I had never intended to settle in NI in the long run and that I was looking forward to wedded life. This seemed to console her, and she asked me to open the chocolates.

"Now I know that you are getting better," I joked. I took the box over to Dimmie who was sitting up in bed. She was obviously in pain but she smiled and took a couple of whirls.

"Congratulations, Charlie. I hear that wedding bells are going to chime. Tricia is very happy."

"Thank you, you are going to get the first invitation so get better soon."

I spent the last ten minutes of visiting time holding Tricia's good arm and telling her how I saw the future. She lay back smiling contentedly, and her eyelids started to droop. I made my goodbyes and then left to drive back to number nine.

I spent a restless night and then switched on for the seven o'clock news. The news was good. The BBC announced that the RUC had matched some of the bullets from a victim of the raid to the victims of other shootings which the PIRA had claimed responsibility for. The RUC now considered that the raid was part of the on-going feud between the PIRA and INLA. The bullets were obviously from my .38, which Alfie had found in a PIRA dump and from the body of the terrorist that Robin had dealt with.

I carried on packing my stuff and cleaning the house. I jumped out of my skin when the door was battered, and I opened it to find two men in dark suits. I nervously scanned the street for the uniformed officers but I was swept with relief when the older of the two guys announced that they had come to measure the house for the estate agent's flyer. My solicitor obviously had not hung about when getting on to his brother. I left them to get on with their work while I nipped up to the town centre to buy more flowers and chocolate. I got back in time to see the estate agents off. They assured me that a quick sale was very likely.

I was starting to feel a lot better as I drove to Coleraine that evening. Tricia looked even better but she told me that she couldn't get stuck into the chocolates because she was fasting. She was due to go into the operating theatre in the morning for a skin graft onto her face. She told me that the surgeons would be taking the new skin from the inside of her thigh. I was tempted to make a joke but I held my tongue. I noticed that Dimmie was deep in conversation with a middle-aged man, and they seemed to be getting along very well. After thirty minutes the nurse informed me that Tricia's parents were waiting to come in, so I made my goodbyes. As we crossed, her mother smiled but her father refused to make eye contact.

I experienced a serious case of the jitters as I drove over to Aunt Sadie's. I dreaded meeting Marcus. Would we part on good terms or would I become a suspected tout as the Provos called their traitors? I had to convince him that I just wanted out of the country and that I held no hard feelings about Tricia's injuries.

I was extra careful about parking two streets away from Aunt Sadie's house, and I stood for two minutes behind a hedge overlooking her street. Just because the RUC had announced that they were treating the raid, as part of the PIRA or INLA feud did not mean that they would not be open minded about other theories. Surely they knew by now about Sadie's involvement with shady characters from the fringes of Loyalism. I didn't recognise any strange cars; I reckoned that I knew all of the vehicles owned by Sadie's neighbours, and car ownership was not high in those days especially amongst council house dwellers.

I pushed my way through a gap in the hedge and entered the front garden of a house in the street above Sadie's. I went through the entry at the side of the house and then down through the back garden. I stopped for another minute at the rear hedge and scanned the back gardens of Sadie's neighbours. I could not see any figures lurking, so I made my way down to her back door and quickly entered the house. Marcus was already there with his massive hands clasped around a mug at his mouth. He put the mug down to reveal the raw scars he had incurred from the splintered door.

"Sit down, young fella, and grab a mug of tea. How's that wee girl of yours? Is she on the mend? I'm truly sorry about her and the other wee lass. I'm not sorry about the farmhand that we shot, he shouldn't have got involved."

I brought them up to speed with Tricia's condition. I assured them that neither her nor Dimmie were in any danger.

"Thank God for that," said Sadie. "Now tell us about your latest plans."

I outlined what I had done to sell my house and to leave my job. I told them about my plans to move to the south of England to find a job and then to bring Tricia over so that we could marry before the baby arrived. I looked anxiously at Marcus.

"Aye, you're best well out of this country. You couldn't marry here if you don't intend to turn. Good luck to you, son. I will be sorry to see you go. You have served us well. I'm going to lie low for a while to see how things go. I'm fairly sure that the peelers are going to treat this as a Republican scrap, and I'm sure that they are not going to waste too much time investigating it. It was a good job that we brought along your old Webley. Harry Weir tells me that it was used to kill Sammy Macauley two years ago in Coagh."

I hid my astonishment that he knew Harry Weir. "Who was Sammy Macauley?"

"Sammy, God rest him, was a Democratic Unionist councillor on Cookstown council. He answered a knock at the door one bitter December night, and he was gunned down like a dog with that old .38 Webley and a 9mm Beretta. The Provos claimed responsibility the next day. The .38 has been used in two other attacks claimed by the Provos, so it is our 'get out of jail' card."

I spent an hour with them, drinking hot whiskies and discussing the general situation, and then I made my goodbyes to Marcus who I didn't expect to see again. I took his best wishes at face value but I resolved to keep my guard up just in case some other hotheads from the NVF were not so sanguine about my leaving to marry a Catholic. I snuck out of the back door and made my way up to the woodie. I drove straight home because I had work to do. College started in a few days' time, and I had courses to plan and lessons to prepare.

The days dragged as I waited for Tricia to come out. The grafting had been a success, and she was back to her usual self. College started and I was soon back into the old routine. Maddenstown was a small place, and word soon started to circulate that I was leaving my teaching post. Linda May cornered me on the tennis courts where I was on break duty.

"I hear that you've left the UDR, and you are giving up your job at the Tech," she accused me frostily. "I suppose, this is all because of your Fenian girlfriend!"

I had never known her so bitter. I tried to explain about Tricia's injuries and our plans to get married but Linda saw through it.

"I suppose, she's up the scoot and you need to get married in a hurry. A quick registry office job in England." I was startled at her crudity. I hadn't realised the depth of her feelings for me. It was hardly a woman scorned. If she had been that keen about me she shouldn't have let my membership of the UDR stand in our way. I can't say that we parted on the best of terms.

Eventually Tricia was released but, of course, she couldn't drive over to see me with her arm still in plaster. She managed to ring me one evening, and I arranged to pick her up at the corner of her road. We went back to number nine where it seemed to hit her when she saw the advanced state of my packing up. I brought her up to speed on my plans. I had a fairly firm buyer and I had been scanning the Times Educational Supplement for jobs in the south of England. I reckoned that I would have no problem obtaining a temporary or even permanent post on the Dorset, Hampshire, Sussex coast. I had already sent off four enquiries.

Tricia had resigned from her job and was due for some compensation for her injuries incurred on bank business. I expected to make a few thousand on the house, so we reckoned we had enough for a deposit on a small house in one of the most expensive areas in Britain. Her mother was resigned to her leaving Ireland; her greatest concern was that we got married in a Roman Catholic Church in good time. Her father refused to speak to her.

We cuddled gingerly on the sofa careful not to hurt her broken arm or to interfere with the dressing on her face. Tricia was in a different world as she outlined her plans for the future going so far as to discuss baby names. I drove her home and arranged to pick her up again each evening.

Chapter 26 - England

A few days later I received invitations for a job interview from a large comprehensive school in Southampton and from a small private college in Chichester. I rang them both and accepted the invitations. Luckily the interviews were only two days apart. I went up to the station and booked my car onto the Belfast-Heysham ferry. I rolled off the ferry at Heysham in Lancashire on a cold, wet dawn and set off down the M6 for Birmingham. I had a break before I merged with the M5 down to Gloucester and another break before I set off across country to Southampton. I had plenty of time to think about marrying Tricia but I had no doubts. I was not so sure about my intention to become an RC. I mentally practised answering the usual questions about teaching Physics and about my reasons for moving to England.

I booked into a reasonable B and B in Shirley, a suburb of Southampton and borrowed the landlady's iron to freshen up my suit and a white shirt. I am not saying that the interview was a breeze but there were only two other candidates, and I was the only one who had bothered to turn up in a suit and with fairly short hair. For fuck's sake neither of the other two had a degree. I managed to appear enthusiastic about the comprehensive system and safely negotiated past a tricky Physics question from the Deputy Head to clinch my grasp of the job. I signed a contract to start after half term, and then I headed into the town with a checklist of things to do.

I rang the college in Chichester and informed them that I would not be coming. I went back to the B and B and negotiated a long-term stay in a bigger room when I came back to start my teaching job. I found out where the Roman Catholic Church was in Shirley and arranged to see the priest that evening. I started to scan the estate agents' boards to get an idea of the housing market. The prices came as a bit of a shock. I had accepted by now that the time had come to get rid of my beloved woodie, so I drove around the secondhand car dealers looking to move up to a younger and better car.

I met Father Farrell in a private study in the parish house. I briefly outlined the situation. Quite frankly, I lied that I was a committed Christian and had always been attracted to the 'high church' wing of the Anglican faith. I told him that I had partaken in the rituals of high Anglicanism while I was at Manchester University. I laid it on thick that I was repulsed by the hypocrisy of some Ulster clerics of all faiths and that, given my need to do the right thing for Tricia, I was considering that it was the time to convert to the Roman faith. He seemed to take it all in but I knew that most RC clerics were not gullible. The outcome was that he would instruct me in an intensive course with the option to convert when I came back to England to teach and that he would be glad to marry Trish and me in good time.

The next morning I completed my trade in of the woodie towards a three year-old Ford Escort Estate with a 1558cc engine. I never thought that I would drive a snot-green Ford but it was the massive luggage room with the rear seats folded that swung it for me. I rushed through the tax and insurance and headed off north for the 7am ferry from Stranraer to Larne. It was the big engine, which allayed my doubts about driving a Ford. It ate up the motorways to Carlisle where I risked an hour's kip then I drove through the early morning past Gretna, now there was an option, and on through the towns of south-east Scotland in good time to get on the ferry.

The weeks passed. I completed the sale of number nine and moved my smaller possessions to my Dad's bungalow, the larger stuff I put into storage. I made my goodbyes at the Tech keeping a low profile. Two nights before I left NI for good, I went out for a farewell drink with Dave. We started off at Brennan's, my local, at the end of Union Street. We had a couple of pints each with Bushmills chasers and were just starting to loosen up. We walked up to the town square and went into the Corporation Arms where we had another pint. It was like a graveyard so we moved on.

Dave knew all about my UDR service but nothing, I hoped, about my membership of the NVF. He also knew about Tricia, so I brought him up to speed about her progress. He fully supported my desire to marry Tricia and accepted that moving to England was the best way forward. He was able to inform me that getting married as a Protestant to a Catholic in an RC chapel was a long drawn out process even in England. Even though the RC church considered Anglicans as misguided deviants from the true religion, my baptismal and confirmation records would have to be checked. Permission would have to be sought at various levels up the Roman Catholic Church, and it would all take up precious time. He had first-hand experience because his brother had married a Catholic in England.

He shocked me when he stated, "Come on, Charlie. I know that you think religion is a load of bollocks, so why don't you just turn and become an RC? It would be a lot quicker."

I was even more shocked at my first reaction when I fleetingly realised that it would save me a lot of hassle and help me build bridges with Tricia's parents.

We moved on down to Limavady Street and, against my better judgement, we went into the Queen's Arms. The irony didn't escape me, considering the conversation we had just had. It was packed. This was the hotbed of Protestantism, although I would have had a good bet that most of the punters hadn't been inside a church in years. We made our way to the bar, which was bedecked with Union, Scottish, and Ulster flags. The shelves behind the bar were divided into sections by small wooden shields from various UVF and UDA battalions. The centrepiece was a large picture of King William III coaxing his horse into the River Boyne as the battle raged around him.

We stood at the bar getting stuck into a couple of pints of the establishment's renowned Guinness when I became aware of Robin Hume making his way past me to the toilets. I started to greet him but he pushed past me without a word. I had heard the expression 'gimlet eyed' but now I saw it personified. When he came back out I noticed in the mirror behind the bar that he made his way to a corner table to sit down beside Sammy Cameron and two other youths.

They were all barely eighteen and dressed alike in faded denim jackets and wide-bottomed jeans with a short tartan scarf tied around their left wrist. I observed that they were deep in conversation and kept looking in my direction. I quickly lowered my pint and went to the toilet. I was halfway through my piss when Cameron stepped up to the next booth. He didn't give me a glance but simply spoke.

"Charlie, Robin Hume's not too pleased with you and your Fenian girlfriend. If I were you I'd get to fuck out of here."

I didn't even hang about to wash my hands. I went back to Dave and grabbed his elbow.

"Come on, we're leaving!"

"But I haven't finished my pint."

I ushered him to the door and set off at a brisk pace towards the town centre.

"There's a bunch of tartan shites in there who've got it in for me and Trish," I told him, "Let's get back to fuck into the town, I'll get you another pint."

There were always taxis waiting at the barricade before the town-centre, so we grabbed one and set off to the Rugby Club. Dave was half cut but I was stone cold sober.

I knew that the IRA were onto me. We had always suspected that they had a mole in the UDR Record and Pay Office in the large army base at Lisburn. They probably knew my home address and my car registration number, so I had always taken precautions. I assumed that the RUC probably had an interest in me because of my relationship to Aunt Sadie who had marched at the front of UDA parades in the early seventies and who used to write inflammatory letters to the local press. Now I had the UDA after me. I was going to have to be extra vigilant in my remaining days in Ulster. I felt totally naked without a gun and I had no contacts for getting one.

We got to the club where the evening was in full swing. I sank another pint of Tennents with a whiskey chaser and started to feel a lot better. Dave wanted to go into the disco, and I followed him reluctantly. I was standing at the fringe like the proverbial spare what's it, deep in my thoughts when Ros grabbed my arm and pulled me into the melee. It was a slow one so we slipped naturally into each other's arms.

"Charlie, you never contacted me," she accused.

"Sorry, Ros, my life has been very complicated lately."

"Don't worry, I know. In fact, I know everything about your girlfriend. My next-door neighbour is a nurse at Coleraine Hospital. She has seen you visiting your girl. I wish things had worked out for us, Charlie," she mused wistfully.

We finished the dance, and I gave her a peck on her brow. "Sorry Ros, I have to go. Don't waste your life thinking about things which might have been."

Dave was standing waiting for me near the door. "Come on, Dave, one last drink, and then I'm on my way."

We went into the bar and tossed off a double whiskey each. Dave told me that he intended to go back into the disco to see what he could pick up - ever the optimist, always on the chase for women. Not like me who waited for them to come to me. I hugged Dave and then went outside. Taxis were always coming and going. I saw a couple of chaps who I had played cricket against, and I asked them if they were waiting for a taxi. They agreed to share it. I didn't fancy walking the two miles to the town centre. God knows whom I would meet. The Ford was parked outside of Dave's house but I knew that I was too pissed to drive it to my Da's house. The taxi-driver was only too glad to carry on to Coleraine after we dropped my companions at the town-centre.

Da was waiting up for me. I assured him that I had enjoyed a lovely evening, and I put on the pan for a midnight fry up ensuring that I did his bacon in a separate pan. We washed it down with large mugs of tea laced with whiskey. I brought Da up to speed with my plans but I left out the bit about becoming an RC. I don't think that he would have cared. I offered to bring him over to live in England as soon as we were settled but he would have none of it. We crawled to bed about three in the morning by which time I had drunk myself sober.

Next morning I felt extremely fragile but I took the bus to Maddenstown and got off at the station. I strolled down to Dave's house avoiding the centre of the town. I kept my eyes peeled for tartan gangs but I reckoned that they didn't crawl out of their pits until after mid-day. I carefully checked under the Ford and then drove away from Maddenstown, I hoped for good. I spent the rest of the day preparing the Escort Estate for the long drive down to Southampton. I packed the rest of my goods and then spent the evening with my Da. At eight o'clock I strolled up to the phone box and rang Tricia. I warned her to be especially vigilant, to stay away from the town and to sell her old VW for what she could get. I promised her that I would be waiting for her as soon as she signed off from the hospital, and then I thrilled her when I told her about my decision to become an RC.

I made my goodbyes to my father and promised him that I would be back. Then it was off to the Larne ferry and down the familiar haul to Southampton. I moved my gear into a much larger room at the B and B, and then my first move was to ring Father Farrell to inform him that I was ready to convert. I had a quick glance at my teaching timetable and then to bed. Teaching in an English comprehensive school came as a cultural shock. The pupils were much more challenging behaviourally than I was used to but most of my Physics examination classes were with really bright teenagers of the type which would have gone to a grammar school in NI. It was the well-behaved kids in my lower set Mathematics groups who I felt sorry for because most of my time was taken up with controlling a few disruptive boys who really did not want to learn. The issue, which most annoyed me, was smart-arses asking me if I was in the IRA. In any case I was relieved at the end of the week when one of the deputy heads told me that I was doing a good job.

I rang Tricia every other evening to discuss our plans for her move to Southampton. When I got a firm date for her arrival, I booked a nice room for her at another B and B in the next street for form's sake. I tried to keep up with the news from Ulster, and I was vaguely aware of a shooting in Maddenstown. I was totally shocked when Tricia told me, in our next conversation, that a terrorist had been shot dead in number nine. It seemed that the guy who bought my house was a Roman Catholic member of the RUC. In the middle of the night he had confronted an intruder who had broken in through the back kitchen door. The intruder was carrying a steak knife and an old Mauser Bolo pistol, so the policeman shot him dead with his Walther PPK. I almost swooned when Tricia told me that the dead terrorist was called Robin Hume and that the police were working on the theory that he had targeted the police officer because he was a Catholic. I knew better but it was another loose end tied up.

Chapter 27 - Adelaide

I am sitting on a recliner on the back verandah of my house, which overlooks the most beautiful city in the world. I had been half-dreaming about events that happened thirty or more years ago in another world when my daughter's voice brings me back to the present. Ciara is tending the barbecue with her husband Tim, and she wants to know whether I want my baps toasted or not.

Ciara will be thirty next February. She is tall and willowy with thick black hair and blue eyes just like a girl that I met at a rugby club thirty-one years ago. Ciara teaches English at a high school in Adelaide but she will be taking maternity leave soon. Tim is one of the better types of Australian men. He is a marine-biologist at the University of Adelaide and he captains our local cricket team.

At the bottom of the garden, my son Edward has his head under the bonnet of an old Honda sports car. When he straightens up he confirms that he neither got his height nor his blue eyes from me. Edward has recently graduated in Modern History from the University of Adelaide, and he is waiting to enter the Australian Federal Police. Tricia thinks that this is a waste of his degree but I assure her that he will get accelerated promotion, if he keeps his nose clean, and that he will be deferred from call-up for military service if the government brings it back. All of his character flaws are inherited from me. His reluctance to give up his toys and his proneness to idleness but he's a far better cricketer than I ever was.

I look sideways to admire Tricia. She is still a stunner for a woman in her mid-fifties. When we go to parties I still have to keep an eye on some of my Australian colleagues when the beer drives them to chance their arm. Tricia keeps her hair long, so that it covers the scars on the left side of her face. I tell her that there is no need to because the scars have faded. She always wears long-sleeved shirts and blouses even in the high heat of the South Australian summer because she is still self-conscious about the scar on her left arm. Tricia works part-time in an estate agency in Salisbury but she doesn't need to. We are comfortably off with my salary as Head of Science at a High School in Elizabeth. Besides, we were very fortunate as we bought and sold houses over the past thirty years.

Ciara brings me a plate piled with veggie burgers in toasted baps. I lash them with French mustard and start to scoff them. Tim and the kids have now joined us on the verandha where the four of them stare at me with bemused contempt while they get stuck into their beefburgers, chicken, and

186

pork sausages. I asked Tim to open me another tinny of Toohey's lager, and I top up my glass before putting it to my lips.

"I just can't get around how you can drink beer while eating veggie food," says Tim. "They're incompatible."

"Carry on stuffing those dead animals down you," I rejoin. "You'll have a thrombosis before you're forty."

Eventually the food and beer catches up with me and my eyelids start to droop. My thoughts, as ever, stray back to the events in Maddenstown thirty years ago. I remember driving to Southampton airport to pick up Tricia and installing her in her own B and B for decency. Tricia's height almost managed to disguise her five-month pregnancy when she stood beside me, before Father Farrell, in the chapel in Shirley. Her parents and her sister had come over for the wedding, and Dimmie was the bridesmaid. She was looking forward to her own marriage to the surgeon who had removed the shrapnel from her legs. Ironically, he is a prod.

My sister Kathy and her husband Duncan had come down from Scotland to represent my side. My father couldn't make it, not because he disapproved, but because he couldn't face travelling. Aunt Sadie sent us a toaster but we didn't get many presents. I got the impression that Tricia's wider family, in the Irish Republic, didn't know much about the wedding. I was particularly pleased that Maddy and Eugene had taken time off to come over for a few days. My personal relationship with Tricia's parents had begun to improve in the couple of days before the wedding. They were present on the day before the marriage ceremony when I was received into the Roman Catholic faith. Tricia's mother was on cloud nine, they had got me to turn and their daughter was being married in a Catholic church to a Catholic before the arrival of Tricia's baby. Although events were not ideal, her parents could hold their heads high back in Ireland. My relationship with Emmett had thawed. I even went out with him and Eugene and Presbyterian Duncan the evening before the wedding. I wouldn't call it a stag night but we had a few laughs.

Tricia and I flew to Jersey for a short honeymoon. Things were looking up. We spent our weekends looking at houses, and Tricia had started to study for her English banking examinations. The money I had made from the sale of number nine had come through, and we decided to look for a house somewhere near Bournemouth. We managed to get a detached family sized house, with a view of the sea, near Christchurch, which left us mortgaged to the eyeballs. Ciara came dead on time without any fuss, a beautiful blue-eyed healthy baby. She seemed to be unaffected by Tricia's trauma and has never had a day's serious illness in her life.

At the end of the year at the comprehensive school I got a better post at a grammar school in Poole. After Ciara's first birthday, Tricia took a part-time job in a bank in Lyndhurst. This allowed her to come home at lunchtime to take over from the child minder. Life was looking good for us, and I rarely thought back to my life in NI although the nightly news bulletins nearly always led with atrocities from that troubled province.

When Ciara was three, I risked taking the family over to Ulster for a holiday to see family and friends. I was shocked by the deterioration in my father's health and braced myself for the inevitable. The security situation had worsened but when we visited Aunt Sadie I found that she had mellowed. She was now a member of an inter-faith peace group. Like many activists from both sides, she had come to realise that the struggle was not with members of a different faith but that they were all up against the socio-economic realities of living in a small province on the fringe of Europe.

Tricia's parents had moved back down south where her father had got another promotion. I didn't risk going over the border but Tricia took Ciara down on a short visit to Galway. I spent the time mostly doing jobs for my father but I did manage to have a night out with Dave Maxwell. I couldn't risk going out on a crawl around my favourite haunts but we had a quiet night at the rugby club. Dave didn't mind that there was no disco that evening because he was now engaged to a young girl whom I had never met. He brought me up to date with the lives of many of my old acquaintances.

Sammy Cameron was doing five years for bottling a man in a bar. Linda May had married a PE teacher at the grammar school and had a baby son. Ros had started a course of teacher training at the university in Coleraine. The old gang still hung about the bookies and Brennan's bar getting fatter and poorer. The bookie, of course, was getting fatter and richer. I dropped Dave home and promised to keep in touch. I had no intention of coming over for his wedding but I didn't let on.

My father died just before Christmas, so I flew over to organise his funeral and to tie up his affairs. He didn't leave much but I made sure that I took care of his medals. As I kissed Aunt Sadie after the funeral I knew that I would never be back in NI. Tricia was not entirely happy about living and working in England. She said that it was a combination of the faster pace of living and the weather but I knew that she had been on the receiving end of snide comments every time a British soldier was killed in Ulster. I gave her a framed photograph of myself wearing uniform to put on her desk but she had had enough.

We decided to take advantage of the rise in house prices in the south coast and to start a new life elsewhere. Ireland, north or south, was out of the question but Australia was looking for Physics teachers. Neither of us had a problem finding well-paid jobs in South Australia, which we chose, mistakenly as it turned out, for the better climate. The equity from the house gave us a good deposit on a bungalow near Henley Beach on the coast near Adelaide. Two years later we were delighted when Edward was born in Adelaide without a problem. We continued to move up the housing market every four years making full use of the reduced rate mortgages that Tricia got through her employer.

Tricia is very active in the local Roman Catholic community. I accompany her to church once a month, and we have even had the parish priest, Father Magee, around for dinner. He must wonder why I never take communion nor go into the confession box but I avoid talking to him about religion.

The news from Ulster often makes the headlines even in South Australia. Over the years it became apparent that successive British governments didn't have the bottle to fully take on the IRA just as it became obvious that the Provos were starting to realise that they couldn't bomb the Protestants out of Ulster. The conflict took on a nasty turn with the tit-for-tat killings of innocent civilians. What really brought the Provos to the table was when they realised that they could not defend their families from the attacks by a new breed of nastier Loyalist terrorists who copy-catted the actions of the IRA who had killed the family members of UDR and RUC men.

After every election in Ulster I expected the province to return a majority of Republican and Nationalist representatives as the Catholics gradually outbred the Protestants but it didn't happen. Anyone with the slightest familiarity of the demographics of Northern Ireland could work out that Catholics were secretly voting for Unionist MPs. Why wouldn't they? Britain had sunk billions into the province's infrastructure and who would want to live in a priest-ridden, all Ireland republic? The better type of Protestants were leaving NI, and their children were flocking to English and Scottish universities. In the future, most Loyalists would come from the ill-educated, unemployed stratum of society; the very people who had nothing to lose by taking to the streets or reaching for a gun if an all Ireland government tried to impose its alien culture on them. Tricia's father Emmett had risen to move in the same circles as realistic southern politicians, and he was able to inform us that privately they didn't want to govern Northern Ireland. Every now and then I search the Internet for stories about the Police Service of Northern Ireland and their Historical Enquiries Team. It reminds me of old times but I notice that they seem to concentrate on the unsolved murders of Catholics. I wonder who sets their agenda.

We have been clearing up after the barbeque, and I have moved into my study at the front of the house to write some letters. Anyhow, I must go now. A large saloon car has driven into the forecourt. Two large men wearing dark suits and carrying documents are walking up to the front door. They are probably Jehovah's Witnesses.